Dedication

To my family: my wife, Karen, sons Chad, Brent, and Troy, daughter-in-law Rebecca, Grandchildren: Alicia Kraft, Violet, Lincoln, and Calvin Urdahl

ISBN: 0-87839-281-5
ISBN-13: 978-0-87839-281-0

First Edition, April 2009

Printed in the United States of America

Published by
North Star Press of St. Cloud, Inc.
P.O. Box 451
St. Cloud, Minnesota 56302

www.northstarpress.com

Retribution

A Novel

by

Dean Urdahl

NORTH STAR PRESS OF ST. CLOUD, INC.

St. Cloud, Minnnesota

Acknowledgements

I would like to thank my wife, Karen, for her advice and editing. She is a partner in all I do.

Thank you to Patrick Coleman at the Minnesota Historical Society for his assistance and to Corinne Dwyer and Seal Dwyer of North Star Press for their skillful work in making my books better.

OUTLINE MAP OF DAKOTA TERRITORY.

Scale $\frac{1}{10,000,000}$

Area of Territory 325,000 sq.mi. area of ceded portion 25,000 sq.mi.

CHIPPEWAS

Long. W. from Washington

MINNESOTA

Red River of the Red
Lake Tr.
Treaty line
Big Stone L.
L. Traverse
Sheyenne R.

L. Sweater

L. Shetek

IOWA

St. Joseph's
Pembina L.

Vermilion R.

Sioux City

YANKTON LAND DISTRICT

Michenakut L.

Sheyenne R.
Geo. Stevens P.R.R. route 1853

Dakota R.

Ft. Pierre
Fool Soldier Village
Ft. Sully
Ft. Lookout
Route of Fool Soldiers

Ft. Randall
Niobrara R.
Keya Paha R.
Elkhorn R.

PONKAS
OMAHAS

Mouse R.

Ft. Berthold
Green River
Ft. Union
Big Knife R.
Ft. Clarke
Heart R.
Cannon Ball R.
Grand R.
Owl R.

KNOX

PossEssions

DAKOTA

MINNETAREES OR CROS VENTRES

White Earth R.
Little Missouri R.

Cheyenne R.
Moreau R.
White R.
Lad
Lands

SIOUX

Ft. Alexander
Chardon's R.
Beaver R.
Powder R.

Black Hills

BRITISH

Clark's Fork
Mash'r-Shed R.
Tongue R.
Powder R. Peak
Crow's Nest

Great Dry Cr.
Yellow Stone R.
Big Horn R.
Rosebud R.

HILLS

DAKOTA TERR.

NEBRASKA

BLACK

FEET

Marias R.

Judith R.

L. Eustis

Ft. Benton
Teton R.
Great Falls
Smith R.

Big Horn R.

Madison R.
Gallatin R.
Wind R.
Sweet Water R.

Rocky Mountains
Fremont's Peak
South Pass

N. Fork or Platte R.
Ft. Laramie

McKenzie Pass
Maria's Pass

Missouri R.

Jefferson R.

CROW'S

Fremont's Peak

UTAH TERR.

Flathead R.
Gibbs R.
Lewis or Clark's Pass
Hell Gate Pass

Root R.

Missouri R.

WASHINGTON

SHOSHONES

FLATHEADS

80 CR

Foreword

This is the story of the darkest period in Minnesota history. There are incidents of heroism and sacrifice on both sides. But overall there is little of which to be proud.

Though I seek to explain fairly and factually what happened near the end and during the aftermath of the war and I use firsthand accounts and trial testimony in that regard, and although much of the dialogue is taken from recorded statements, there is some fictional conjecture, as with the Fool Soldiers and the story of JoAnna and Jesse.

Wherever I could find a record of an event, I used it. Very little is "made up." That said, in telling this story I found it necessary to be graphic in some accounts. Murder in this war was gruesome, and there were atrocities on both sides, but, while events were horrific, I tried to help the reader to understand why things happened. I made up no description of any violence or atrocity. They came from first-person accounts.

My overall goal is that this novel will help to further understanding of this pivotal moment in Minnesota history and guide how we relate to our present and future with all people of Minnesota.

Dean Urdahl

ॐ ॐ

Preface

The Minnesota River Valley was awash in blood. On August 17, 1862, four young warriors—hungry and resentful over broken treaties, unkept promises and mistreatment—had murdered five white settlers near Acton in central Minnesota.

This isolated, unplanned and random event swept like a wildfire ravaging the prairie. From the two agency reservations to Fort Ridgely to towns and settlers' cabins, the rampage spread from the Valley and spilled onto the prairies north and south of the river.

Hundreds of whites were killed. Estimates ranged as high as eight hundred dead. No one knows for sure how many died. Much of western and southern Minnesota was depopulated. The question was how many had been killed and how many had just left never to return? Indian dead were left uncounted.

One thing was clear. Most of the dead were settlers, not soldiers. The Santee Dakota fought a total war. Men, women and children were killed. Many died as their killers feigned friendship. Most were unaware that an uprising of the Santee had even begun. The Native Americans fought for revenge and to repel invaders. They fought to reclaim their land and they fought to right perceived injustices It was a war for survival that became an ethnic cleansing.

There was mercy among the merciless. While many Sisseton and Wahpeton Santee aided Little Crow, many others did not. John Other Day led Upper Agency whites to safety. There were many instances of Indians risking their own lives to save white friends. It was Little Paul and Red Iron who demanded that the white hostages held by Little Crow be freed. It was they who offered sanctuary to them.

Even as America was in the midst of a great Civil War, there were divisions among the Santee. Some had adopted the white man's ways as urged by the missionaries. They had cut their hair and wore clothing styled like that of the white pioneers and become farmers. Others chose to retain traditional Indian garb and customs.

Four tribes comprised the Santee Dakota. The Mdewakantons and Wapekutes of the Lower Agency, also called Redwood, were led by Little Crow. The war was started and carried by them.

The Upper Agency, or Yellow Medicine Santee were led by Christian chiefs and comprised the Sisseton and Wahpeton tribes. Farther to the west across the border into Dakota Territory were the Yankton and Yanktonais tribes of Dakota.

The farthest west Dakota tribes were the seven bands of the Teton Dakota. They were the Oglala, Black Foot, Minneconju, Brule, Hunkpapa, Two Kettles and Sans Arc. They ranged primarily from the Missouri River west. Different dialects of the same language separated the tribes and the three major groupings of Teton, Yankton and Santee.

The Dakota Conflict of 1862 was the bloodiest of all Indians wars west of the Mississippi River. It spawned a series of wars that lasted until Wounded Knee in 1890. But because America was simultaneously embroiled in the great Civil War that threatened to tear our country apart, events in Minnesota have largely been covered by the sands of time.

The Dakota Conflict of 1862 was a defining moment in the state's history and in the nation's expansion. What happened when the guns stopped firing was equally riveting.

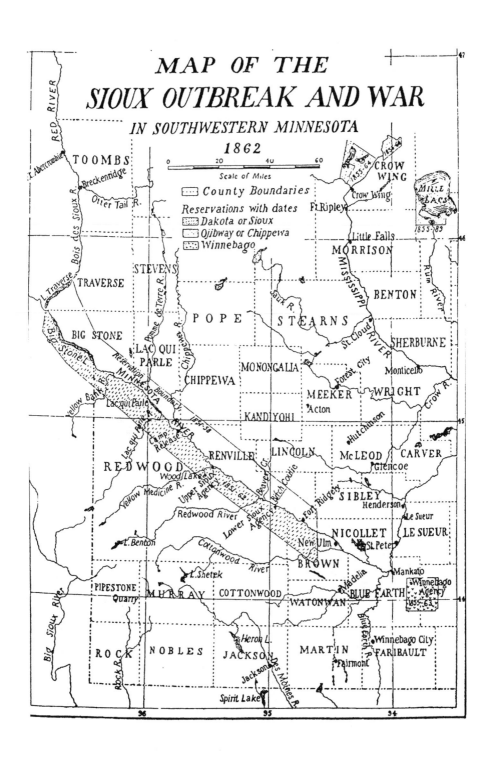

1

THE NORMALLY BUSTLING RIVER town of St. Paul, Minnesota, appeared subdued. An early morning rain left the dirt streets sticky with mud. The muck made smacking sounds as it sucked at the booted feet that crossed it.

The sun shone brightly by mid-morning when small clusters of men gathered outside a telegraph office. Some still wore soggy jackets that steamed as the warm rays evaporated their moisture. The day would be hot, but the weather, normally an endlessly entertaining topic for Minnesotans, was the last thing on their minds.

The office door flung open as a white-shirted man burst into the crowd.

"They attacked New Ulm yesterday!" he shouted. "But they drove the devils off! Lower Sioux Agency got sacked and burned, Marsh and his men got ambushed at the ferry. They might all be dead. It's worse than we heard last night. They's fightin' and killin' all up and down the river valley!"

"Vat are ve goin' ta do?" an old Norwegian immigrant wailed. "Vat is Ramsey doin' 'bout dis?"

"Quiet and I'll tell you!" The command burst from a tall, blue-uniformed man in the doorway of the telegraph office. "I am Colonel

Stephen Miller." He stood ramrod straight and waited for silence, rubbing his dark, white-flecked beard. "I have here a proclamation from Governor Ramsey. It will be given to the newspapers, but I shall read it to you now."

Miller balanced a pair of spectacles on his nose, cleared his throat, and began to read:

> The Sioux Indians upon our western frontier have risen in large numbers, attacked the settlements, and are murdering men, women and children. The uprising appears concerted, and extends from Fort Ripley to the southern boundary of the state.
>
> In this extremity, I call upon the Militia of the Valley of Minnesota, and the counties adjoining the frontier to take horses, and arm and equip themselves, taking with them subsistence for a few days, at once report separately or in squads, to the officer commanding the expedition now moving up the Minnesota River to the scene of hostilities. The officer commanding the expedition has been clothed with full power to provide for all exigencies that may arise.
>
> Measures will be taken to subsist the forces so raised.
>
> This outbreak must be suppressed, and in such manner as will ever prevent its repetition.
>
> I earnestly urge upon the settlers of the frontier that while taking all proper precautions for the safety of their families and homes, they will not give way to any unnecessary alarm. A regiment of infantry, together with 300 cavalry, have all been ordered to their defense and with the voluntary troops now being raised, the frontier settlements will speedily be placed beyond danger.

"That sounds real good," someone yelled from the crowd. "Now tell us what it means!"

"All right," Miller answered, "I'll put it on the drumhead for you. Governor Ramsey has sent Colonel Sibley and four companies, three

2

hundred men, to the Minnesota River Valley to put down an uprising of the Sioux. More troops will be joining him soon. I, myself, will be heading out tomorrow. You are safe here. We will secure the frontier."

"An Indian-lovin' politician's gonna save us?" a man with a scruffy beard shouted derisively.

"Colonel Sibley is a fair man and was a good governor," Miller replied. "It's true he worked as a fur trader dealing with the Sioux, but that only helped him to know them better, how they think. He will do what needs to be done to end this crisis."

SEVERAL BLOCKS AWAY a row of newly constructed homes stood adjacent to a muddy street. A hand-painted sign, erected upon a ridge at the end of the roadway, announced "Summit." The Mississippi River flowed behind the Summit houses and beneath a nearby bridge.

In a sun-splashed parlor, a young couple sat at a small round table drinking coffee from china cups. Lieutenant Jesse Buchanen, handsome in a new blue militia uniform, gazed with earnest affection at the pretty young woman across from him. Dark curls framed her fair complexion. She dabbed tears from deep-blue eyes.

"Jesse," she implored, "you're a lawyer. You don't have to do this. The army needs lawyers. You don't have to fight Indians. What about us? Don't I make any difference?"

"Of course you do, my darling JoAnna." Jesse smoothed back his straight, dark-blond hair. "But try to understand. You know that I had to enlist, the Union needs men, and soon I'd have been sent south to fight the Confederacy. Now war has come to Minnesota. I have to do my part.

"Your father was a lumberman." He gestured at a family portrait hanging over the fireplace mantle. "Now he's a militia colonel heading west, too. It's our duty."

"Duty!" JoAnna replied brusquely. "Too many men die for duty and honor. My father's company's helping to build the towns of Minnesota. Isn't that enough?"

"Cutting down trees and providing lumber is important, but it's not the same, JoAnna. Your father had a dream of building something out of this wilderness when he came from Maine. Now it's time to protect what men like him began."

JoAnna shook her head in exasperation. "But what about us, Jesse? What about us?" she repeated, more softly this time.

The young soldier leaned forward and enveloped JoAnna's right hand in both of his. Solemnly, yet tenderly, his eyes locked with hers. "Tomorrow we leave, but this shouldn't take long, and when it's over, I'll come back here."

He paused to put his words in order in his head. Then he looked deep into her beautiful eyes. "The future's uncertain after that. I'm sure that eventually I'll be sent south. But before that happens, if you want me, even though this may be unfair to you . . . Joanna, would you please become my wife?"

JoAnna's expression registered a startled joy. She leaned forward, wrapped her arms around Jesse and whispered passionately into his ear, "Oh, yes, Jesse, I'll marry you! But I don't want to wait for the Civil War to end. It'll be hard enough to wait for this Indian thing to end!"

Jesse returned his fiancee's loving embrace. As their lips eagerly met to seal the pact, the sound of the front door opening echoed down the hallway to the parlor. The couple hastily separated just as Colonel Stephen Miller entered the room.

Jesse scrambled to his feet and unfolded to his full six feet, two inches. He snapped a salute at his commander and remained at attention.

"Father, have you news?" JoAnna said, trying hard to contain the joy of her own secret news. "We didn't expect you back so soon."

Probably not, Miller thought, noticing the reddish tinge to his daughter's complexion and the obviously embarrassed soldier. "At ease, Lieutenant. Sibley's left Fort Snelling with about 300 men. We leave tomorrow with a thousand more. We should catch Sibley before he gets to Henderson."

"Yes, sir," Jesse said.

"I want to go with you," JoAnna announced. "I've read in history books that women often go with armies."

"Not with this army," her father answered, "and the type of women that have historically followed armies are not those that I would permit you to associate with."

"Please." JoAnna wiped tears from her eyes. "I want to be with both of you."

"Now, now, JoAnna," her father tried to reason. "People are being killed up and down the valley. I will not risk harm to you." He gestured at the portrait of himself, JoAnna, and his recently deceased wife. "Your mother, God bless her soul, would never rest if I permitted you to go into danger."

"What about when the fighting is over? I know they'll keep you out there longer. Can I come out then? Please, Father?"

"When it's safe, maybe. I'll see," Miller answered.

JoAnna broke into sobs. "Promise me, Father. I must be with you and Jesse. No maybes?"

"If it's safe, all right, you can come then," Miller relented.

The tears disappeared as JoAnna grabbed a sheet of paper from the table before her and brought it to her father.

"You'll be out west and who knows what communication will be like. To make it easier, please write down what you just said."

"What!" Miller exclaimed. "I'll do nothing of the sort!"

In spite of the situation, Jesse smiled, knowing that Miller was doomed eventually to relent to his only child's wishes.

"Please, Father." The tears came again. "It'll make things so much easier. Please?"

Miller shrugged and glanced sidelong at Jesse. "Are you sure you know what you're getting into with this one?"

Then he took the paper, sat down and wrote. "My daughter, JoAnna Miller, may travel to join me after hostilities with the Indians have ceased and a military escort is provided for her safety." He signed it, "Colonel Stephen Miller."

"I better not regret this," Miller said as he handed the missive to his daughter.

JoAnna tucked the note inside her bodice, then hugged her father and planted an enthusiastic kiss on his cheek. "Of course you won't. You two will end this war quickly, and we'll all be happy together. I just know it."

She stepped over to Jesse and squeezed his hand tightly. "Don't let anything happen to him, Father."

"I won't, but this is war, JoAnna. It's not all about cheering as men march off." Folks had lined the streets to sing and cheer as men left Fort Snelling to go south to fight in the Civil War. The men looked sharp as they marched onto the riverboats in brand-new blue uniforms with shiny buttons.

"It's not about civilians waving big hats and dressed in finery. The shine fades off soldiers' buttons quickly. War is a dirty business, whether we're fighting Indians or rebels. Remember that and pray for us."

Miller turned to the younger soldier. "Jesse, we leave at five in the morning. You have men to see to and preparations to make. Say your goodbyes."

With her father gone from the room, the newly betrothed couple held each other close. JoAnna rested her head against Jesse's chest, then gazed up at him with a look of pure love in her deep-blue eyes. The intensity of his feelings made Jesse feel weak-kneed. He longed for the day when she would become his wife.

Then JoAnna turned more serious. "Don't do anything foolish, Jesse. I want a husband, not a dead hero. I'll come to you as soon as I can."

"Are you sure you should? Your father's right about his concern for your safety."

"When I go, it'll be safe, like the note from Father says. And, of course, I'll be there in the morning to say goodbye."

After another tender, lingering embrace, Jesse left the house on Summit to join his company. JoAnna's feelings of regret at Jesse's imminent departure were tempered by the note she pulled from her bodice.

She read it again with satisfaction. Yes, it was her ticket to reunite with Jesse. And she would use it sooner rather than later, she vowed.

She tucked the note back into her bodice. She would stash it there to ensure its safe keeping. Then JoAnna drifted into delicious memories of her handsome fiance's embrace, his tender whispers in her ear. She would see to it that they soon became the embrace and whispers of her husband. *Oh, how dashing Jesse looked in his new uniform!*

The next morning in the pre-dawn mist, 1,000 soldiers marched from Fort Snelling to the Minnesota River and began their journey west to end a rebellion, not of southern rebels as they expected when they enlisted, but of Indians.

The image of JoAnna standing in the fort's high tower and waving as he passed burned into Jesse's mind. *Leaving her behind*, he thought, *is harder than the fight ahead*.

But he knew it was best that she stay. Total war was raging in the river valley and points north and south of it. Risks were great, and the scythe of death didn't play favorites.

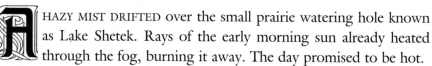

2

A HAZY MIST DRIFTED over the small prairie watering hole known as Lake Shetek. Rays of the early morning sun already heated through the fog, burning it away. The day promised to be hot.

Green- and purple-hued grass undulated like a great inland sea around the five-mile-long lake. But on the eastern edge, a narrow band of green-topped trees hugged the shoreline.

Scattered among the trees were a half-dozen cabins. Smoke drifted lazily like feathers from their chimneys into the stillness of the bright blue sky. A lone horseman trotted along a trail through the woodland.

Eighteen-year-old Charlie Hatch was new to the Shetek settlement, but he came with big dreams. With his brother-in-law, Will Everett, he planned to build a mill to grind grain into flour. But he needed oxen for the project, and the Hurds had a pair.

Charlie was about midway between the two ends of the lake when he passed the John Eastlick cabin. Eastlick paused from digging potatoes in his garden to wave at the passing horseman. Charlie returned the greeting, thinking it good that Eastlick had come back home from helping another settler with harvest. Five children and a wife shouldn't be left alone out here, Charlie thought, even if no Indians had been around for months.

"Ya jes never know what can happen out here," he mumbled to himself.

Suddenly, the horse lunged forward. Charlie jerked back in the saddle before wrenching hard on the reins to bring the animal under control.

"Tarnation, you beast!" he exclaimed. "Scared of your own shadow, are ya? Never shouldda got such a frisky colt."

Charlie gently kicked the horse's sides with unspurred boots and continued toward the northeast end of the lake.

Lavina Eastlick poked a fork into the slab of ham that sizzled on a flat iron in the fireplace. "Almost done," she said cheerily to the three children sitting expectantly at an oak-plank table. Lavina was twenty-eight years old. Her pleasant face was framed by thick, long, dark-brown hair. Neatly wound into a bun, it otherwise tumbled three feet down her back.

Cries sounded from a cot in the corner. Lavina stooped to pick up two-year-old Johnny.

"Now, now," she cooed to her toddler. "Time to eat." She paused before a calendar fashioned from an old flour sack, hanging on the wall. The day was Wednesday, August 20, 1862.

Lavina sat down at the table with Johnny, her youngest, in her lap. Frank, age ten, Freddy, five years old, and Giles, three, waited impatiently.

"C'mon, Ma! Can't we eat?" Frank pleaded.

"Your pa and Mr. Rhodes'll be in shortly. Merton, too. Then we'll eat. Pa's bringin' in more taters."

As if on cue, John Eastlick, tall and slender with bushy blond hair, entered the cabin with his new hired man.

"Merton's cuttin' up more spuds. We'll get started," John said.

As a bowl of sliced ham and fried potatoes was passed around the table, Lavina commented, "John, I fergot to tell ya. We got Indians back on the lake. Haven't seen any since spring, but Pawn and five other men, with their squaws, were at the Everetts' when I brought 'em some butter.

"Pawn seemed friendly. He said he was gonna camp by the Wrights' cabin and wait for some others and then go west on a hunt."

"I might a run inta the ones he's waitin' for," John replied. "When I got back on Sunday, I seen sixteen of 'em out on the prairie. They was naked and all painted, but I'm sure they don't have no mischief in mind. They're cut-hairs from the Upper Agency, ana-way."

"What'cha mean, 'cut-hairs'?" Frank asked.

"They's friendly to the whites. Wear their hair short like we do. Most of 'em are farmers. A lot have been converted by the missionaries. We don't need be scairt of 'em."

Lavina looked at Jim Rhodes as he filled his mouth with a big forkful of ham. "We always treat 'em good here, Mr. Rhodes. If they's hungry and need food, we don't turn 'em away. Some folks do, though."

Rhodes swallowed hard and drank from a cup of cool water. "To be fair. Seems the reds don't think they're bein' treated good. Up at the agencies they's still waitin'. Government promised 'em food and money in the treaties. Money's still tied up in Washington. No money, no food."

"Leavin' hungry Indians mad as hornets," John added.

"Is it 'cause a the war that the money ain't come?" Lavina asked.

"Hard tellin'," Rhodes answered. "Some say the Union's out of gold, and they want to send paper money. Mebbe they just got too many things goin' on ta worry 'bout redskins in Minnesota."

"Oh, John, I hope we don't have no trouble here."

"Don't worry, Lavina. There's strength in numbers. I don't think they'd do nothing ana-way, but we've got what, fifty-some people livin' 'round the lake. They won't cause no trouble here."

"And, Mrs. Eastlick, they know that your husband's a mighty fine shot, one of the best on the frontier."

"He's the best!" Frank exclaimed.

Rhodes smiled. "Well, boy, like I said, your pa's good. There's another fella I know that's purty good, too. Lives up by the Kandiyohi lakes. Solomon Foot's his name, the 'Daniel Boone of the Lakes' he's called."

10

"I still bet he's not as good as my pa," Frank insisted.

Rhodes smiled and then noted, "Nice solid house, John."

"Thanks. We'll put another floor on later. We're a little cramped. Only the Wrights have a two story. Just added it. The roof shingles are still green wood."

"At least we got a log house," Lavina said. "I've lived in a soddy. Never again! Mud and dirt fallin' from the roof onto the table, bugs hatchin' outta the dirt and overrunnin' the house. If this was a soddy, you'd be here alone, John Eastlick."

"We got a stand of trees here that comes in handy fer buildin'. That's one thing this lake's good for," her husband replied.

Jim Rhodes wiped ham grease from his plate with a slice of bread. "Mighty fine breakfast, ma'am. Ya don't see many trees out here on the prairie. Ya gotta use 'em when ya can."

"Papa, why ain't we got more trees?" little Freddy wondered.

"Fire, Freddy. It burns through the prairie in the summer sure as snow comes in the winter. The wind blows the fire from the southwest, sometimes northwest. It hits a lake, and the fire divides. It joins up on the other side, but them fires burn so fast they usually miss the trees near the lakeshore. That's why the east sides of lakes mostly got trees. And that's why we live on the east side of Lake Shetek."

"Ma! Pa!" Eleven-year-old Merton burst through the doorway and shouted between quick breaths, "Charlie Hatch's comin' fast as he can run!"

John, Lavina, and Rhodes hurried outside just as Hatch sprinted into the yard and up to the cabin. Pale and out of breath, he stood before the three adults and bent over with his hands on his knees.

"Charlie, what's wrong?" Lavina felt an awful forboding.

"It's started!" Hatch gulped a mouthful of air before more words tumbled out. "The killin'. It's started! They kilt Voight over at Hurds'!"

"Who kilt Voight?" John demanded. "What's going on?"

"I left my horse at Kochs' ta walk ta Hurds' to get oxen. Phineas Hurd and Bill Jones, they're still gone, ya know. But Hurd left Voight behind ta tend ta things fer Mrs. Hurd."

11

Charlie had to catch his breath, then continued. "When I got there just now, I seed the dog dead in a pool of blood. The house was all tored up, and then I saw Voight shot dead in the yard. I couldn't find the woman and her baby.

"I went back ta Kochs'. When I got close, I heard a shot and saw Indians all around. They had my horse, but the shot scared 'im, and he took off like a bat outta hell. When the reds chased after my horse, they wasn't lookin' my way, so's I sprinted through the clearing and made it here.

"People gotta know what's hap'nin'! You gotta git outta here!"

"Mommy, what's happenin'?" Frank asked.

"Merton," Lavina said urgently, trying to control the emotion she felt, "git the children inta the house now. We'll be in soon."

The oldest child dutifully herded his siblings into the cabin as the adults continued their discussion.

"I need a horse," Hatch said, "I've gotta tell the others."

"I've got an extra one by the stable. Take it," Rhodes quickly volunteered.

"Tell folks ta meet up at Wrights'," John instructed Hatch. "It's the biggest, strongest building around.

"Lavina, git the children. Let's git on the road. I need my rifles. Hurry, there ain't no time ta get anything more."

As Hatch furiously galloped Rhodes's horse south, the seven Eastlicks and Rhodes hurried by foot among the trees lining the shore. The Smith cabin was next in line. The little party approached cautiously.

"Don't look like nobody's around," Lavina observed.

Her husband nodded. "Looks quiet."

"Smith! Smith!" the men yelled.

"No one here," Rhodes decided. "Let's keep goin'."

Soon Wrights' cabin came in sight. White settlers, including Henry and Sophia Smith, were in the yard. Nearby, Indians were camped and sitting around a fire.

Lavina recognized them at once. "It's the band what was with Pawn on Monday."

John watched intently. "People're walkin' 'round like everything's normal. Let's go in."

Julia Wright, who was in her early thirties, rose from a chair when John and Lavina entered her house. She calmly walked to Lavina and embraced her.

"Don't worry," Julia reassured the younger woman, "it'll be all right. Pawn said there're some bad Indians about, but he'll protect us. Most of the neighbors are here. I'm glad they're here 'cause my husband left two days ago for Mankato.

"I seen the Meyers family gallopin' by in their wagon. Didn't know what was up then. I guess we know now. Mariah Koch's here, poor dear. They kilt her husband, Andrew. Will Duley and Tom Ireland came without their families. The Indians were shootin' at Tom, so he run off, leadin' them away from his wife and children," Julia continued. "Will's wife's played out and couldn't keep goin'. He left her and the children hidin' in bushes and came ta get help.

"Pawn offered ta help git them. Him, Will, Tom, and some squaws went off lookin' fer the women and children. I hope they git back soon!"

They did return a short while later with the Irelands, Duleys, and Mariah Koch. Meanwhile, the men of Shetek prepared the Wright cabin for defense by chipping out chinking between the logs to use as loopholes for rifles.

John Eastlick took charge. "Move the high-backed furniture in front a the winders. No lamps lit in here tonight. Make sure you've all got at least two good places ta shoot from."

He paused and spoke softly to his wife. "Lavina, we got axes, hatchets, and butcher knives on that table there." He pointed to the dinner table. "Make sure the other women and older boys all git somethin' and then head upstairs. Keep the children quiet an' keep a lookout from the windows."

13

John kissed Lavina, and she wrapped her arms around him in a quick, hard embrace. Then he called to the women.

"Ladies, please come here. I got some things fer ya."

～ 3 ～

WILL DULEY SMOOTHED BACK the nervous sweat in his black hair and peered through a crack in a wall. "Look at 'em. They're over at Smiths' lootin' the place."

"Ya sure they're not friendlies, the ones Pawn was waitin' for?" Will Everett wondered.

"No, these're different," Charlie Hatch answered. "That fella on that horse there, ridin' inta the field, I saw him at Kochs'."

"Look," Edgar Bentley warned, "someone's coming!"

"It's Pawn," Duley said. "Open the door a crack."

The Indian stood about ten yards in front of the door. Pawn was past middle age, and the years were showing in his lined face. He wore his hair long in the traditional style, dressed in breech clout and leggings. His face reflected concern.

"White men, we want to help you. Give us guns, and we will come inside to fight the bad Indians with you."

Duley considered Pawn's words and turned to his friends. "You trust 'im?" he asked.

"Not as far as I can throw the red devil," Smith muttered.

"Me neither," Bentley agreed.

15

Duley nodded. "All right, gimme a coupla rifles, not the best ones."

Everett walked to the wall where weapons had been stacked and selected two, which he brought to Duley. Will opened the door and walked out.

"Pawn, this here's the best we can do. Here are two rifles and some ammunition. Go to the stable. You can make your stand there, and we'll make ours here in the house."

"All right. But when the bad Indians come, let us both fire together at the same time. It will scare them away."

"Okay," Duley replied, "git ready and follow my lead."

Within a half hour, dozens of Indians approached the Wright cabin. They had painted faces and lots of weapons. But the walls of the house bristled with protruding rifle barrels. From chinks in the stable wall, more weapons appeared.

Duley peered down the sight of his rifle, then yelled, "Ready, Pawn! It's time!" He squeezed his trigger slowly, as did others, and a dozen miniature explosions erupted from the cabin. The interior dimmed with acrid gunsmoke.

Lavina hurried to her husband's side. "John, I was watchin'. Them Indians in the stables, they didn't fire. Their guns are still loaded. Don't shoot your other rifle yet. Wait."

"Pawn!" Duley screamed, "what in hell are ya doin'? None of ya shot, and the Sioux are still there."

The old Indian strode from the stable. "I will go talk to them."

The occupants of the Wright cabin watched as Pawn walked toward the group of marauders.

"I think they planned on shootin' us when we shot first, but they got too yella," Charlie Hatch suggested.

"Let's see what happens," Duley said. "There's a buncha Sioux ridin' to meet Pawn. Looks like they's talkin' now. I hope somebody's being reasonable."

The wait was just minutes but seemed like an eternity to the anxious settlers in the house. Finally Pawn turned from the Indians and came back at a run. He stopped in front of the cabin door and gathered his breath before speaking.

"They are Santee from the agency. Two hundred will be here soon, and they have bad blood. They want this land back that you took. They say if you go away peacefully now, they will not harm you," Pawn reported. "If you stay in this house, they will burn it over your heads. You have only a short time to decide what to do."

"We'll let ya know," Duley answered.

He turned to the refugees in the cabin. "Well, you heard 'em. Whatcha think?"

Bentley looked around nervously. "How many of us are there?"

"Thirty-four," Duley said, "looks like eleven men, the rest women and children."

"Let's try to hold 'em off," Charlie implored. "We can't just give up. We can't just walk out there. I don't trust 'em."

"But they can burn us out, or starve us out," Will Everett pointed out. "Even with green shingles, I don't like our chances. Nobody knows we're in this fix. We can't count on bein' rescued. If 200 armed Indians start pepperin' this house with shot, purty soon they'll get us all, women and children, too. I hate to say it, but leavin' here might be our only chance. Let 'em have the land today. Leave peaceably. Troops'll come back and get this settled. Then we can come back."

Duley looked uncertain. "Can we trust 'em?"

"Like Will said," Henry Smith replied, "we ain't got much choice. Keep yer guns ready, though. Will, you were in the Mexican War. You're the only one here that's been in the army. We'll do what ya thinks best."

A quick discussion ensued. No one seemed happy with their choices. Finally, everyone had had a say.

"All right," Duley said, "is that what you wanna do? If there's an objection, tell me now."

He paused and waited for a negative response. When none came, he shouted out the door. "We're comin' out. Don't shoot!"

Then he turned to his wife. "Laura, get Mrs. Wright and Mrs. East-lick. Bring the other women and children out with us. Stay tight together."

The little party assembled at the cabin door. Julia Wright voiced the question on most everyone's mind. "Where are we goin'?"

"New Ulm," Will Duley answered with conviction. "It's the closest settlement of decent size. But it's a hundred-mile walk."

"Will, we're mostly women and children. Some might not hold up too good," Julia pointed out.

Almira Everett spoke up. "We got a wagon at our cabin. If it's still there, it could haul most of the women and children."

"Rhodes, Hatch, go get it and catch us on the trail," Duley commanded.

"Git some flour and quilts from inside, too," said Julia. "We'll be spendin' nights on the prairie. We'll need 'em."

Julia looked around the yard, and then cautiously stepped from the shelter of the house. The others followed her, and they started the long trek to New Ulm, to the promise of safety.

The sun scorched their backs like a fire ball. Unprepared for a hazardous journey, most had only the clothing on their backs, some of it already ripped. Several, including Lavina, had no shoes and thus walked barefoot on the tough, sharp prairie grass, but their fear blunted the pain. Babies cried and children whined, sensing their peril or their parents' tension.

Hearing someone approach from behind, Julia quickly turned around, momentarily terrified that the Indians were coming, but she saw, to her great relief, Hatch and Rhodes rolling up in the open wagon. She and Lavina helped the other women and children board the rattly wagon. Julia, Lavina, and Lavina's two oldest sons, Merton and Frank, walked, keeping watch for any sign of movement about them. The eleven men, guns held at the ready, ringed the wagon as they trekked across the prairie.

⅏ 4 ⅑

OR ANOTHER MILE the Shetek clan continued on their route. Then a cry rose from a woman in the wagon.

"Look back! They're comin' and Pawn's with 'em!"

The men quickly convened while their eyes swept over the approaching scene. Dozens of Indians galloped after them.

"Damn Pawn!" Smith exclaimed. "He's with the bastards."

"We got no protection, nowhere ta go and a wagon full of women and children," John Eastlick bemoaned. "Any ideas?"

"Everybody in the wagon!" Duley hollered. "Men in the back with rifles. Mrs. Smith, Mrs. Eastlick, drive the teams hard. We gotta move!"

Many women and children in the wagon screamed and sobbed as terror etched their faces. Some simply hung their heads and trembled. Sophie Smith gripped the reins tightly and held on as Lavina lashed the horses with all her strength.

The animals bolted forward, and the wagon lurched behind them. The nearing Santee let loose with blood-curdling screams, urging their mounts to greater speeds. The poor horses pulling the wagon were overloaded. Even as their muscles strained and became sharply defined under their hides, they couldn't muster much more than a fast walk. These were farm animals used to a slow plod.

"It's hopeless!" Tom Ireland yelled as the screaming Indians closed on them. "We can't outrun 'em! They're almost on us!"

"Mebbe they just want the horses," Bentley hoped desperately. "Let's git out and let 'em have 'em. We can't stop 'em anyhow."

"Stop the horses!" Will Duley cried. "Women and children, run for the slough yonder! Hide in the tall grass. Men, follow 'em and give cover."

"Should we shoot at 'em?" asked Will Everett.

John Eastlick responded without hesitation. "I'll plug the first one that touches that team of horses."

The Santee were just on the fringe of musket range, around a hundred yards away. Led by Lean Bear and White Lodge, they had spent the summer some twenty miles to the northwest on Lake Shakotan.

* * *

THE SANTEE WARRIORS knew something that the whites didn't. Just a few days before, on the morning of August 18, frustration and desperation had exploded into an uprising. Little Crow had led an attack at the Redwood Agency. Twenty white people had died in the attack, another ten were captured, and nearly fifty escaped to Fort Ridgely.

The afternoon of August 18, soldiers under Captain Marsh arrived at the agency ferry to bring order. They were ambushed and twenty-five were killed. The Yellow Medicine Agency was attacked in the evening.

By the time the Shetek settlers sought shelter from the Santee in the tall slough grass, war had begun raging throughout the Minnesota River Valley. New Ulm had been attacked, hundreds killed. That same afternoon Fort Ridgely's defenders were being attacked by a force of Santee nearly four times their number. The isolated settlers of far western Minnesota hadn't had the chance to learn of those events.

Lean Bear, the younger of the two leaders, turned to White Lodge, a veteran chief with white hair and an arthritic limp. He pointed a war lance at the fleeing whites. "See them run like sheep before us."

"Yes, Lean Bear, and we can kill them like sheep. We are near gun range. Spread the young men out in a long line and ride into them. Fear no one."

"The white men have guns," said Lean Bear.

"Shoot them. It is a good day to die."

The Santee galloped across the prairie toward the Shetek refugees. They whooped, screamed and tremeloed cries of war. Once in range, the Indians fired at the whites but hit no one. Lean Bear made a running leap from his horse and grabbed the bridle bits of the wagon team horses. As the Santee jerked the horses' heads around, John Eastlick and three others blasted shot at him. The Santee chief fell heavily onto the sod, instantly dead.

The Santee reloaded after their first volley while Jim Rhodes and Henry Smith sprinted down the road, deserting their friends. Three Santee tried to catch them but were driven off by rifle fire from the two whites. Rhodes and Smith got away without a scratch. Sophia Smith was left behind.

The settlers desperately charged into the slough grass, but they couldn't elude their pursuers. The Santee rained bullets at them. Lavina Eastlick took an early shot in the heel. Nor were her children spared. Little Juliana Ireland was hit in the leg, eight-year-old Emma Duley took a bullet through the arm, and her brother Willie's shoulder was shot to pieces.

The long grass only hid the little band from sight. It didn't protect them from the heavy balls and bullets fired at every movement in the grass. For hours the Santee blasted shot into the vegetation.

John Eastlick was the best marksman with the best gun, but his rifle kept misfiring, and he spent a frantic hour trying to fix it.

The others kept shouting, "Shoot, John, there's one, shoot, you can git 'im."

But John couldn't. His rifle wouldn't work. The women huddled apart from each other with their children. The men tried to spread out to fight back.

Will Duley shouted to whoever could hear him, "Don't waste shot. Squeeze the trigger carefully! Make every shot count."

"Will," John answered, "there's gotta be 'bout 200 of the savages out there. We've got what, six-eight men left? It's gonna take a lotta squeezin'."

"We die either way," Tom Ireland called to them. "Let's fight!"

The day was hot and sticky, but in the far west a bank of dark clouds rose ominously and a low rumble echoed from the western horizon. A storm was coming at them across the prairie, but it wasn't here yet. For now, they had to contend with the hail of bullets picking off the members of the scattered party.

Lavina tried to move away from her children, thinking they might be safer.

"Mommy, I wanna stay by you. We'll be safer by you," little Freddy begged.

Groans and shrieks of pain mixed with the sounds of shot while a hail of bullets snapped through the vegetation, as if the scythe of the grim reaper were sweeping through the slough. Occasionally a thud indicated that a bullet had found a target.

Almira Everett screamed, "Lavina, my neck, my neck! It's bleedin'!"

An instant later Lavina felt a hard blow to her side. She reached down and held her hand tight on her abdomen as blood oozed between her fingers.

"John, John!" she cried, "I'm hit!"

"How bad?" he asked with trepidation.

"John, I . . . I think it'll kill me." Lavina paused to muster strength to continue. "Stay where ya are. You can do more good with yer rifle."

Gritting her teeth against the pain, she longed desperately for the comforting arms of her spouse. Yet Lavina forced herself to discourage

John from seeking her. "If'n ya move ta come ta me, they'll see ya and kill ya, too."

Lavina looked in the direction where she supposed her husband to be. Another blow slammed her head hard to the ground as though she'd been kicked by a horse. Groggily, she probed her injuries. Her fingers discovered a ball lodged between her skull and her scalp.

She had barely made this discovery when John called out, "Lavina, I think they're on to where I'm hidin'! I've gotta move. I'm loaded and ready ta shoot."

Then Lavina heard the telltale thud. "John!" she said urgently, "are ya all right? Are ya hurt, John?" The only answer was two faint, heart-wrenching groans.

"Hold on, John, I'm comin'."

"No, Lavina!" Mariah Koch warned. "It's too late for 'im. You can't do no good."

"He's hurt, Mariah! I've gotta git to 'im."

"For God's sake, Lavina. Think! If ya stir from this spot, you and yer children will all be kilt. John's dead already. You can't do nothin' fer 'im. I beg ya. Stay here with yer children."

"Y're right, Mariah, I'll stay. My children are all I got left."

The firing stopped, but the rumble of the distant storm clouds grew louder. Pawn and two others rose from the grass and walked toward the slough.

The old Indian cried out, "Women, bring your children and come out. No harm will come to you. We fight only men!"

"Then why are dead women and children all around me?" Everett shouted.

"Will Everett, I know the sound of your voice," Pawn responded. "Come out of the slough. We will not hurt ya."

"I can't, Pawn, I'm shot. Why don't you come ta me?"

"You lie. You can walk if you want to." The other two Indians opened fire in the direction of Will's voice. One bullet shattered his elbow.

Tom Ireland stood in the grass and pleaded, "Kill us men if ya want. But not the women and children. Let 'em live. They done nothin' to ya."

Two Santee galloped to Ireland. Without speaking, they raised their rifles and fired point-blank into his body.

Tom stumbled to the soggy earth and groaned, "Oh, God, I'm kilt."

Seven shots had hit him. Two passed through his left lung, one through his left arm and the rest lodged in his body.

Will Everett held tightly to his arm and grimaced with pain as he spoke to his wife through clenched teeth. "Almira, tell 'em I'm dead, that all the men are dead. It's our only chance."

Almira Everett rose like a ghost from the swampy ground. "Pawn, you kilt my man. All the men be dead. What do ya want?"

"You must all come out. We will hurt no one more, but I want you and Julia Wright for my squaws. Come now."

Will Everett whispered to his wife, "Look, if we stay here, they'll kill us all fer sure. You got a chance, go with 'em, obey 'em, then look fer a chance to get away. Either you escape or the army'll find you and get ya back. There ain't no other choice."

"Lavina," Almira asked, "do ya want ta come with me?"

"No," she answered, "not yet. Take Julia. She speaks Sioux."

Almira and Julia walked with trepidation to Pawn.

"How many are left?" their supposed protector asked.

"I don't know," Julia said. "The men're all dead."

"Tell the rest to come out of the grass. They will not be harmed. Then I want you to gather up the men's guns and bring them to us."

"Why don't ya get them yerself," Almira countered.

"No, someone might still shoot. You get them."

The two women returned to the slough as the three Indians waited back on a small rise. Julia approached Lavina. Sophia Smith and Laura Duley joined them as their children huddled nearby.

"They say come out. They say they won't hurt us," Julia said.

24

Will Duley crawled toward them, leaving a crimson trail of blood in the dry grass. "Go with them," he urged. "If you don't, they'll start shootin' again. Then everyone's gonna die. We'll get ya all back. I promise ya."

Laura bent over to stroke her husband's hair, her hands lingering on the contours of his cheeks. As they exchanged a kiss in the privacy of the tall grass, tears welled in her eyes. Then she stood, squared her shoulders, gathered her children and began walking toward Pawn.

"Come," Almira yelled, "all you women and children. We'll be safe if we go to Pawn."

Scattered all through the slough, the dispirited and bloody survivors stood and slowly struggled their way out in a state of shock. Many could walk only with the support of another. Lavina limped heavily, wounded in the side and the head, a musket ball in her heel. She turned and staggered away from Pawn.

"Where're ya goin'?" Sophie Ireland asked in a state of half-panic.

"I've got ta see my husband one more time. Children, stay with Mrs. Ireland."

Lavina hobbled to where she had last heard John. She found him there, lying on his side, one hand across his face, the other holding his rifle with a death grip. She knelt by his side. No blood showed. Alone with him in the grass, surrounded by murderers and her dead and dying friends, Lavina tenderly said good-bye to John.

Lifting her husband's stiffened hand from his head, she clenched it, brought it to her lips and kissed it gently. She lovingly caressed his brow, his cheeks, his lips. "Rest in peace, my love. We had twelve blessed years. Ya gave yer life for yer family. Good-bye, my dear husband, good-bye."

She stumbled back to her children. From there, Frank and Giles helped her walk to the others who were gathering on the rise with Pawn. Merton carried little Johnny.

"I cain't do much," she told her oldest boy. "It's up ta you ta take care of Johnny."

She walked between the two boys and eased the weight off her foot by placing her hands on their little shoulders. They were almost out of the long grass when they came upon Tom Ireland. Bloody froth oozed from a hole in his chest.

Sophie Ireland fell to her hands and knees. As she struggled to speak, Tom's words came in a hoarse whisper first. "Good-bye, Sophie, I love ya. Tell the little ones."

Tears stained the dirty faces of five-year-old Sarah and three-year-old Juliana, who cowered nearby.

Julia Wright reentered the slough as the Eastlicks and Irelands emerged from it. Passing near Lavina, she told them, "Pawn sent me back fer the guns."

Julia came upon Tom Ireland first and picked up his rifle. He was near death.

"Shoot me. I can't stand the pain," Tom begged, blood dripping from the corner of his mouth.

"I would if'n I could." She choked out the words of apology. "But I cain't pull the trigger on a friend. Not even to end his sufferin'. Please forgive me."

Julia then continued on through the grass, picking up guns from the dead. In doing so, she encountered several other victims alive and in better condition than Tom Ireland. Will Everett, Ed Bentley, Charlie Hatch, John Rose, and Will Duley were all wounded but alive.

Duley handed a rifle to Julia. "Take this, but I'm keepin' my other gun. Same wi' the other men. If'n they have an extra gun, take it. But we gotta be able to defend ourselves if we need ta. Take from the dead. And, Julia, tell my wife again, we'll find a way ta rescue you."

Julia struggled from the grass with a heavy stack of rifles that she dropped at Pawn's feet. Three more Santee had joined Pawn, and they stood over the bloodied and forsaken lot that huddled on the ground before them.

Sophia Smith was shot through the hip and nearly immobile. Almira Everett held her hand to her neck; the right side of her clothes had become drenched in red before the bleeding subsided. Tiny Juliana Ireland, shot in the lower stomach, was pale and whimpering softly. The little girl's face was blotchy, and froth ran from her lips. Death was near.

A bolt of sharp lightning split the sky as thunder cracked overhead. The heavens released rain in torrents. Several more Indians appeared and caught their horses to leave for shelter.

"They'll take us all now," Lavina whispered to Laura Duley.

Indeed one warrior already had Mariah, and another took up the other little Ireland girl to ride with him.

Before Laura could comment, a young warrior strode between the two women, grabbed their hands and roughly pulled them along.

Lavina jerked her hand free and turned back to her children. "Follow me," she shouted over the thunder of the storm.

Little Freddy rose at her command. As he did so, an old Indian woman, her face lit with rage, clubbed the boy from behind. She struck Freddy several more times over the head with her heavy club. Blood running from his nose, mouth and ears, the boy struggled to his feet only to have the old hag grab him by his clothing, raise him over her head and fling him hard onto the prairie sod. She then raised a knife high and thrust it into his chest.

Lavina tried to rush to her son's aid, but her Indian captor grabbed her from behind in a viselike grip. She struggled, twisted and screamed to no avail. The Indian dragged her away through rain and mud, but Lavina's eyes stayed riveted on the horrific scene behind her.

"Mother, Mother!" ten-year-old Frank cried in agony as he, too, was attacked. The boy was already on his knees, blood streaming from his mouth where four teeth had been shot out. Blood poured from his stomach and leg. It was too much. He crumpled face first onto the muddy sod.

Lavina was paralyzed by the murder of her sons and was oblivious to what befell the others. More Indian women fell upon the settler women and children with knives and clubs.

Almira Everett broke away and ran back toward the slough where her husband lay wounded. A young brave raced to catch her and, just as he closed in, a shot blasted from behind. Almira tumbled to the earth, mortally wounded by a bullet in her back.

Laura Duley stood numbly in the midst of the mayhem. Her wet hair hung limply to her shoulders as rain mixed with tears spilling down her face. She cradled her two-year-old in her arms. Jefferson, six, plastered himself to his mother and gripped her dress as his older brother, Willie, ran to join them. Two bullets ripped into Willie, and he rolled to a stop at their feet.

Shock and terror fixed on Laura's face as she turned to Pawn. "Please," she pleaded desperately, "Don't kill us. Please, don't murder my babies!"

"Stay near me," Pawn replied evenly. "You will not be harmed more."

Lavina shouted at the chief, "What about me? Are you gonna kill me?"

"No," Pawn replied as he leaned upon his rifle. "Go, hurry on!"

Suspicious, Lavina hesitated. She watched as Julia Wright, Laura Duley and their surviving children were led away. Other prisoners were fast disappearing like specters through the sheets of rain. She wondered if any of the men were still alive.

Lavina started back toward the slough. Fear had driven away the pain, and she limped along at a rapid pace. She glanced over her shoulder and saw that Pawn was reloading his rifle. Cold terror swept over Lavina as she struggled over a small slough and onto a trail. Then a bullet thudded into her back on the left side. It exited her body on the right just above the hip and went through her right arm between elbow and wrist.

Lavina crumpled face first onto the trail. Afraid of being trampled by galloping horses, she frantically pulled her mangled body off the side of the roadway. In minutes she heard steps approaching and held her breath, praying her assailant would presume her dead and pass by.

The Indian stood over Lavina and watched her intently. Then, just as the thunder rolled again, he raised his rifle and beat the woman on the head several times with the butt of his weapon.

Lavina's head bounced off the sod with each stroke as she desperately tried to hold her breath feigning death. It was no use. The muddy sod and grass so suffocated her that several times she had to gulp air. Supposing she was in her death throes, the man left her muddy and bloody in the swampy grass. As blackness swept over her, the last Lavina heard was Merton's voice calling for his mother.

❧ 5 ❧

Lavina awoke late in the afternoon. The rain still washed over her as she struggled back to consciousness. She had been lying face first with her hand under her forehead. Her fingers were congealed with dried blood. The head wound, which had bled freely, had been washed clean by the torrential rain.

As she struggled to free her mind from a labyrinth of terror, heart-wrenching memories floated back to Lavina. Her last memory was of a child's voice crying for his mother. Was it Johnny? What had happened to Merton? Were they with the wounded men still in the slough?

The woman pushed herself up onto her knees and then slowly and painfully struggled to her feet. Gingerly she touched her fingers to her head. Strangely, pain was minimal there, but as Lavina turned her head from side to side, a grating sound indicated a fractured skull.

"How could I have lived through this?" she mumbled. "My hair, my long, thick hair, it musta blunted the force of the blow." She remembered more. "I gotta find my children."

With great effort Lavina took a step. As she dragged her other foot forward, her whole body throbbed with pain. The next step was difficult, but easier than the first. Lurching forward, still in misery with each stride, Lavina moved into the tall grass around the slough. After a few steps she heard, "Mother, Mother."

Parting the high stalks of grass, she saw young Willie Duley, grievously wounded. He cried plaintively, "Mrs. Smith?"

Lavina was sickened but knew she could do nothing to help him. She forced herself to press on without speaking to the boy. The cries of another child spurred the woman on in hopes of finding Johnny. But it wasn't her boy that she came upon. Two-year-old Charlie Everett lay dying in the rain. His six-year-old sister, Lilly, leaned over him as she tried to shield him from the storm.

"Lilly," Lavina called softly.

Startled, the girl snapped her head around. "Mrs. Eastlick, the Indians ain't kilt us yet?"

"No, Lilly, but there ain't many of us left."

"Mrs. Eastlick, will you take care of Charlie?"

"I can't. My Johnny is out here somewhere. He'll die unless I can find him and keep him warm."

Crestfallen, Lilly pleaded, "Will you give me a drink of water?"

"Lilly, it's not even in my power to do that fer ya. Look at me. There's nothing I can do fer ya. I'm sorry."

Lilly raised her eyes to Lavina. "Will there be water in heaven?"

"When ya git ta heaven, you'll never suffer from thirst or pain."

Lavina turned and stumbled on into the growing darkness. She found the bodies of Sophia Smith and Sophia Ireland. Three-year-old Juliana Ireland lay upon her mother's breast, life slowly ebbing away.

Sadness overwhelmed Lavina when she found Giles. Her little boy was on his back, shot in the chest. It seemed like a small smile played at his cold lips.

"An angel must be with him," Lavina sobbed.

She left Giles and dragged herself to the sound of heavy breathing. In the darkness she found the body of a child lying face down. When Lavina turned him over, to her anguished horror she realized it was Freddy. The rattling sound in his throat told her that the end was near.

"Why didn't I find 'im dead?" she despaired. "Why don't I just fall down and die with 'im?"

Then she answered her own question. "No, there still be somethin' ta live fer. Merton and Johnny might still live, hidin'. They'll be hungry, cold and fearin' Indians or wolves. I gotta find 'em."

There was more hard breathing nearby. It was Almira Everett, shot through the lungs. The telltale rattling, gurgling sound told Lavina that there was nothing to be done for her.

Still, Lavina asked, "Almira, Almira, can ya hear me?" But Almira was beyond hearing.

* * *

WHILE LAVINA HAD BEEN UNCONSCIOUS and presumed dead, the surviving men gathered after the Santee had left. Rhodes, Smith, and now Duley had already made their escape. Tom Ireland, barely clinging to life, crawled out of the slough grass. Charlie Hatch and Ed Bentley supported the crippled Will Everett between them.

"I think they're all dead, dyin' or the Indians took 'em," Charlie assessed. "Let's see if we can get ta New Ulm."

The three men started east. Lavina Eastlick wandered the prairie through the cold, driving rain, calling for Merton and Johnny. When morning came, the rain stopped, and she crawled into weeds to hide in case Indians returned. Come back they did.

Shots and screams echoed through the bright sunlight. The Santee braves were finishing off what they had started the day before. Lavina squinted her eyes tightly shut and clamped her hands hard over her ears. Even though it made her right arm throb, it was less painful than enduring the children's agonized screams.

Of the thirty-four who left Shetek, thirteen lay dead in the grass around the slough. Eleven were captured and taken away by the Santee, and ten managed to escape the killing field. John Voight lay dead at the Hurd cabin. Andrew Koch was face down in the mud of his barnyard.

Lavina, failing to find Merton and Johnny, knew that her only hope was to get to New Ulm. She turned east and started the long journey.

❧ 6 ❧

ON THE MORNING OF AUGUST 21, a sodden band of Santee guided a forlorn little cluster of captives across the rolling prairie of southwestern Minnesota. Their destination was Lake Shakotan, near the Dakota border and the village of White Lodge.

Julia Wright and Laura Duley walked trancelike, their eyes staring unseeing into the distance, like sleep walkers. Their dresses were ripped and bloody. Their shoes had been taken, and they now walked in old worn moccasins.

Laura held her baby Frances to her breast. Emma, eight, and Jefferson Duley, six, trudged behind their mother. Eldora, five, and George Wright, four, clung to their mother's dress on either side.

Three other children had no parent to hold onto. They had trouble keeping up and were tossed into a travois, a conveyance consisting of two long lodge poles pulled by a pony. One end was attached to the animal by leather thongs. The other end, which dragged in the dirt, was connected by hides that stretched from pole to pole, making a platform. Camp belongings were piled on top and pulled like a sled by the pony. Rose Ann Ireland, eight, her little sister Nelly, six, and Lilly Everett, also six, rode on the travois. When the Santee had returned to the slough,

34

they'd found Lilly near her brother's body. Her life spared, she was now a prisoner.

"Mrs. Wright," Lilly whimpered, "we're hungry. Is there any food, please?"

"Did you see our Pa?" Rose Ann cried. "We din't see him when they took us."

"What about our sisters, Sarah and Julianne?" Nelly cried.

"Girls," Julia looked at them over her shoulder, "we can't do nothin'. We're prisoners. Pray, it's all that's left for us ta do."

"I could hardly watch 'em last night, out there dancin' in the rain and screamin' like demons," Laura whispered to Julia.

"At least we were outa the rain, in Ireland's cabin." Julia paused, a pained look carved into her face. "I saw Sophia dead, Tommy was hurt bad. I guess he's gone, too."

Tears welled in Laura's eyes. "So many are dead, my children, Willie, Belle, so many others. Why? We didn't do nothin' to 'em. Why?"

"I heard 'em talkin', Laura. There's killin' all over. Up and down the Minnesota Valley. We took their land. We din't pay for it, and they want it back."

"But, Julia, they're killin' women and children."

"I guess it don't make no difference to them. White is white. I heard one say they would rub us out like we weren't ever there. Remember, some of us mebbe made it. Your husband, Will, I saw him when they sent me ta get guns. He said people would come fer us. They will, I know they will."

"You speak Sioux, don't you?"

"I picked it up over the years. It'll help us, I think."

"Julia, they'll take us, you know. We'll become squaws and the children will be adopted by the Sioux."

"Laura, if we want ta live, we have ta do what they want. We're all the children have."

"Where are we goin'?"

Tiredly, Julia breathed, "Wherever they take us."

35

Two old leaders, White Lodge and Pawn, rode in the front as the procession headed west. Pawn turned to White Lodge. "It was a bad thing we did. But blood was hot and now there is no turning back."

"This is the last chance for the people," White Lodge replied. "Riders from Redwood told us what happened at the Lower Agency. Once the four young men killed whites at Acton, our path was set. The whites would not settle with just punishing the four. All Santee would have to pay.

"It was right that the agency was attacked and the soldiers killed at the ferry. The whites fight each other way off. The time will never be better for us," White Lodge concluded.

"Why don't Red Iron and Little Paul lead us?" asked Pawn

"They are old women!" White Lodge snapped. "They hold some of the Sisseton back. They want to farm and pray to the white man's god. They don't understand that our people must fight to survive. The whites are taking our way of life from us."

Pawn frowned. "Some of them signed the white man's paper that took our land."

"We lost our land to more than paper," White Lodge countered. "The whites bribed our leaders and made us sick with devil water."

"And our chiefs were greedy," Pawn continued, "but the Mdewakantons said kill all. We killed many. The whites will never let this go. We killed women and children."

"It happened throughout the valley. If we are to survive, all whites must die or be driven away. Our children were starving and dying while the warehouses were filled with food that the agent would not give us. Our women sickened and died. They took from us everything that let us care for our people. They murdered first. We only responded in kind. We fight to survive."

Pawn hesitated, then said thoughtfully, "What do we do? What about the captives we have taken?"

"The soldiers will come, Pawn, and their vengeance will be hot like the burning coals of a fire. They will try to rub us out. The white women and children will be our shield. I will take the one who speaks Santee. She will be my squaw. We go to the setting sun. To the land of the Teton. We will join them and be safe. Let Little Crow and the Mdewakantons fight in the valley. We must keep moving."

7

ieutenant Jesse Buchanen and the militia from St. Paul caught up with Sibley's force on the Minnesota River town of St. Peter. Jesse was with his future father-in-law when the colonel met Sibley in a dingy hotel barroom. A black-haired, dark-complexioned man rose from a table with Sibley as the others entered the room.

"Good to see you, Stephen!" Sibley exclaimed. He was tall with straight black hair retreating slightly across his forehead. His mustache drooped at the ends above a patch of whiskers that sprouted below his lower lip.

Sibley makes a commanding impression, Jesse thought. *Indians respect him*. Sibley had been governor of the state and knew the language and customs of the Sioux. Jesse worried, though, about his lack of military experience. *But leading men is what it's all about. Sibley can do that all right.*

"This is Lieutenant Jesse Buchanen," Miller acknowledged, and then, with a crook of his lips, "my future son-in-law."

Sibley brightened. "Lucky man! I met JoAnna. This," he pointed to the dark man at his side, "is Jack Frazer. He got through from Fort Ridgely. Jack's the main reason we slowed down and waited for you before marching into Ridgely. Tell them what you told me, Jack."

"In the first coupla days after the fightin' at the agency and ferry, the Indians swarmed like yellow jackets on both sides o' the river. I bet they kilt near fifty in Milford Township outta New Ulm. They coulda took the fort that first day, but they tried New Ulm instead. After that din't work, they tried the fort on the twentieth. By then some reinforcements with Sheehan and Galbraith had got there, and they beat the red devils back."

"How many men are in the fort?" Miller asked.

Frazer looked pensive for a moment. "Hard tellin', maybe a little over a hundred soldiers all tole. There was a lot more Sioux, I'll tell ya that. They really hit 'em hard on the twenty-second. But the big guns, the cannons, drove 'em back. They's real scart of them cannons. Now the scairt soldiers at Ridgely are just hangin' on, waitin' fer ya."

"Why did you wait, Colonel?" Miller asked Sibley.

"There are maybe a thousand Sioux warriors within miles of us. It seemed prudent to wait for more supplies and the reinforcements that you brought. Now we will move to Ridgely. Tomorrow, we'll advance. Colonel McPhail will lead with his cavalry. They should be able to relieve the fort by the twenty-seventh."

Jesse looked beseechingly at Miller, and the colonel understood. "Colonel Sibley, Lieutenant Buchanen leads a troop of cavalry. Do you mind if he accompanies McPhail."

"We can never get enough good cavalry. Shortage of horses, you know. Seems Lincoln wants them all."

Two days later, to huzzahs and cheers from 150 defenders and over three hundred civilian refugees, Jesse accompanied McPhail's cavalry into the wall-less fort.

Jesse gazed at the wooden and stone buildings that made up the perimeter of Ridgely and the barriers with earthworks dug for protection between them. Wagons were tipped on their sides and along with barrels and logs filled the gaps between the buildings.

"Captain Northrup," he called to an officer from Minneapolis riding next to him, "how do you suppose they managed to hold this place against overwhelming numbers?"

"Cannons, my boy, look around." Northrup pointed to each of the corners of the fort where cannons pointed outward. "I'm told they only had one regular army man here, the rest was just green recruits. But Sergeant Jones, he drilled 'em to shoot cannons. It paid off. We got lucky."

"There would have been hell to pay if the fort had fallen," Jesse agreed.

"The whole valley to St. Paul would have been open to 'em, Lieutenant. They'd be knockin' on the gates of Fort Snelling by now."

"I hope we move out after the Sioux soon," Jesse offered. "This needs to end quickly."

"I've been around Sibley for a while," Northrup answered. "I worked for him with the American Fur Company. He's a good man, but he takes his time. The colonel wants to make sure that things are right before he acts. We'll go after the Sioux, all right. But not tomorrow. The time will have to be right."

"Captain, I sure hope that those still being killed and taken captive will understand that. I think they're in a hurry."

"Time will tell, Lieutenant, time will tell."

JoAnna read the newspaper accounts of both the Civil War and the Dakota war with rapt attention. Stories of the battles in Virginia horrified and fascinated her. There were reports that Lee would attempt to invade the North, maybe move through Maryland.

But it was news from the Minnesota frontier that consumed most of JoAnna's interest, though good information on that front was harder to come by. There had been stories about the massacre at Lake Shetek and the attacks on Fort Ridgely and New Ulm, though.

Individual horror stories had been recounted by survivors and printed in the paper. What she read frightened her. Fears for Jesse and her father's safety chilled JoAnna like a blast of cold night air.

"God protect them," she prayed silently. "Soon I'll be able to join them. I just know it'll be safe soon."

$\mathcal{so}$ 8 $\mathcal{os}$

ittle Crow's bands left the ruins of the Lower Agency on the Redwood River and retreated upriver toward the Upper Agency. Their hostages included 107 whites and 162 mixed-blood. Half-naked, clothing shredded, and many with cuts on their feet, they trudged in a five-mile-long convoy of wagons, buggies, and carts. The Santee were weighed down with tents, clothing, pots, pans, and loot from white cabins. The hostages, only four men among them, shuffled listlessly along the dusty path. The sun's rays seared them with relentless choking heat.

Sarah Wakefield stumbled as she looked for her two young children. She wiped the sweat from her eyes, reassured that they were just behind her. "Lisa, James, keep up. Don't lag behind," she told them.

"When will we see Father?" five-year-old James asked plaintively. He had asked this many, many times.

"Is he dead, Mommy?" little Lisa asked for what seemed like the hundredth time.

"No, dears, I don't think he's dead. I've heard Chaska and others talk. John Other Day saved many lives at the agency. I believe your father was with them. Besides, he was a doctor, good to the Indians. The Indians knew that. They had no reason to kill him."

"They had no reason to kill Mr. Gleason, either. But they did," James answered.

The memory swept over Sarah again. With the news of killings at the Lower Agency, her husband, questioning the veracity of the report but fearing the worst, had sent his wife and children to safety with Assistant Agent George Gleason. They didn't get far. Two Santee, Hapa and Chaska, had stopped their wagon on the road to Fort Ridgely. Hapa had killed Gleason and turned his rifle on Sarah.

Chaska had stopped him. His words still echoed in her head. "No," Chaska had said. "I am going to take care of them. You must kill me before you kill any of them."

Tears welled in Sarah's eyes as thoughts of the past weeks plagued her. Was her husband safe? What of her friends and neighbors? She knew many were dead and thanked God for the refuge provided by Chaska and his mother.

They were walking back along the very trail where she and her children had been captured. Just ahead George Gleason had been killed. Sarah spied his decomposing body and tried to press her eyes shut, but she had already seen too much. Gleason had been stripped of his clothing, save underwear. His head had been crushed by a rock.

"Don't look!" Sarah commanded her children as she turned their heads away from the grisly sight.

Susan Brown, mixed-blood wife of former Indian Agent Joe Brown, picked up Lisa and held her face against her shoulder.

"She saw him killed. Once was enough," Susan said, tears flowing.

"Thank you," Sarah replied. "You're related to Little Crow. He talks to you. Have you heard anything?"

"Rumors, Sarah. Only rumors. Some want to kill us all when we get to Yellow Medicine. But Little Crow won't let that happen."

"But can he stop them?" Sarah said with alarm. "His men listen to him only when they agree with him. I've heard Little Crow tell his men to fight like the soldiers do and not kill women and children. But that doesn't stop them."

"The Santee need us. If the captives are killed, all Santee will be hunted down. The prairie will not be big enough to hide them. We will be used to keep the Santee safe."

The women and their children struggled forward under the weight of fatigue and the sun that scorched them mercilessly.

Sarah wiped more sweat from her brow, leaving a white streak through her dust-coated forehead. Her long brown hair hung dirty and limp at her shoulders.

"Susan, it's not true, you know. What they say. It isn't true."

"What, Sarah, what do you mean?"

"I know what the other captives think. They think I'm Chaska's woman. That I've betrayed them. But it isn't so. Chaska saved our lives when Hapa killed Gleason. That night Hapa was drunk. He came into Chaska's family's lodge and was going to take me. Chaska stood up to him and said that he had lost his wife and was taking me. He laid down next to me on the robes so that Hapa would believe him. When Hapa left, Chaska got up. He never touched me. We decided to let the ruse continue so that other Indian men would leave me alone. Now we are like a part of Chaska's family. His mother watches over us. But I'm not his woman, and I will never be."

Susan shook her head sadly. "Do what is right to keep your family safe. My relationship with Little Crow keeps me safe."

A band of six Santee trotted on horseback past the women and children. They were adorned in clothing looted from the whites. Some wore feather bonnets, two had gold watches tied to their ankles, another a crepe shawl around his head. Brightly colored pigments were smeared upon their faces.

In spite of all the tragedy she'd faced, Sarah smiled. "Look at the poor creatures, Susan. They don't even know that they're wearing women's clothing. They look more like a troop of monkeys than anything human."

The five-mile procession wound over the baked earth throughout the day and most of the next. Cattle bawled, children cried, and dogs barked as the pitiful whites stumbled and supported each other on the trail. It was the afternoon of August 27 when they arrived at the Upper Agency near the confluence of the Minnesota and Yellow Medicine rivers.

News of the attack on the Redwood Agency had reached the Upper Agency, or Yellow Medicine as many called it, by 8:00 a.m. on August 18. By noon they knew that Captain Marsh and nearly half his command had been killed at Redwood Ferry. While the Yellow Medicine Santee debated whether or not to join in the war, many of the agency whites deserted Yellow Medicine or sought safety in the large brick warehouse there. On the morning of August 19, as the traders' stores burned in the valley below, a Sisseton named John Other Day led sixty-two whites to safety across the prairie.

Other Day had addressed the nearly 100 Sisseton and Wahpeton as they struggled with their decision on joining the war. He warned them, "You might easily enough kill a few whites—five, ten, or a hundred. But the consequence will be that our whole country will be filled with soldiers of the United States, and we will be killed or driven away. Some of you might say you have horses and may escape to the plains, but what will become of those who have no horses?"

No clear-cut decision was reached on joining Little Crow. While some rode off to attack Fort Ridgely with him, others attacked the outer buildings surrounding the Upper Agency. Still others refused to take part.

The latter, called "friendlies," then took up residence in the agency buildings after the whites had escaped. It was there, in Dr. Wakefield's house, that Little Crow sought Little Paul Mazakutemani, a Christian Indian and Speaker of the Upper Sioux.

"These houses must be burned," Little Crow insisted when he reached Yellow Medicine. "The soldiers will come and get into them if they are not burned. Get out. If you do not, we will burn you with the buildings. We are building a new camp to the north over the creek. Join us there," Little Crow commanded.

As the "farmer" Indians, who had remained friendly to the whites, packed and moved north, Little Crow's warriors put the torch to the agency buildings.

45

Little Paul rode with Akepa on the agency trail. Buildings flamed on either side, and their horses skittered in fear. On the edge of the compound huddled the hostage captives. Women and children stared at the two Santee leaders with blank despair in their eyes. Many were barefoot and bareheaded in the hot sun and were still wearing the clothing that hung in bloody shreds from their backs. Blood oozed from cuts on their legs and feet where the tough prairie grass had sliced.

Akepa shook his head. "If these prisoners were only men instead of women and children, it would be all right, but it is hard that this terrible suffering should be brought upon women and children."

"My heart is sad," Little Paul replied. "I am almost sick. We must do something to save these people."

The Yellow Medicine Santee placed their camp apart from their Redwood brothers. Little Crow sent warriors galloping before Little Paul's lodge to demand that they come to a council with the Lower Sioux band.

Little Paul, Iron Walker, Akepa, Red Iron, and Simon Anawangmani crossed the creek to Little Crow's village. Little Crow strode from his tipi to meet them. "Join us in a circle." He pointed to where Cut Nose, Red Middle Voice, Medicine Bottle, Shakopee, and Mah-ka-tah were sitting in a semicircle. The Yellow Medicine leaders completed the circle.

Little Crow raised a pipe to the heavens. Then he handed it to Cut Nose to smoke and pass on. Little Crow looked haggard. His black hair, streaked with white, hung straggly at his shoulders. Lines seamed his face more deeply than they had just weeks before.

"We have come here because it is not safe near the Redwood. The Long Trader, Sibley, has reached Fort Ridgely. Soon he will move on us. We must be ready, and you must join us. Only 400 Sisseton and Wahpeton attacked the fort with us. We need you. You must decide if you are Indian or white."

Mah-ka-tah glared at the Yellow Medicine leaders. "A Soldiers' Lodge is formed. The young men are fighting and dying while you live here in the white man's houses, safe and well-fed. Join us or we will destroy your lodges."

Akepa shot back, "You started this war. Now you come to our land without being asked. We would rather fight you and die on this spot than follow crazy people in a war that cannot be won."

"Cowards!" Cut Nose shouted, his one nostril flaring. The other was deformed, bitten off in a fight years before. "Sibley is coming. We must join together now. We must kill the captives. They slow us down."

Iron Walker leaped to his feet. "You should be fighting only the men! Let the women and children go back to their people. This is what we ask."

"No," Red Middle Voice countered. The four Acton murderers were members of his Rice Creek band. "We know that the soldiers are strong and that they will drive us from the valley. But let the captives suffer or die with us."

"Let us kill all the American settlers and then make friends with the British to the north. Maybe they will help us," Shakopee suggested.

Anger grew in Red Iron as he listened carefully. He faced the Redwood Santee and spoke slowly but resolutely. "Brothers, it is good you are camped here between the villages of Christian chiefs. There is danger for you to the north. When the whites come for you, if you try to escape across the lands of the Upper Agency with these captives, the northern Dakota will kill you. Go west or south, do not look north for safety or support. Do not look to us."

Mah-ka-tah's eyes flashed hatred. "Cut Nose is right. You are cowardly women. We will fight you when we have finished with the whites!"

Little Paul stood and stretched to his full height of five-foot-four. While small of stature, the Yellow Medicine chief stood tall among the others. His eloquence was well known among the Santee. He brushed his uneven cut hair and looked defiantly at Little Crow.

"I want to speak to you now of what is in my own heart. Give me all these white captives. I will deliver them up to their friends. You

47

Dakotas are numerous. You can afford to give these captives to me. I will go with them to the white people. Then, if you want to fight, when you see the white soldiers coming to fight, fight with them, but don't fight with women and children. Or stop fighting." He paused and looked at the faces around him.

"The Americans are a powerful people," he said. "They have much lead, powder, guns, and provisions. Stop fighting, and now gather up all the captives and give them to me. No one who fights with the white people ever becomes rich or remains two days in one place, but is always fleeing and starving. You have said that whoever talks in this way shall not live—that you will kill him. Stop talking in that way, and if anyone says what is good, listen to it."

Mah-ka-tah jumped erect. "If we are to die, these captives shall die with us. The braves will not give up these captives. We are men, and will fight the whites as long as we live."

Little Crow stared daggers at Little Paul. "We shall die bravely, and though the captives die along the way, I don't care. Don't mention the captives anymore."

Amid catcalls and insults, the Yellow Medicine Santee stood and mounted their horses to leave. As they slowly rode from the Redwood Santee's camp, Little Paul spoke firmly, yet softly to Akepa. "Call together the Sisseton and Wahpeton. Send word to Standing Buffalo. We must prepare to defend ourselves. Little Crow is a greater danger than the whites."

Akepa considered Little Paul's words, then replied, "They want us to join them in their war. We must not. It would be death to us. We must drive the Redwood braves off our land. It is better to die in battle than become slaves, even of our own people."

The call was spread to the surrounding villages of the Upper Santee. Hundreds of braves streamed into Little Paul's village. They painted themselves, prepared their weapons and erected a large tipi near the center of the camp. It was a Soldiers' Lodge dwelling built in opposition to the Redwood Soldiers' Lodge of Mah-ka-tah. If necessary, they would fight their brothers to defend their land.

The next morning, August 29, three hundred Redwood Santee thundered into the Yellow Medicine camp. They hurled insults, chanted, and fired their guns into the air. But they refused to attack the Soldiers' Lodge built in the camp's center.

Red Middle Voice wrenched his horse's neck and jerked the animal to a halt before the lodge. He called out, "Mah-ka-tah, let us attack these cowards now and burn this village."

"No, it is not the right time or place. There is still time for them to think like us. But not if we kill them. We must return across the creek."

As the Lower Santee retreated, hundreds of Yellow Medicine braves followed the Redwood warriors back to Little Crow's village. They stormed into the camp, galloping among the tipis, firing their rifles into the air and screaming at the Lower Santee.

Little Paul led his men in a race around the Redwood Soldiers' Lodge. A cloud of dust raised by horse hooves billowed into the air. Little Paul leaped from his horse and and stood before Little Crow.

"You took wagons and horses that belonged to Wahpeton and Sisseton. We come for them."

"Take what is your people's," Little Crow said resignedly. "I will not fight my brothers and the whites at the same time."

Little Paul turned to his warriors. "Form a line and face the Redwood band."

The two Indian factions stared at each other with hostility, their eyes boring with hatred like hot cinders from a stirred fire.

Little Paul strode between the two lines of Indians. Midway he stopped and turned back to his warriors. "Soldiers and young men of the Sisseton and Wahpeton! I told the Mdewakanton that they commenced war upon the whites without letting us know anything about it. Why should we assist them? We are under no obligation to do so. They have never interested themselves in our affairs. When we went to war against the Chippewa they never helped us. The Mdewakanton have made war upon the white people and have now fled up here. I have asked them

49

why they did this, but I do not yet understand it. I have asked them to do me a favor, but they have refused. Now I will ask them again in your hearing."

The small man straightened his body and drew back his shoulders. Standing erect, he turned to face Little Crow and his band of Santee. "Mdewakanton, you are fools. We want nothing to do with you. Why have you made war on the white people? The Americans have given us money, food, clothing, plows, powder, tobacco, guns, knives, and all things by which we might live well. They have nourished us even like a father his children. Why then have you made war upon them?

"I want to know from you whether you were asleep or crazy. In fighting the whites, you are fighting the thunder and lightning. You will all be killed. You might as well try to bail out the waters of the Mississippi as to whip them." He paused before beginnning again.

"You did not tell me you were going to fight with the white people, and how then should I approve it? No, I will go over to the white people. If they wish it, they may kill me. If they don't wish to kill me, I shall live. So, all of you who do not want to fight with the white people, come over to me. I have now have hundreds of men. We are going over to the white people. Deliver up to me the captives."

When no one moved, he said, "Your young men have brought a great misfortune upon us. Let them go and fight the soldiers. But you, who want to live and not die, come with me. I am going to shake hands with the whites. I hear some of your young men talking very loud, boasting that you have killed so many women and children. That's not brave; it is cowardly. Go and fight the soldiers. That's brave. You dare not.

"When you see their army coming on the plains, you will faint with fright. You will throw down your arms, and fly in one direction and your women in another, and this winter you will all starve. That is the wrong path. Go back from the lands of the Sisseton. They have not buffaloes enough for themselves and cannot feed you. Fight the whites on your reservation if you are not afraid of them. Make your boasts good and stop your lies!"

The faces of the Mdewakanton flushed red with rage. Loud cries of "Kill him," "Kill Little Paul!" rose from their ranks.

Little Paul was not deterred. "Some of you say you will kill me. Shout away. I am not afraid. I am not a woman, and I shall not die alone. There are 300 around me who you will also have to kill before you have finished. Now as many of you as don't wish to fight with the whites, gather yourselves together today and come to me."

A young brave walked directly from Little Crow's band to the Yellow Medicine warriors. Then more followed, a few bringing captives with them. They were not many in number, but to have any join Little Paul was a grave disappointment to Little Crow.

The Mdewakanton leader shook his head wearily. "You who join those friendly to the whites betray your people. I will not give up this war. We fight to reclaim the lands of our fathers. We were meant to live here, to roam the prairies as we will, to hunt in the woodlands."

Then Little Crow turned to those gathered around, and his voice rose. "Paul wants to make peace. It is impossible, even if we wanted to. The whites have hung us for minor things. Now we have been killing them by the hundreds in Dakota, Minnesota, and Iowa. If they get us into their power, they will hang every one of us. As for me, I will kill as many of them as I can and fight them till I die."

He faced Little Paul. "Do not think you will escape. There is not a band of Indians from the Redwood Agency to Big Stone Lake that has not had some of its members in this war. We must fight and perish together. A man is a fool and a coward who thinks otherwise and who will desert his nation at such a time.

"Don't disgrace yourselves by a surrender to those who will hang you up like dogs, but die with guns in your hands like warriors and braves of the Dakota."

Little Crow spread his arms wide. "Do you forget how the whites have cheated us. The treaty we signed said that we should be paid in gold and food for our land. They try to turn us into farmers, but when the crops fail and there is no food to harvest, the agents still will not give us food, even though the warehouses are full. They say they cannot because the gold has not come from Washington. They must pay food and gold together, they say. The traders who sit at the pay tables and read their accounts against us must be paid first they say."

The words began to burn like bitter gall in Little Crow's mouth. "But the traders keep the books. If we say they charge too much or that we did not put something on account, the agent believes the traders and we pay. When it is over, the traders get the money, and we get some food. But this year the only food we got was what we took by force from the agent here at Yellow Medicine."

He turned again to his adversary. "Little Paul, your people were starving, as well. It was the warriors from Redwood who came here and forced Agent Galbraith to release food. If they had not done that, you would still be waiting and starving."

Little Crow spoke matter of factly. An orator rivaled only by Little Paul among the Santee, but this time his voice showed little emotion. "It is likely that I will die in this war. But they will not take me alive. I will not be caged like an animal, and they will not place a rope around my neck."

For the first time his voice rose that all could hear. "No white hand will touch me so long as I live!"

Standing Buffalo, chief of the Upper Sisseton, responded. "I have always felt friendly toward the whites. You have brought me into great danger without my knowing of it beforehand. By killing the whites, it is just as if you had waited for me in ambush and shot me down. I know that my people killed no whites. But we will have to suffer for the guilty. I was out buffalo hunting when I heard of the outbreak. When word came to me, I felt I was dead. I feel the same now. You know we need the aid of the white man to live. I have made up my mind that Paul is right. We stand with him."

A warrior in Crow's band shouted, "Paul asked for the prisoners. Don't ask anymore. We are determined that they shall die with us."

Discouraged, Little Paul turned to his people. "Return to our village," he ordered. Then he turned to Akepa and said, "This will end badly for us all. Yet we must free the captives, unless Little Crow kills them first."

The Mdewakanton and Wahpekute Santee of Little Crow left the Yellow Medicine two days later. They divided their forces. Little Crow would lead a band to the north to raid Hutchinson and Forest City. Gray Bird and Big Eagle would move down the Minnesota River Valley to the south to plunder and loot. Other warriors were left behind to watch the captives.

The Sisseton remained apart in their own camp, watching and waiting.

∞ 9 ∞

The tall man rose from his desk and stared through the window behind his high-backed chair. In his large gnarled hand he held a sheaf of papers. A young man sat respectfully and expectantly across from the desk. Abraham Lincoln, sixteenth president of the United States, gazed down at the papers. He slid his reading glasses down his nose and began to read aloud.

"Listen, Hay, this one's from Governor Ramsey. 'The Sioux Indians of our western border have risen, and are murdering men, women, and children.'"

Lincoln shuffled the papers and read another. "This is from the Minnesota Secretary of State, Baker, 'A most frightful insurrection of Indians has broken out along our whole frontier. Men, women, and children are indiscriminately murdered, evidently the result of a deep-laid plan, the attacks being simultaneous along our whole border.'"

The president turned to face his youthful personal secretary. "It seems that Mr. Baker shares a conviction held by at least some of my cabinet officers. At our last meeting, Secretary Smith had no doubt that the Rebels were behind the uprising in Minnesota. He stated that southern emissaries were known to be agitating among the Sioux."

"John hasn't said anything about that and he's there." Hay referred to John Nicolay, Lincoln's other personal secretary, who had been sent to Minnesota prior to the outbreak to negotiate a treaty with the Chippewa.

"No," Lincoln replied, shuffling papers again, "this is what I got from Nicolay. 'We are in the midst of a most terrible and exciting Indian war. Thus far the massacre of innocent white settlers has been fearful. A wild panic prevails in nearly one-half of the state.'"

"What are you going to do, Mr. President?"

"Well, some things we wait on to see what plays out. But upon others we can act. Ramsey wants Minnesota's allotment of recruits suspended. We can do that for now. He also wants more troops sent to Minnesota. That is more difficult. Little Mac already complains nearly daily that Lee outnumbers him. If by some magic I could reinforce McClellan with 100,000 men today, he would be in ecstasy over it, thank me for it, and tell me that he would go to Richmond tomorrow, but when tomorrow came he would telegraph that he had certain information that the enemy had 400,000 men, and that he could not advance without reinforcements. When I gave him the command of the Army of the Potomac, McClellan told me that he could do it all. Maybe he can, but he does it very slowly."

"It seems he can do everything but fight," Hay responded.

"I thought it advisable to divide the command. That's why I put Pope in charge of the Army of Virginia."

"I come to you out of the West where we have always seen the backs of our enemies," Hay intoned. "That's what he told you. Then he loses at Second Bull Run. What a disaster! Two generals commanding our main forces, one filled with arrogance, the other a braggart, and neither can win. Besides, they hate each other. What are you going to do with them?"

"Here's an answer." Lincoln looked at another letter. "Ramsey wants me to create a new military department in the Northwest, he means Minnesota, to deal with the Indian insurrection. I'll leave

McClellan here, give him one more chance to finally win, and I'll send Pope to Minnesota. Ramsey asks for 3,000 guns, 500 horses and wants more men. I can't do that. We have a war here, too. But I can send Ramsey a general."

"Pope won't like that," Hay replied. "He'll feel he's been demoted, and he already blames McClellan and everyone else possible for his defeat."

"He'll just have to accept it, Mr. Hay. Tomorrow I'm ordering General Pope to Minnesota. Let him see Stanton first. My 'God of War' will help Pope to see that the Indian wars require the attention of a military officer of high rank."

"Mr. President, he still won't like it."

ಹ 10 ಐ

ROM LAKE SHAKOTAN, White Lodge's band and Pawn joined Lean Bear's and Sleepy Eyes' bands. They fled with the captives into Dakota Territory just across the southwest corner of Minnesota.

The Sisseton Santee camped at Two Woods Lake, home of Lean Bear, who had been slain by John Eastlick at Slaughter Slough, as Lake Shetek was now referred.

White Lodge creaked to his knees and then folded to a sitting position, joining Pawn, Sleepy Eyes, and Red Owl in a circle on the banks of the lake. From a small campfire in the center, White Lodge lit a pinkish-colored, long-stemmed pipe, offered it to the heavens, and passed it to the others.

"May Wakan Tonka guide us and keep us safe," the old chief intoned.

"We must keep moving," Pawn commented. "The soldiers will come."

Sleepy Eyes looked toward the setting sun. "We should follow the muddy river that the whites call Missouri. It will bring us into the lands of the Yankton and Teton. They will give us refuge."

"What about the captives?" Red Owl asked. "Should we kill them?"

"No," White Lodge said adamantly, "the Wright woman is mine. She speaks Dakota and is a good cook. The children are all in the lodges of others. Kills When Running has taken the other woman. When the soldiers come, the hostages will keep us safe. Until we reach the Yankton, we will travel with the moon. No fires can be lit."

"White Lodge," Pawn asked, "how will we feed these people?"

"Small bands must hunt while we rest during the day. Women must gather berries, nuts. We must do what we can until we reach the Yankton. We will stay here until the moon rises. Then our journey begins."

Laura Duley lay on buffalo skins in a tipi. As she had done each night since they left the Ireland cabin, she wrapped a blanket around her head and tried to blot out the cries coming from a nearby lodge. But it was no use. The cries and screams came from her baby Frances, who had been taken from her on the second day after Slaughter Slough. "Why?" she whispered. "Each night they torture my baby. Why? Why?"

Laura wrapped the blanket tighter and pushed against her ears as tears of anguish poured from her eyes. But the cries still reached her and tormented her. Laura wanted to die, yet knew she must try to be strong. She had seen her children Jefferson and Emma from a distance that afternoon. Each had been "adopted" by Santee. She must live to get them back.

Julia Wright slept in White Lodge's tipi. She wept softly into the soft fur of the buffalo robe beneath her. Her son, George, had never recovered from his wounds at Slaughter Slough and had died. Eldora, her little girl, had been taken from her by a Santee woman.

Julia was left to cook and care for an old arthritic man, White Lodge. But, like Laura Duley, she was determined to survive the pain, hunger and abuse that were sure to follow.

The Santee struck their eighty tipis as the sun set and transformed the lodge poles into travois. It took the women about fifteen minutes to take down three foundation poles, twenty support poles, and the twelve sewn-together buffalo hides that formed the covering. Two women could put it up again in an hour. While White Lodge and Red

Owl watched, the older chief remembered to his younger friend, "Grandfathers told me of the time before the horse, before the God Dog, when dogs were all we had to pull the travois."

"The lodge must have been much smaller," Red Owl commented.

White Lodge snorted. "They were the size of a full-grown man. Now a man can stand on another's shoulders in a tipi and reach up and still not be close to touching the top. The horse changed our lives. It let us move from the valley and onto the plains when we wanted. It let us follow *tatanka*, the buffalo."

"Now the buffalo are gone. They have gone to the Teton."

"And we must follow them," White Lodge concluded.

The Santee band pushed west onto the Corteau des Prairies, a rolling grassland interspersed with high hills, some reaching 900 feet. They moved through it as they followed the Missouri River north in the moonlight. The band rested in the daylight, but men still had to hunt each day while women searched for nuts, berries, and edible roots.

White Lodge and Pawn were resting beside their lodges when a young Santee brave galloped into camp. He leaped from his pony and breathlessly explained, "Yankton, they are near, just upriver. I saw their camp."

White Lodge attempted to rise, struggled and then reached up to the brave, who helped his chief to his feet. "Pawn, let us go to the Yankton. Help is near."

A small party of Santee led by White Lodge and Pawn trotted their horses into the village of the Yankton Dakota, brothers of the Santee. Several warriors strode out to meet the visitors.

"We are Santee, from Minnesota," White Lodge proclaimed in greeting. "We have traveled many miles since fighting and killing many whites. My people are hungry. We need the help of our brothers, the Yankton."

"I am Broken Bow. This is my village. We know what is happening in the valley of the Minnesota. We have smoked and talked about it. The whites have done nothing to us. We have decided to take no part in this war. The soldiers will come after you. We know you have white captives with you. If you stay with us or if we help you, the whites will know it, and they will come after us, too. You must pass by. We cannot help."

White Lodge was stunned by Broken Bow's words as surely as if he had been struck across the face. "My people are hungry," he insisted. "We must have food."

"We have none to spare," Broken Bow replied, "and you are the cause of it. Santee from Minnesota come to our land and take our buffalo, our food, and drive *tatanka* farther to the west, to the Teton."

"We needed food. We had to follow the buffalo. You must help us. The Teton must help us."

"Sitting Bull of the Hunkpapa Teton has sent riders to us. He feels as we do. You are a danger to us all. You took our food and now you want us to give what little we have to you. We can't. Stay away from the Yankton and the Teton."

Hot anger flashed from White Lodge's eyes. He twisted his pony's head around and grimaced in pain as he kicked the animal's ribs and trotted downriver to the Santee camp. The Minnesota band and their captives were on their own.

White Lodge was sure that the survival of his people depended upon their staying on the move and somehow reaching a herd of buffalo or Dakota that would help them. He was sure that the white soldiers could not be far behind.

✂ 11 ✂

OANNA MILLER MADE REGULAR visits to Fort Snelling. There were benefits to being a colonel's daughter, especially when it came to gaining information and keeping up with the latest gossip. JoAnna's appetite for news from the battle front was insatiable, and this day looked to be of even greater interest. A notice in the newspaper announced that refugees from Fort Ridgely and the agencies would meet and address the public in the Fort Snelling commissary.

Perhaps they had details about Jesse or her father that couldn't be gleaned from the letters she received from them. The guards at the front gate, accustomed to JoAnna's visits, greeted her warmly.

"Here for the meetin' at the commissary?" a young corporal smiled.

"Yes, Corporal. I'm sure it will be interesting."

"Those folks bin through a lot, Miss. They're lucky they got here at all."

"I'm eager to hear their stories."

JoAnna hurried across the parade ground to the large limestone building that served as mess hall and meeting room for the soldiers. The fort was a beehive of activity as soldiers marched and drilled, cleaned stables and cut wood. The rhythmic *tap, tap, tap* of the post blacksmith echoed a metallic refrain heard throughout the post.

The building was crowded with soldiers and civilians as JoAnna entered. She found a seat near the back and sat down just as Post Adjutant General Oscar Malmos stood at the front of the hall.

"Welcome, all," Malmos began. "It's a warm day for September and even with all the windows open, I fear it will get sticky in here. So we'll get right to our presenters. This is John Other Day."

Malmos motioned to a tall, slender Indian dressed in a dark frock coat and black pants. "John is a real hero of the uprising. A full-blood Sioux, he is a Christian from the Yellow Medicine Agency who brought sixty-two whites to safety."

The young Indian man stood to warm applause.

"Tell us your story, John," Malmos instructed.

John Other Day began slowly in what was very good English. "When we heard about the attack at the Redwood Agency, we Wahpeton and Sisseton met to decide what to do. I spoke for peace, but no final decision was made. The braves could decide for themselves. I was determined that my white friends would be saved, and I warned the people of the Yellow Medicine Agency that an attack was coming soon. Some had already left but most hadn't. I gathered the people in the brick warehouse and stood guard through the night. On the morning of the nineteenth, while the traders' stores in the valley were attacked, looted and burned, we loaded into wagons, crossed the river and climbed onto the prairie to the north."

He paused, drew in a long breath, then continued his story. "Some wanted to go to Fort Ridgely. I told them that if we went to the fort, we would all be massacred. We needed to cross the prairie to the northeast and then turn toward St. Paul, a hundred and twenty miles away. After three days of hard travel with little food we reached Cedar City in McLeod County. It took us five days and four nights to reach St. Paul. We hid in the grass and by lakes at night. We never saw an Indian on our journey."

He turned to another man next to him and said, "Many of you may know Dr. Wakefield, who was with us. Listen to him."

The room remained quiet with rapt attention as a slim, fair-skinned man stood to address the audience. "I was the Yellow Medicine doctor. When I heard that there might be trouble, I took no chances and sent my wife and children with George Gleason from the agency about noon on the eighteenth. The Sioux caught up with them. I'm told that Gleason was killed and that my wife, Sarah, and our children were taken captive. I don't know what happened to them." Wakefield paused, bowed his head and swallowed hard. "I only pray that we find them safe soon."

As a woman took her turn speaking, JoAnna heard a middle-aged lady directly in front of her sob deeply and wipe tears from her eyes. JoAnna laid her hand comfortingly on the woman's shoulder. "Were you there?" she whispered to the distraught person.

"I'm Alice Gleason. George was my husband. He's the one murdered when he was helping the Wakefields. He should have waited and gone with us."

"He was brave, Mrs. Gleason, risking his life for others."

"Brave and dead," Mrs. Gleason answered sharply as she wiped more tears from her eyes.

JoAnna sat back as sensations of fear and dread prickled her body. The words were eerily like those she had last spoken to Jesse. She wanted a live husband, not a dead hero. She had hoped to be uplifted by the testimony from the survivors, but JoAnna left Fort Snelling filled with apprehension.

๑ 12 ๏

IGH ON A HILLTOP IN THE LAND of the Teton, a young Sans Arc brave from Two Kettles' band sat cross-legged as he raised his hands to the heavens. White clay covered his body. His name was Waanatan, Charger, and he was on a vision quest.

Through four days and nights Charger had fasted, prayed and waited. He had first prepared himself through purification in a sweat lodge and conferred with the grandfathers. Now he waited for the vision to come to him from the Great Spirit.

It might not happen, an elder had told him. Visions do not always come. Sometimes the seeker is not ready. Sometimes the Great Spirit chooses another time. "Pray, think pure thoughts and be patient," he was advised.

It was near the end of the fourth day. The quest would soon be over. Suddenly, as if struck by a lightning bolt, Charger grew rigid and fell back onto the ground. Then he saw it. As plain as memories of yesterday, a vision played through his mind. Charger saw an unkempt contingent of people walking alongside a great river. Then bright light shone upon some of them, and he knew that these were not Indians; they were white. Ten times faces were lit up. Two adult women and eight children. As the vision continued ten elk cows were followed by ten bull elk.

A black crow flew overhead, circled and landed next to Charger. It spoke to him. "Waanatan, it is not right that these ten have been taken. It is your mission to form a soldiers' lodge, find these people and bring them back to their world. This is the answer to your quest."

The crow cawed loudly, spread its wings and flew away.

In moments, the young man on the hill jerked awake and opened his eyes, rubbing them in bewilderment. Then Charger's mind cleared, and he knew what he must do.

He walked down the hill to where his pony was tethered near a stream. He mounted and galloped home toward Two Kettles' village. The young man saw dust kicked up by another pony in the west.

It must be Kills Game, he thought. His good friend had also sought a vision. Soon their paths intersected.

"Hiya," Kills Game shouted excitedly. "I had a vision. I saw white women and children. An eagle said we must save them."

Charger gasped in startlement. "My friend, the vision is true. I had the same one. White people are coming. I don't know where or when. But we must be ready, for this is the path Wakan Tonka has chosen for us."

He reached across and held out his right arm to Kills Game. They each grasped the other's forearm. "Let us swear to Wakan Tonka today," Charger told his friend, "that we will not rest until we have fulfilled the charge given us in this vision. I swear, do you?"

"Yes, Charger. This is our destiny. Let us go to Two Kettles together."

The two galloped into the Sans Arc village of Two Kettles on the Missouri River. They reined their ponies to a halt in front of Two Kettles' lodge. Their chief rose to meet them. "Was your quest successful?" he asked.

"Yes," Charger answered. "Wakan Tonka has given us a great mission. We are to form a society and free white captives."

Charger and Kills Game detailed their visions for their chief. Two Kettles listened, with apprehension and skepticism. When they had finished, he said, "You should have considered your visions and talked and smoked with elders before swearing a promise to the Great Spirit. The Sans Arc and the other six councils of the Teton take no side in the Minnesota war. We must not interfere in anything that our Santee brothers have done. It is not our way."

A crowd of villagers gathered around the three and listened to the exchange.

"Two Kettles," Charger answered, now a little uncomfortable, "we have sworn to fulfill our vision. When the time is here, we must do as we promised."

An old man spat on the ground near them. "You are Dakota, and you want to free whites taken by your Dakota brothers? You are fools!"

The remark brought laughter from the onlookers, but determination froze on the faces of the two vision seekers. They had sworn to the Great Spirit.

OVER THE NEXT FEW WEEKS, most forgot about the vow made that September day. Villagers did notice that wherever Charger went, Kills Game followed. They also noticed that Swift Bear was often with them and that other young men were listening to Charger's words.

Each day the three friends visited Primeau's store. The establishment was a trading post that the Frenchman had built above the abandoned Fort LaFramboise and old Fort Pierre on the Missouri River. Some still called it Fort Pierre, but the Frenchman, disregarding modesty, preferred Fort Primeau.

Charger and Kills Game told the story of their vision to Primeau. The Frenchman encouraged them.

"Sometimes I hear about what ees happening on zee river. Eef news comes to me about white captives I weell tell you. What weell you do until then?"

Charger looked resolutely at the trader. "We cannot do this alone. We must form a soldiers' lodge to help us."

"A soldiers' lodge? What ees that?"

"The Dakota have many warrior societies. Most come through visions or dreams. Our purpose comes in that way. We are warriors, the vision tells us how to dress, how to act and what we are to do. A lodge can be of hunters, those who take power from animals, like the Bear Cult. They can be dancers, singers, holy men. There are many kinds. We are sworn to form a lodge that is different. We are sworn to help the whites."

"May God be weeth you," Primeau uttered.

∾ 13 ൽ

URING THE SECOND WEEK of September, two weary bands of Santee returned to their camp at Yellow Medicine. Battles had been fought by both. Little Crow and Gray Bird had each won battles. At Birch Coulee, Gray Bird had attacked the burial detail sent out from Fort Ridgely. Twenty-five soldiers were killed and eighty horses lost before Sibley's reinforcements arrived and the Santee left.

Little Crow's warriors moved into the Big Woods forty miles to the north of the valley. There the Santee attacked a force of the Ninth Minnesota and defeated them in a running battle along the west side of Long Lake, near Acton. But subsequent raids on Forest City and Hutchinson were failures.

As they gathered to council near the Yellow Medicine River, there was little to celebrate. The soldiers were closing in.

The four bands of the Santee, friendlies and hostiles, were all represented in a great circle. A bubbling pot of dog stew gurgled nearby, and occasionally an Indian would ladle some into a bowl and eat.

Gray Bird handed a paper to Little Crow.

"This was found on a stick after the Birch Coulee fight. It is a message from the Long Trader, Sibley."

Little Crow examined the paper and handed it to Joe Campbell, a half-breed who read English and acted as Little Crow's driver when the chief chose to ride in a wagon.

"What does it say?"

Campbell squinted and scrunched up his face, then read haltingly, "If Little Crow has any proposition to make, let him send a half-breed to me, and he shall be protected in and out of camp."

Little Crow considered Sibley's words carefully. Then he spoke to the Santee leaders of both factions. "Sibley seeks a peaceful way out of this war. Maybe it is possible."

Santee of both sides shouted out, some in agreement, others in anger.

"Give up the captives now! That will show our good will toward the whites," Akepa shouted above the throng.

Mazzawamnuna, young and powerfully built, shouted back. "I speak for Shakopee and Red Middle Voice. You men who are in favor of leaving us and delivering up the captives talk like children. You believe if you do so, that the whites will think you have acted as their friends and will spare your lives. They will not, and you ought to know it. You say that the whites are too strong for us, and that we will all perish. By sticking together and fighting the whites, we will live, for only a few more days, perhaps. By the course you propose, we would die at once. Let us keep the prisoners with us and let them share our fate. That is all the advice I have to give."

Wabasha had been involved in the war from the beginning, but never with a whole heart. The powerful leader of the Santee now spoke for peace. "The time to fight is gone," he pleaded. "We must seek peace. The captives must be freed. You failed to listen to Little Crow when he called for a war of soldier against soldier. Many of you made war on women and children. Now we must pay. We will pay more dearly if the captives are not freed unharmed."

Wabasha's own son-in-law, Rdainyanka, then rose to answer. "Ever since we made treaties with them, their agents and traders have robbed and cheated us. Some of our people have been shot, some hanged, others placed

69

upon floating ice and drowned, and many have been starved in their prisons. It was not the intention of the Dakota Nation to kill any of the whites settlers. Then the four men returned from Acton and told what they had done. When they did this, all the young men became excited and commenced the massacre. The older ones would have prevented it if they could, but since they signed the treaties that took our land, they had lost all their influence. We may regret what has happened, but the matter has gone too far to be remedied. We have got to die. Let us, then, kill as many of the whites as possible, and let the prisoners die with us."

Little Paul climbed atop a wooden barrel to make sure that he was heard. He shouted at the Redwood Dakota. "By your involving our young men without consulting us, you have done us a great injustice. I am now going to tell you something you don't like. You have gotten our people into this difficulty through your actions, and I shall use all the means I can to get them out of it without reference to you. I am opposed to their continuing this war, or of committing further outrages, and I warn them not to do it."

Everyone was listening. Forcefully, he said, "I have heard a great many of you say that you are brave men and can whip the whites. This is a lie. Men who cut women's and children's throats are squaws, cowards. You say the whites are not brave. You will see. They might not kill women and children, as you have, but they will fight any of you who hold weapons. I am ashamed of the way you have acted toward the captives. Fight the whites if you desire to, but do it like brave men."

Dark Bird replied to his chief, "I am a Sisseton. I fought the whites at Lake Shetek. Paul is my chief, but I do not do what he advises. I hope our people will not agree with him. We must all die in battle or perish with hunger. I say let the captives suffer what we suffer."

Little Crow turned to Big Eagle. "It is time to form a reply to Sibley. It is plain that the Redwood Dakota will not turn the captives over to Little Paul to be given over to the whites. We will use the captives to bargain with as we try to reach an agreement with the Long Trader. Sibley asks for proposals, we have none without the prisoners."

70

The friendlies and the hostiles haggled over the wording of Little Crow's reply to Sibley. After many changes it was given to Joe Campbell to put into English.

Dear Sir,

For what reason we have commenced this war, I will tell you. It is on account of Major Galbraith. We made a treaty with the government, and beg for what we do get and then can't get it till our children are dying with hunger. It is the traders who commenced it. Mr. A.J. Myrick told the Indians they should eat grass or dirt.

Then Mr. Forbes told the Lower Sioux that they were not men. Then Roberts was working with his friends to defraud us out of our moneys. If the young braves have pushed the white man, I have done this myself. So I want you to let Governor Ramsey know this.

I have a great many prisoners, women and children. It ain't all our fault. The Winnebagoes were in the engagement, and two of them was killed. I want you to give me an answer by the bearer all at present.

Yours truly,
Friend Little Crow

Little Crow turned to two mixed-bloods, Tom Robertson and another man with a very similar name, Tom Robinson. "Take this message to Sibley. Take the buggy and mule and leave this afternoon."

Tom Robinson was apprehensive. "They will shoot us as soon as they see us."

"No, Sibley promised safe treatment to the bearer of my message, and Tom is the son of Andrew Robertson, the agency teacher. You will be unharmed."

Reluctantly the men climbed into the buggy and headed down the river.

$\mathcal{so}$ 14 $\mathcal{os}$

ENRY HASTINGS SIBLEY SAT on a chair behind a small desk in his office at Fort Ridgely. Two men, Robertson and Robinson, stood before Sibley. Sunlight shone through two windows. An officer, Colonel McPhail, and two soldiers stood alongside them.

Sibley was smartly dressed with the bars of a colonel sewn onto his blue uniform blouse. He looked down at the wrinkled note in his hands and read it again. Then he cleared his throat before speaking to the mixed-blood couriers before him.

"Does Little Crow have anything to add?"

Robinson answered, "That the war is not our fault and that Little Crow did not want it. We have prisoners and want to keep them safe for you. We want peace but will fight until we are all dead if we must."

"I have the message." Sibley held up the letter from Little Crow. "Privates, take this one out," he pointed to Robinson. "You, Robertson, I believe? Stay."

The two enlisted soldiers escorted Robinson out the door. Sibley addressed McPhail. "Colonel, I'm told that you questioned both of these men before you brought them to me. It seems that this one had a more interesting story."

"Yes, Colonel Sibley, Mr. Robertson tells a different account regarding the Indians at Yellow Medicine."

Sibley's hard gaze turned to Robertson. "Tell me."

"The peace chiefs, Little Paul and Red Iron, they told me to tell the Long Trader that all do not follow Little Crow. They wish to form a peace lodge. Many are friendly to you and want to free the white captives. "

"Can they do that?" Sibley asked.

"Not yet. Little Crow's warriors are many and strong. They will fight you if you come to the Yellow Medicine. They fight well and are determined to battle until they have destroyed you or can fight no longer."

Sibley considered a moment and then began to scribble a note on a small sheet of paper. He wrote:

Little Crow:

You have murdered many of our people without any suffi-cient cause. Return to me the prisoners, under a flag of truce, and I will talk to you like a man. I have sent your message to Governor Ramsey.

H. H. Sibley
Colonel Commanding
Military Expedition

"Here, Robertson." He folded the note and handed it the messen-ger. "Take this to Little Crow. I knew your father. He was a great man."

Tom paused, then spoke directly, "They took me prisoner early in the war. Crow made me go to the second battle at New Ulm and Fort Ridgely, but I didn't fight. Then they made me a messenger and inter-preter. That's why I'm here."

"Do you want to stay here?"

"No, I must return with your note. Maybe by doing this I can help end the fighting."

As the Santee departed to join Robinson, Sibley motioned to McPhail to remain. "Colonel, it seems that there is dissension among the Santee. If they fight among themselves, they can't fight us very well. It's just a matter of time. When we get more horses to replace those lost at Birch Coulee, we'll move on them, and it will be over quickly."

"What then?" McPhail wondered.

"Peace on the frontier. But there will be change, and the Sioux will find life much different. Governor Ramsey isn't going to speak of treaties or council with them or smoke a peace pipe. Listen to this from the *Pioneer Dispatch*." Sibley took a folded newspaper from his desktop and read. "These are Ramsey's words:

> The Sioux Indians of Minnesota must be exterminated or driven forever beyond the borders of the state. The public safety imperatively requires it. Justice calls for it . . . The blood of the murdered cries to heaven for vengeance on those assassins of women and children. They are amendable to no laws, bound by no moral or social restraints, they have already destroyed every pledge on which it was possible to found a hope of ultimate reconciliation. They must be regarded and treated as outlaws."

"It seems that revenge will be the driving force when this is over," McPhail noted.

Sibley nodded. "And a degree of revenge is necessary. They have committed atrocities. Now Lincoln has appointed General Pope as commander of the new Northwest District. I hope he will be amenable to our needs, I've already sent a request for more bread, bullets, blankets, clothing, mules, oats, hay, pork, and horses. If we aren't better supplied soon, we may have to fall back and not advance."

"The newspapers would crucify you for that. They already call you a turtle and the state undertaker. You said we'd move out on September 19. All hell will break loose if we don't."

"It is still my plan, Colonel McPhail. But we must be prepared. For now, let's see what Little Crow does."

∞ 15 ∞

hen Robertson and Robinson arrived back at Yellow Medicine, they found Little Crow and his warriors preparing to leave. Robertson handed Sibley's note to Little Crow. The Santee chief glanced at it and handed it back.

"What does it say?" he inquired.

Robertson slowly translated the missive into Dakota.

Little Crow wearily looked at his people packing belongings and dismantling dwellings. "It is right that we move farther up the river. We go to Lac Qui Parle where the Chippewa enters the Minnesota. We will put another twelve miles between us and Sibley. Even Little Paul's bands will go. They cry that they are friends of the whites and that we should free the captives, but they still don't trust the white army. You two, stay with us. I may have more use for you later."

Once again the five-mile procession of wagons, Indians and their white captives set off across the prairie. The day was stifling hot, and the convoy raised a great cloud of dust that choked them every step of the way.

Sarah Wakefield and Susan Brown limped along the trail together, their feet leaving bloody tracks in the dirt. Lisa Wakefield whimpered and tugged at the rags that were Sarah's dress.

"Mommy, I can't walk. It hurts."

As Sarah reached down to pick up her daughter, she grimaced in pain.

"Let me," a young man offered. Susan's seventeen-year-old son Samuel stooped down and picked up the little girl. "I'll carry her for a while. We can't let her git behind us."

Sarah managed a grateful smile and hobbled forward.

"Sarah," Susan said, walking close to speak confidentially, "Little Crow spoke to me again. He's worried. The young men don't listen to him. They do what they will, like when they attacked New Ulm when they could've captured Fort Ridgely. He'll keep fightin' and kill as many whites as he can. But Little Crow doesn't care if he dies in battle. He just doesn't wanna be caught and hanged. He's going to send another message to Sibley."

It was late afternoon when the long column reached the mouth of the Chippewa River, also the site of Red Iron's village. As Little Crow's Santee approached, the Sisseton chief and 150 of his warriors blocked the path to the north. They fired their guns into the air as a warning.

Red Iron strode from his men to stand before Little Crow and the warriors who gathered behind him. "We warned you that you could not go to the north beyond my village. This would leave the Sisseton to stand against Sibley and vengeful whites. When they come looking for you, they will find us. They won't care that we have been friendly. They will only care that we are Dakota and see the color of our skin."

In answer, the Redwood Santee fired shots into the air and above the Sisseton. No one was hit.

Little Crow raised his hands and shouted for quiet. "Do not fire your guns at your brothers! We are all Dakota. Red Iron, call your chiefs. We must council."

In a short time both Redwood and Yellow Medicine leaders gathered at the confluence of the rivers. Red Iron did most of the talking.

"You commenced the outbreak and must do the fighting in your country. I cannot bear the thought of everything of mine being destroyed because of you. Therefore I shall stay here where I belong until General Sibley comes here, and I will shake hands with him, and then he may do what he pleases with me."

One of Red Iron's lieutenants supported the words of his chief. "I live by the white man and the buffalo. These people who have done this act have destroyed everything I have, the treaties with the whites and everything else, and for that reason I shall object to their going across my land."

Wacouta and Taopee shattered Little Crow with a surprise announcement. They stepped forward together. Wacouta addressed Little Crow.

"We and our people shall camp with the Sisseton and Wahpeton. We will not remain with those who have killed women and children. The white army will show no mercy to you."

Little Crow's expression flashed from anger to depression as thunder follows lightning. "Do you think they will show mercy to you because you claim not to have harmed any whites? Do you think Sibley will care if you tell him you didn't join in the uprising? If you think so, you are fools. But we will not cross your land, Red Iron. We will go west or south as we need."

Little Crow turned and walked back amongst his throng of warriors. Red Middle Voice and Shakopee accosted him.

"You give up too easily!" Shakopee accused. "We could beat them. Let us fight."

"It would be a fool's war. We cannot fight Sisseton, Wahpeton, and Sibley. And now some Mdewakanton led by Wacouta join them. They think that if they didn't fight the whites they will be left alone. That it will be as it was. The whites will treat all Santee the same."

"When Sibley comes," Red Middle Voice added, "then the Sisseton will know. Then they must fight to help us."

Little Crow sighed. "If Sibley gets this far, it will be too late. We will have failed to stop him. But the Long Trader was my friend. I will try one more time for a peaceful end to this. Send Campbell, Robertson, and Robinson to me. Tell Campbell to bring writing tools."

Little Crow sat alone under a tree by the river. He gazed at the swirling waters and knew that they couldn't be stopped, just as he knew that the rushing rivers of white settlement could not be stopped. When Red Middle Voice and the others had come to him after the killings at Acton, Little Crow had resisted their call to war. He had been to Washington, had signed the treaties and knew the power of the white army. But they had come to him as their leader, the young men who demanded war, and Little Crow had pledged to fight and die with them.

Change was coming and his people had resisted change. Now it would sweep over them. Grief hung over him like an ominous cloud.

Shakopee, Red Middle Voice, and Medicine Bottle approached from the village. His letter writer and the two messengers were with them.

Little Crow remained sitting and looked up first at Campbell. "Write these words. It is for Sibley." The chief considered thoughtfully for a moment. "'We have in Mdewakanton band 155 prisoners. They are at Lake Qui Parle now. The words that I sent to the governor, I want to hear from him also, and I want to know from you as a friend what way I can make peace for my people. In regard to prisoners, they fare with our children or ourselves just as well as us.' Sign it, 'Your truly friend.'"

He looked at Robinson and Robertson. "Tomorrow at dawn take the letter and go to Fort Ridgely again. See that the Long Trader gets it."

Tom Robertson lay alone in his tipi that night. It was difficult to sleep. Heat and thoughts of his mission kept him awake. He lay on his back, eyes closed but wide awake. Suddenly he felt a hand close over his mouth and heard a voice whisper in his ear.

"Don't be alarmed. It is me, Good Thunder, I wish to talk."

Tom sat up and saw the dim form of the Sisseton leader. He was a Christian farmer from Yellow Medicine who, with his wife, Snana, had been among the first married by the missionary John Williamson.

"I want you to carry a message to Sibley for me as well."

"What message, Good Thunder?"

"I have paper and a pencil. I will tell you what to write."

"I can't see to write in here and any light will be seen and attract others."

Good Thunder paused, then suggested, "Here, I have a candle, put your buffalo robe over us and we will write beneath it."

Good Thunder leaned over the smoldering ash from a small cook fire. The candle wick took hold and flickered a low flame. The two men draped the robe over their heads. "Now," Good Thunder said, "write these words: 'You know that Little Crow has been opposed to me in everything that our people have had to do with the whites. He has been opposed to everything in the form of civilization and Christianity. I have always been in favor of, and of late years have done everything of the kind that has been offered to us by the government and other good white people. He has now got himself into trouble that we know he can never get himself out of, and he is trying to involve those of us in the murder of the poor whites that have been settled in the border; but I have been kept back with threats that I should be killed if I did anything to help the whites. But if you will now appoint some place for me to meet you, myself and the few friends that I have will get all the prisoners that we can, and with our families go to whatever place you will appoint for us to meet. Return the messenger as quick as possible. We have not much time to spare.' Sign it, 'Wabasha and Taopee.'"

ॐ **16** ॐ

ENRY SIBLEY WALKED the parade ground at Fort Ridgely with State Adjutant General Oscar Malmros. They stopped near the flagpole in the center of the post.

Malmros shook his head and remarked to Sibley, "It was amazing they held this place when the Santee attacked. No walls, no well, outnumbered four to one. But they held."

"The cannon drove them off, Malmros, cannon and the brave men who defended this place. Ravines are on three sides. The Sioux were able to use them and literally appear out of nowhere to attack. If they had taken this fort, we couldn't stop them until they got to St. Paul. God help us if that had happened."

"When are you moving out, Colonel?"

"Soon, maybe a couple days. More horses have arrived. Pope pushed hard for them. Since he got to St. Paul, he's tried to get us more of everything we need. Last week we received 50,000 cartridges. More rations and clothing have arrived. And now the Third Minnesota, 250 combat-experienced veterans, are under my command. Finally more horses were sent. We still need more, but I've received orders from the general. He wrote, 'I cannot urge upon you too strongly the necessity of marching as rapidly as possible upon the Sioux.'"

"What do you have, 1,600 men?"

"Yes, but most are infantry. My mounted force is twenty-five men. If I had 400 to 500 cavalry, I would bring this campaign to a speedy conclusion. Our chief scout is John Other Day. He could be invaluable. He knows his people, and he knows Little Crow."

"What do you hear of the Sioux?"

"They are near the Yellow Medicine, and they are divided. I received missives from both friendly Sioux and Little Crow. Little Crow begins to quake. I expect to reach him and fight him within a week. Wabasha claims friendship to us. That may be true, or it may be a trick. I'll remain vigilant. I wrote Wabasha that those who have not been concerned in the murders and expeditions should gather with all the prisoners. If they raise a white flag, we will raise one, too. Then they may come forward and be under my protection."

"What did you write to Little Crow?"

"I offered him no charity or terms. I reminded him that he has not given up his prisoners and that he must do so before we talk. I admonished him that since his first letter, he has continued to allow his young men to commit murder and that is no way to make peace. Little Crow is in a box, we'll nail it shut soon."

17 ⌘

Fter six weeks of terror and bloodshed, the war in Minnesota was reaching a climax. Sibley's army was finally on the move, up the Minnesota near the Yellow Medicine Agency.

John Other Day led the way. He rode alone ahead of the main army through the great sea of tall prairie grass, its six-foot-high stalks rippling in the breeze like waves.

His horse pranced through the grass. A gaudy red headdress attached to its bridle bobbed up and down like a lure in a lake. Other Day stood tall in his saddle and looked over the shimmering grass for signs of Santee. Riding farther along the trail, he found moccasin prints in soft dirt. A small pile of discarded plum pits lay alongside the road. Other Day dismounted and felt them. They were still damp. It couldn't have been more than an hour since Santee had eaten plums here.

The warring Santee were near. John Other Day had to tell Sibley.

The Long Trader was bivouacked at Lone Tree Lake, mistakenly called Wood Lake by some whites. The Wahpeton scout reported to him outside his tent.

"Colonel, I saw signs of warriors ahead of us. They are close."

"Did you see any, John?"

"No, but they are near."

"I'll put out more pickets for tonight, but I'll keep them in close. No sense getting them out in the tall grass. It might not be safe. But from the messages I've received, I don't think Little Crow plans an attack this soon and not here. We must outnumber him two to one, and they are divided as it is."

"Watch carefully, Colonel, you know Little Crow. He is a great warrior."

"He's had his chance, John. It's over for him. They should run away now before we close in on them and run them down."

Other Day was silent a moment and then replied, "They will not run. They have one big fight left, I know it."

"Time will tell, time will tell, John."

"Maybe tomorrow."

❧ 18 ☙

John Other Day was right. Little Crow planned one more fight. The great Santee chief stood before his warriors on the plain east of the Chippewa River. He wore his finest headdress and skins. Long-fringed leather sleeves concealed his thin, withered lower arms and wrists injured long ago in a fight with the Chippewa.

Little Crow held his arms high. The Santee silenced.

"Listen, warriors, listen to your chief one more time. Every brave fit to fight must join in this battle. We know where the Long Trader camps at Lone Tree Lake. We can crush them like locusts descending upon a field of corn. There will be honor for whoever brings to me their flag or the scalps of Sibley and the traders who ride with him. I have tried to convince Sisseton and Wahpeton to help us. But the blood between us is bad and few will join us. Little Paul's people have left us to camp west of the river.

"Brave Santee, Sibley is only two miles from the agency. Tomorrow when the white army starts on the road toward the Yellow Medicine, they will be like a long snake. We will wait in the long grass of both sides of the road. We will attack the snake from the sides and not allow it to coil. Fight bravely, my warriors. It is our last chance to save the land of our fathers."

85

Chaska went to his lodge, where Sarah Wakefield remained with his mother. They were separate from the captive camp and the friendly Indians. "I must go," Chaska told Sarah. "If I don't ride to fight Sibley, I will be shot, and you will be in danger, too. Stay here with my mother. Do not try to leave for the camp of the friendlies while we are away. Stay away from the half-breeds and white women. It is not safe otherwise."

"What will happen to us, Chaska? What does Little Crow plan?"

Chaska said nothing. He turned his back and left to join the other warriors. His mother stood near Sarah and spoke in a low voice. "Little Crow will attack the friendlies' camp when he returns," she warned Sarah. "Everyone there will die. You must stay here."

Soon after, the Mdewakanton left Lac Qui Parle and headed back down the Minnesota. It was fourteen miles to Sibley to take up positions for the coming fight.

Early the next morning, on the west side of the Chippewa, the friendly Santee gathered their leaders together to council. A dozen Indian men sat in a circle. A low fire surrounded by stones slowly tendrilled smoke into the hazy blue sky. Nearby the Chippewa River emptied into the Minnesota on the wild frontier prairie. From far off a rumble sounded, but there were no rain clouds and it wasn't thunder. It was the distant sound of cannon.

Little Paul, Christian chief of the Sisseton band, stood and looked at the tired, careworn faces of his leaders. Cloudman, Akepa, Simon, Good Thunder, and Red Iron were among them.

"Listen, my chiefs. Hear the big guns roar," said Little Paul. "The battle is fought, one more time."

"Little Crow says they will kill the soldiers, like they did at the ferry." Red Iron looked into the fire as he spoke.

"Red Iron," Akepa replied, "no matter what happens, we must deal with Little Crow when they return. If they have won, they may attack us and kill the captives. If they lose, they still may kill the white captives."

"I have been told that is right," Good Thunder said. "No matter what, they will kill the prisoners."

Big Eagle arose and spoke gravely. "I have ridden with Little Crow for much of this war. There are conflicts within him. He wanted this fight to be army against army, but his warriors would not let that be. They killed some women and children, and they took others captive. Now he must decide what to do with them. Whatever he chooses, he will not let them get in the way of his people's well being. He will use them if he can. If he can't, they may be killed."

"See there." Red Iron pointed across the river to the hodge-podge of tipis that housed the captives near Little Crow's camp. "Only a few braves are left to guard them. The rest are away fighting. Let us cross the river, take the captives and bring them here."

"Then we must surely be prepared to fight Little Crow when he returns," Little Paul answered.

Simon had been silent. Now he spoke in agreement. "Bring the captives here. Dig trenches and pits to fight from. We will save these people and drive off Little Crow. Then maybe the whites will remember that we did something good."

As the sound of the fight down the river echoed up the valley, the Sisseton and Wahpeton warriors closed in on the village where the captives were held hostage. In short order, they took them across the river and fortified their position. Then they waited for Little Crow.

ഇ 19 ൙

ibley's army camped at a place called Wood Lake just miles from the Upper Agency. The Santee planned to ambush the soldiers as they marched strung out along the road.

A foraging detail left camp without orders, bound for potatoes in the abandoned agency gardens. The soldiers detoured off the road and into the tall grass concealing Santee warriors. The battle began there, prematurely and without design.

The Third Minnesota, led by Major Arnold Welch, rushed into the fray to assist their comrades. The soldiers pushed the Santee back until an order came from Sibley ordering a retreat back to camp.

Welch turned to Lieutenant Olin, "Blast it! Why does he want us to retreat? We've got the upper hand here."

"Because it wasn't planned, Major, there's no sense of order to this. Sibley likes order. Look, the fight is becoming every man for himself."

"Bugler," Welch ordered. "We've got orders to follow. Sound the retreat."

As the bugle sounded and the men moved back, Little Crow ordered a steady volley to cut off their path of retreat. When the soldiers crossed an outlet stream from the lake, the Santee flanked them on both sides and charged the Third Minnesota from the rear.

On high ground between the stream and lake, Welch ordered his men. "Form up here. We'll make a stand. Help will come! Fire at will!"

Back in camp, James Gorman, Lieutenant of the Renville Rangers, ordered his men into the fight. The Rangers consisted of some fifty mixed-blood volunteers bound for the South. The Rangers fell in with the Third Minnesota to stave off the onslaught. Jesse Buchanen raced to join them, along with a young one-armed civilian.

Welch raised his sword and yelled, "Pour it into 'em, boys! Push 'em back!" Then the young major grabbed his leg and crumbled to the ground.

"I'm shot!" he cried. "Take me in!"

A young corporal, Ezra Champlain, was quickly at his side. The one-armed man joined him and both helped the major to his feet. They struggled to assist Welch as bullets whizzed past them.

Jesse shouted above the din of battle, "I'll cover your backs. Let's move!" He aimed his carbine and fired. Then he drew his revolver and shot repeatedly. There was no time to fire at a particular target. The lieutenant just pointed his pistol at the mass of Indians before him and let go.

As they neared camp, three soldiers fleeing the battle raced past Welch and those assisting him.

Welch screamed at them, "Go back and fight, you white-livered cowards! Go back and fight, or I'll shoot you!"

The men kept running. The wounded major drew his pistol and fired a shot just over the head of the middle soldier. The three stopped and turned back, terror set in their pasty-white faces. Welch pulled back the hammer on his pistol and pointed it at them.

"I said get back there, boys, and I mean it!"

The frightened soldiers headed once more into the fight from which they had sought escape.

Welch was left on a small hill near the camp.

"Don't you want to be left by the wagons?" Jesse asked.

"No, I want to watch what's happening," Welch answered.

"Nathan Cates, what on Earth are you doing out here?" the major asked the one-armed man. "You're not a soldier."

"I once was, Major. It looked like you needed some help."

"Look," Jesse pointed, "the Sixth and Seventh are moving in. Cannons are rolling into position, too."

"Looks like Sibley changed his mind about retreating." Welch grimaced as Champlain tied a rag around his wounded leg. "It's about time we win this thing."

Jesse Buchanen and Nathan Cates raced back into the battle as reinforcements poured in from behind and cannon shot blasted overhead. Olin ordered a counter charge into the center of the Indian lines, and the Santee broke.

The battle was over. Jesse and Nathan remained unscathed.

≈ 20 ≈

Little Crow and Wabasha rode slowly and despondently in an open wagon back to the village on the Lac Qui Parle. Their beaten and dispirited warriors followed. Little Crow's driver, Joe Campbell, flicked the reins over the exhausted horses' backsides.

"It is over, Wabasha. There is no more fight after this. We should have won today."

"Your plan was a good one. It was the wagons that turned off the road to take a shorter route to the agency that made things go bad. Our braves were lying in wait for Sibley's men to string out on the road. But when the wagons rolled on top of them, our braves could not wait. They shot too soon."

"Yes, Wabasha, the ambush plan was ruined, and we could not get enough of our warriors in place to concentrate against the soldiers. It was our last chance, and it went bad."

"We lost Mankato. He refused to move for a cannon ball that he said was spent. It killed him. Mah-ka-tah died in the grass, too."

"We have lost everything. We must leave this place and head onto the prairies of the Dakotas. Maybe even Canada. I will leave at dawn. Will you come with me?" Little Crow asked.

91

"No, I will stay. Will you release the prisoners? It will go better for us all if they are freed before the Long Trader arrives. Maybe they will let us live in peace on the reservation."

"Friend, they will drive all Dakota from Minnesota," Little Crow said.

As the two rode into the camp, they were met by Red Middle Voice, his face scarlet with rage. "The friendlies have taken the captives. Little Paul holds them in his camp. Let us attack and take them back."

"Yes," Little Crow answered, "we may need them. We'll take them back."

"Wait," Wabasha interrupted, "we have already lost one battle today. Let them be. If there are captives still in your camp, free them, too. If you attack Little Paul, brother will fight brother and captives may die in the crossfire. Sibley will certainly be even more vengeful then."

Hapa supported Red Middle Voice. "The Sisseton and the Wahpeton have betrayed us. We must punish them. If the whites get in the way and are killed, it was meant to be."

"Do what you will. I must leave this place." The Santee chief, full of despair, went to his lodge to prepare for the journey west.

21

Little Crow and his four wives hurriedly threw packs of food and belongings into a wagon as several of his friends gathered to bid farewell and plan for the future. Joe Campbell, who was his interpreter and cousin, along with Red Middle Voice, Hapa, Shakopee, and Big Eagle stood before their leader's lodge.

The afternoon sun shone brightly from the blue sky, but it couldn't brighten the mood of the defeated warriors. "I will leave in the morning," Little Crow told his friends. "The Yankton and Teton will give me sanctuary. The Long Trader would like to put a rope around my neck. I will not give him the chance."

Campbell answered, "They never hanged anybody before. I don't think they will hang anybody now."

"No, cousin. It is different now. Too many women and children have been killed. If only men had been killed it would be different. We could make peace now. Let any remaining captives go. Take some to Sibley if you wish. Too many have died already."

Chaska opened the flap of his tipi and entered the dim, smoky dwelling. Sarah Wakefield sat on a buffalo hide mending a worn moccasin. She smiled when she saw him. He tossed her a wadded-up ball of clothing.

"It is your dress. Now you look like an Indian. It is better if you are dressed like a white woman when the soldiers come."

Sarah rose and stood before Chaska. "Is it true? Is it all over?"

"Yes, the Long Trader is near, the Santee are beat. You must join the other captives, and I must leave this place."

"Leave? Why, Chaska?"

"Sibley will kill all who fought the whites."

"Oh, no, I'm sure he won't. I've heard he sent a letter saying that he would punish only those who are guilty of crimes against us, those who committed murders and massacres. He was governor of the state once. He'll keep his word."

Chaska slowly and sadly shook his head. "I will stay. But if I am killed, the blame is yours."

In the morning 100 men gathered to accompany Little Crow to the Dakotas. Many of the worst perpetrators of murder, rape and other crimes done in the name of war were among them.

Red Middle Voice, Hapa, Shakopee, and Medicine Bottle accompanied the four who had started the uprising at Acton. Others joined them, now ready to head west to escape the white man's vengeance.

"The old ways are gone. We will go to the Grandmother's Country, Canada," Shakopee said. "Maybe we can live in peace there."

"There are whites there, too," Big Eagle replied. "Why will it be different? Whites always try to make the Indians give up their life and live like they do—go to farming, work hard—and the Indians did not know how to do that, and did not want to anyway. . . . If the Indians had tried to make the whites live like them, the whites would have resisted, and it was the same way with many Indians."

"True words," Shakopee replied, "but we cannot stay here."

They gathered close around Little Crow's wagon. Their chief stood in the wagon box to give his last speech.

"I am ashamed to call myself a Dakota. Seven hundred of our best warriors were whipped yesterday by the whites. Now we had better all run away and scatter over the plains like buffalo and wolves. To be sure, the whites had wagon guns and better arms than we, and there were many more of them. But that is no reason why we should not have whipped them, for we are brave Dakota, and whites are cowardly women. I cannot account for the disgraceful defeat. It must be the work of traitors in our midst."

The disconsolate band of Santee rode north across the Minnesota River and up out of the valley. From a high bluff, Little Crow turned his horse to gaze sadly one last time at the beautiful panorama that had long been home to his people.

Tree leaves were beginning to change color. Shades of red and yellow mixed with green near the river. On the flood plain, lush greenery mixed in with undulating big blue stem grass as the valley seemed to wave a silent goodbye.

"We shall never go back there," Little Crow muttered. Then he faced northwest again.

❧ 22 ❧

ENRY SIBLEY WAS IN NO rush to leave Wood Lake and journey to the Indian camp. He could have marched his army there in one afternoon. Instead, he waited three days. His men had just won a big battle, he reasoned. Let them rest. The wounded needed some time to mend.

After Little Crow left, Joe Campbell brought a message from Wabasha to the Long Trader.

Campbell was ushered into Sibley's large field tent. The flaps remained open, allowing a light breeze to blow in freshness off the lake. Sibley sat upon a stool behind a small field desk. He looked up at Campbell, who stood between two blue-coated soldiers.

"Talk to me," Sibley ordered with clipped words.

"I'm Joe Campbell. Wabasha, he sent me to tell you that the captives are now in the hands of friendly Indians. Those who made war on the whites are gone. It is safe to go the village. Little Crow's prisoners are waiting for you."

Sibley silently turned over Campbell's words and then began to scratch with a pen upon a sheet of paper. He wrote: "My friends. I call you so because I have reason to believe that you have had nothing to do

96

with the cruel murders and massacres that have been committed upon the poor white people who had placed confidence in the friendship of the Sioux Indians. I repeat what I have already stated to you, that I have not come to make war upon those who are innocent but upon the guilty. I have waited here one day and intended to wait still another day to hear from the friendly half-breeds and Indians because I feared that if I advanced my troops before you could make your arrangements, the war party would murder the prisoners. Now that I learn from Joseph Campbell that most of the captives are safe in your camp, I shall move tomorrow, so that you may expect to see me very soon. Have a white flag displayed so that my men may not fire upon you."

Once Campbell brought the letter to the Sioux camp, word swept among the captives like the rising waters of a flood. George Spencer, one of four captive men, shouted, "Our salvation is here! In a few hours we'll be saved!"

The Santee walked among the captives and gave them clothing that had been looted from white settlements. Chaska led Sarah and her children to the middle of the Santee camp, where the whites gathered near a high flag with a large American flag fluttering atop it.

"Maybe the soldiers won't be so angry if the whites are dressed as whites and not as Indians," he said, but he was still uneasy.

"Chaska, you and your mother have been so kind to us. You saved our lives. I'll speak to Sibley, I'll write a letter for you. Don't worry. Nothing will happen to you," Sarah assured him with deep gratitude.

"I wish I could be sure. Revenge is a strong feeling. It runs deep like the water of rivers in the spring," he replied.

Sibley didn't come the next day. The Dakota and the captives waited anxiously. Each sound downriver, each swirl of dust raised expectations and excitement in the village. Still no soldiers came. Excitement turned again and again to tension. It was a very difficult time.

Night passed into another day. Sarah Wakefield waited with her children and other women in a hastily constructed makeshift tipi. All looked out of place in clean new dresses. She tried not to wonder where they had come from, if the women who owned them had been killed.

Margaret Cardinell's dirty face was streaked by tears. "Why don't they come?" She sobbed. "Oh, where is Sibley?"

Martha Classen patted Margaret's dirty hair. "I heard a Sioux say that Sibley made only eight miles yesterday. He's close. But he should be here soon."

"Don't they realize what's happenin'?" Margaret cried. "Young girls're still bein' raped."

Nancy Faribault spoke in a trembling voice. "Last night twenty or thirty Indians came in with a young sixteen-or-seventeen-year-old white girl. They'd had her. I know it. She could hardly speak. All this while Sibley ain't doin' nothin'."

"Maybe he's afraid," Sarah said. "Chaska's worried that Little Crow might come back if Sibley doesn't come soon."

"No! He can't!" Margaret's voice rose in alarm, and her eyes went wild. "Sibley *must* come."

"Look at the funny man, Ma." Lisa pointed out the open tent flap. A disheveled Santee warrior was visible through the opening. He was tossing three apples into the air and juggling them effortlessly. Sarah quickly pulled the flap shut.

"It's Tazoo, honey. He was a bad man. Stay away from him."

"He's the one what raped Mattie Williams. I was there," Margaret whispered.

Martha shook her head sadly. "Mattie's had it rough. I wonder what's happened to her and the other three after White Dog took them off?"

"Mattie and that teacher, Emily West, are strong willed. I'm more worried about what's happened to Mary Schwandt."

"Yes, Margaret," Sarah replied, "But with White Dog, they're all in a bad place. Pray for them."

"Savages!" Margaret exclaimed. "I hope Sibley hangs 'em all!"

"Not all. Some have helped us."

"You had your protector, Sarah Wakefield. Most din't. It was real bad for lots of us."

"It wasn't like you think, Margaret. It wasn't easy for me, either." Then Sarah fell silent. She knew that after six weeks, their minds were set about her and about all Santee.

Another day passed while Sibley edged closer. When the village came in sight, the Long Trader ordered a halt and called his officers to the front of his 1,600-man column. Then Sibley stood stiff in his stirrups and addressed a dozen of his highest ranking men.

"There it is." He pointed up the river to the ratty-looking village. "We shall call our bivouac Camp Release. I have delayed moving thus far to recover from the battle, to make sure that the captives will not be caught in a crossfire, and to await orders. A messenger has brought me this from General Pope in St. Paul:

"'The horrible massacres of women and children and the outrageous abuse of female prisoners, still alive, call for punishment beyond human power to inflict. There will be no peace in this region by virtue of treaties and Indian faith.

"'It is my purpose utterly to exterminate the Sioux if I have the power to do so and even if it requires a campaign lasting the whole of next year. Destroy everything belonging to them and force them out to the plains, unless, as I suggest, you can capture them. They are to be treated as maniacs or wild beasts, and by no means as people with whom treaties or compromises can be made.'

"Well, gentlemen, we know our task. The Santee are supposed to be friendly. I've asked that a white flag be flown by them to acknowledge surrender. But be vigilant."

✂ 23 ☙

T TWO O'CLOCK ON THE AFTERNOON of September 26, six weeks after the conflict began, Henry Hastings Sibley and his escort of two companies of soldiers marched into Camp Release.

Drummers beat a rhythmic cadence as fifers piped a shrill melody. Regimental flags fluttered alongside the majestic Old Glory. As the procession entered the camp, bayonets glistened from the soldiers' rifle barrels.

A large American flag was displayed on a pole near the center of the camp. But just to be certain of safety, white rags were fastened to the tips of nearly every tipi pole. They were also on wagon wheels, tied to sticks stuck in the ground, and on various other objects.

A Santee brave sat stoically upon a black stallion. He had woven white cloth into the horse's tail and wrapped an American flag around his body.

Some bit of white cloth was worn by nearly every Indian as a sign of surrender.

Little Paul, Traveling Hail, Wabasha, and other friendly chiefs gathered beneath the large flag to await the Long Trader. Sibley marched expressionless and resolute at the head of his men.

He halted before the Santee. The drums silenced. Sibley was abrupt and to the point.

"Santee leaders, I demand that the prisoners be delivered to me instantly. They will go to my camp. If there are parties among you guilty of depredations against white citizens, I want them surrendered to me. I assure you that all Santee guilty of war crimes will be pursued, overtaken and punished."

Little Paul walked apart from his chiefs and stood before Sibley. The Santee raised his arms until all was quiet. Then he addressed the soldiers.

"We will release the captives to you. Taking them was Little Crow's doing and not ours. But first I must speak. I have grown up like a child of yours. With what is yours, you have caused me to grow, and now I take your hand as a child takes the hand of his father. My hand is not bad. With a clean hand I take your hand.

"I know whence this blessing cometh," Little Paul continued. "I have regarded all white people as my friends, and from this I understand this blessing has come. This is a good work we do today, whereof I am glad. Yes, before the great God, I am glad."

Instantly the mass of Indians parted, revealing the hostages. Rushing forward to the waiting soldiers were 107 whites and 162 half-breeds, nearly all women and children. Many wore new clothing from looted cabins, but many others were still half-naked, wearing shredded remnants of the clothing they had worn when captured.

Nearly all wept for joy, tears making mud of their dirty faces. Protruding ribs and sunken cheeks were tangible evidence that starvation had been a way of life for most. They pressed in upon Sibley and his officers, touching them and grabbing hold of the men's hands and arms, feeling only relief that their horrible ordeal was at an end.

Jesse Buchanen, who had fought valiantly at Wood Lake, whispered out of the corner of his mouth to Lieutenant Olin. "Look at their faces, woeful, half-starved. But some just have a blank stare like they've been through so much that nothing matters. Not even rescue."

Olin wrested an arm free from a beseeching woman. "It makes your heart sink. It's like they think the red devils will come back for 'em."

Sarah stood on the edge of the mass of captives with Chaska and his mother nearby. The Indian woman tore her shawl in half and gave one piece to Sarah. The two women tearfully embraced and held each other tight until Chaska placed his hand on Sarah's shoulder.

"I shall take you to the Long Trader. He knows me from his days with the fur company." Chaska paused and looked into Sarah's bright blue eyes. "You are a good woman. You must talk to your white people, or they will kill me. You know I am a good man and did not shoot Mr. Gleason, and I saved your life. If I had been a bad man, I would have gone with those bad chiefs into Dakota."

"Chaska, you're trembling." Sarah placed her hand upon the Indian's arm. "Don't worry. They won't harm you."

The Indian and the white woman approached Sibley as he freed himself from overwrought refugees.

"Long Trader," Chaska said, "this is Sarah Wakefield, wife of Dr. Wakefield from the Yellow Medicine Agency. "

"Colonel Sibley, we are grateful. This man, Chaska, saved my life and the lives of my children," Sarah explained in a rush. "We would not be here save for him. I trust he will be treated fairly."

"I know Chaska," Sibley answered. "If what you say is true, he has nothing to fear."

"What of my husband? Do you know anything?"

"Mrs. Wakefield, it is my pleasure to tell you that he was among those brought to safety in St. Paul by John Other Day. You may be together soon."

Weeks of worry and dark dread eased off her shoulders, almost making her weak with joy. "Thank God, Colonel! But I must ask, why did it take you three days after your victory at Wood Lake to get here? Didn't you realize what was happening here? Women were still being violated. We lived under constant fear that Little Crow would return.

God watched over us and kept the savages back. He deserves the honor and the glory. But not you."

Sibley was taken aback. He considered her words before he replied. "Mrs. Wakefield, you are still under great strain. You are safe now, and the criminals will be punished."

ɛɔ 24 ଔ

The next morning, September 27, 1862, dawned with a chill in the air. A smoky cloud drifted across the river from the Indian camp toward nearby Camp Release. Over 1,200 Dakota awaited their fates, and that number continued to swell as more and more left the prairie to surrender.

Henry Sibley looked fresh, his hair neatly combed and his mustache trim. He gingerly sipped at the tin cup of steaming coffee in his hand while gazing at the distant Dakota village before turning his attention to the blue-clad officers standing before him. They were the "brain trust" of his regiment: Colonel William Marshall, who commanded five companies in the battle of Wood Lake; Colonel William Crooks, who led the Sixth Minnesota Infantry at Birch Coulee and Wood Lake; Captain Hiram Grant, commander at Birch Coulee; Captain Hiram Bailey; Indian Agent Thomas Galbraith; Major George Bradley of the Seventh Minnesota; St. Paul attorney Isaac Heard, who advised Sibley and fought at Wood Lake; and First Lieutenant Rollin Olin, another veteran of Wood Lake, also an attorney.

"Gentlemen," Sibley began, "we now begin the next phase of our operation. I can tell you this. The cry for vengeance is resounding.

Newspapers cry for the extermination of the Dakota. One writer wants the government to treat them for all time to come as outlaws who have forfeited all right to property and life."

Sibley paused, then said, "Even our friend, the Reverend Stephen Riggs, speaks of the 'wail and howl for retribution.' We can ignore all of that. But we are soldiers and these words by our commander, General Pope, cannot be ignored."

Sibley reached into his pocket and unfolded a letter. He stared at it a moment, cleared his throat and read, "'The atrocious behavior of the Sioux calls for punishment beyond human power to inflict. There will be no peace in this region by virtue of treaties and Indian faith. It is my purpose utterly to exterminate the Sioux if I have the power to do so. Destroy everything belonging to them and force them out to the plains unless, as I suggest, you can capture them. They are to be treated as maniacs or wild beasts.'"

"Colonel Sibley," Thomas Galbraith said, sweeping a hand over his forehead before continuing. "What do you propose? There are so many of them."

"And more coming all the time," Captain Grant added. "They know winter is coming. They have no food. Women and children are out there, too. They'll starve or freeze to death. Bad as it is, we're all they've got. We could see another thousand surrender."

"Will you arrest them all?" Marshall wondered. "You said those who committed no atrocities have nothing to fear. How do we sort them out?"

"Bull!" Olin spat the word like a rifle shot. "They're all guilty. If they fought, they were part of the killin'."

Sibley looked evenly at his officers and spoke his mind. "We will arrest the worst of them tomorrow. I will announce a Military Commission to hear the evidence and pronounce verdicts. You will try summarily the mixed-bloods and Indians engaged in the raids and massacres. I have already considered this, and I want Marshall, Grant, Bailey, Crooks, and Olin to serve on the commission."

Bill Crooks shook his head slowly as his lips tightened. "I'd be glad to do as you order, Colonel, but this is a mighty task. None of us speak Sioux. How can we sort this out? I suspect that the worst of the savages have already headed west. We get stories even from the captives about 'good' Indians."

"They'll all be good when we get ropes around their necks," Olin shot back emphatically.

"Do you realize," Sibley replied, "we have one handsome woman who is so infatuated with the redskin who took her that she said she would not return to her husband were it not for her children. Then there is Harriet Adams from Meeker County, an exceedingly pretty young woman, who claims that she was not molested but protected as a sister by a brave."

"We got that Wakefield woman," Galbraith added, "claims that Chaska saved her life. Chaska and Hapa killed Gleason, my assistant. I don't care what the woman says. Chaska's gotta swing."

"That brings me back to my main point," said Sibley. "You raise good concerns. We don't know the language, and we've got to sort this out. Find out who to punish and who not to."

"Colonel," Heard began hesitantly. "I've got an idea. The first dozen or so might be easy. But then it gets harder to, as you say, sort it out. Stephen Riggs has been a missionary here for decades. He speaks their language and knows these people. Let him question the captives, gather evidence and bring the guilty, er, accused, to the commission."

"Kind of like a one-man grand jury," Sibley mused. "I like it. Will he do it?"

"I took the liberty of asking him to be helpful in a general sense. He agreed. I think he would do this."

"Good, gentlemen. Mr. Heard, talk to Riggs. It all begins tomorrow. One more thing. I have submitted my resignation to General Pope. My task was to end the hostilities and free the captives. I have done so. Now I think a more military man might be better suited for what remains to be done. That's all."

106

❦ 25 ❧

TEPHEN RIGGS WAS UNCOMFORTABLE in his black coat. The morning was cool, but it wasn't the temperature that caused him to draw the garment around himself like a cocoon.

Riggs gazed at the dusky Indian village with a heavy heart. The prospect of the duty thrust upon him by Isaac Heard was overwhelming.

He exhaled a frosty mist, unusual for late September, and shuddered through his fifty-year-old bones. His friend and longtime colleague Dr. Thomas Williamson stood alongside and shook his head in sympathy of the task before them.

"Stephen, who'd have thought it would come to this? Twenty-five years, save the year you went East to supervise the printing of the Dakota language translation. Twenty-five years among the Dakota in Minnesota. We've seen a lot of change in that time. Do you ever wish you'd stayed in Ohio? What would you have done?"

Riggs brushed back his graying hair and then thoughtfully stroked the short beard that framed his face along his chin and the bottom of his cheeks. "Thomas, I suppose I would have still have gone to college and then the Presbyterian seminary. Probably would have still married Mary and settled down to some small parish on the Ohio and preached my Sunday sermons. But you called me, Thomas. That's why I came."

"And you've been a godsend, Stephen. My mission needed someone like you, skilled in language to help me reduce the Dakota tongue to a written form to transmit the Gospel."

"'Just a little west of Fort Snelling,' you wrote me." Riggs smiled in spite of himself. "But it was a 200-mile, back-breaking trip up the Minnesota to your Lac qui Parle mission. Mary was about ready to leave me and go home."

"She's been an invaluable partner to you, Stephen, to us all."

"She's in St. Paul yet. Thank God, she was safe from the slaughter."

"But she followed us through it all. To each mission up and down the river: Lac qui Parle, Traverse des Sioux, Kaposia, and finally my Pajutazee and your Hazelwood mission at Yellow Medicine."

"Thomas, did we do right? The Episcopalians, Catholics, the government all wanted to change them. Make the Indians farm, send them to school, teach them English. Bringing them to Christ, the reason we became missionaries, became secondary to enculturation. If only we could have educated more of them. Those who could read and understand the Gospel would not commit savagery. We forced them to change. Men devoted to the life of hunter-warrior we asked to farm, to take on roles traditionally left to women."

"Change was inevitable, Stephen. These are people just out of the Stone Age. Bishop Whipple would agree. Before we could bring them down the path to eternal salvation, they must first learn to walk for themselves. Civilization and Christianity: these are the Siamese twins of our mission policy."

"And now they ask me to help kill them."

Williamson's bald pate reddened in the cold, and he wished he had his fur cap. But it had been left behind when he escaped Pajutazee mission, just ahead of marauding Santee on the eighteenth of August.

The medical doctor/missionary rubbed his scalp and softly reassured his friend. "Stephen, if this is to be done fairly, you are the best one, the only one for this ugly business. You speak Dakota fluently. You know many of them by name. You've witnessed depredations yourself and you'll be able to interview both Indian and white to ascertain who is guilty of crimes and who is not."

"It's a heavy responsibility. By my words men will be charged and tried. My words will cause the death of many men. I fear this is a terrible necessity. The demand for justice by the public will require that the great majority of those who are condemned be executed."

"If they have sinned against God and man, they deserve to die. Remember, an eye for an eye. A tooth for a tooth. There were many atrocities, especially in the Beaver Creek region and near New Ulm."

Riggs looked disturbed, then replied, "The soldiers here, they've seen so much destruction, they've buried the mutilated corpses. These soldiers are greatly enraged. Their officers have told me that they're afraid they won't be able to hold the men back once they confront the Santee. I've already heard revelations from the white women. The indignities performed upon them by the Indians will further enrage the soldiers. How can any fair decision be reached?"

"You have a heavy responsibility, Stephen."

A long sigh forced from deep in Riggs' lungs hung in the frosty air. "I will do what they have cast upon me. A tent will be set up. Heard will help take down testimony, and I will listen to stories of mayhem and horror. I pray to our Savior that I will be able to do what is right."

"God be with you, Stephen. He will guide you."

❧ 26 ❧

L ATER THAT MORNING Sarah Wakefield was troubled as she walked from Camp Release to the Indian village. She had left belongings in Chaska's tipi and wanted to retrieve them. Word had already spread through the camp that Indians would be arrested and tried for war crimes. Sarah feared for Chaska's safety.

She crossed the village and sensed apprehension creeping like a contagious disease through the people. When she reached Chaska's dwelling, she found her protector squatting near the opening, poking a stick at a dying campfire.

He stood to greet Sarah as hot embers drifted into the sky. His face was drawn, and his eyes reflected the anxiety he felt.

"The soldiers are rounding up the warriors," Chaska said pointedly. "They will come for me soon. I will die. I know it."

"No, Chaska, they musn't." Sarah stood directly in front of Chaska and stared into his fearful brown eyes. "I was wrong when I told you to stay. Leave. Leave now. I will see to your mother."

"No. I am not a coward." A look of resolution strengthened his face. "I am not afraid to die. All I care about is my poor old mother. She will be left alone. I should not have listened to you yesterday. Then I

110

could have escaped safely. Now it is too late. Now I will stand here and die if I must."

The flap of the tipi opened, and Chaska's mother stepped into the sunlight. Spying Sarah, her eyes narrowed and flashed like a stormy sky.

"White woman, my son listened to you. Now they will come to kill him. He saved your life. Now he will pay for bad things he never did. It is your fault."

Sarah Wakefield flushed red with shame and hurt. Tears welled in her eyes as she proclaimed, "Chaska, I'll still help you. No matter what happens. I'll fight for you."

Her belongings in the tipi now seemed trivial to Sarah. She turned back to Camp Release, leaving them and her friends behind.

A fire blazed near the center of Camp Release. Private Dan Buck gently placed a fresh log on top of those already flaming. The setting sun cast long shadows as twilight turned into dusk. Captain Hiram Grant drew up a campstool and joined officers, soldiers, and former captives to bask in the relaxing warmth of the campfire.

"Well, men, we've had a good day." The captain's face glowed orange, reflecting the flames. "Seven of the black devil redskins are in custody, and we'll hang 'em tomorrow. Then we'll round up some more. Then we'll hang them, too."

Jesse Buchanen cleared his throat. "What about trials? And haven't most of the real criminals like Little Crow, Red Middle Voice, and others already gotten away?"

Grant stared hard at Buchanen, then smiled. "Lieutenant, I've been appointed to the trial commission. We'll hear their stories about how innocent they are, how all the bad Indians are gone. We'll listen real good. Then, we'll hang 'em. They'll get about as much mercy as they gave Marsh at Redwood Ferry or my men at Birch Coulee. Reverend Riggs is gonna sort through things for us tomorrow. I think he needs a little help. Lieutenant Buchanen, I hereby give you the task of being the reverend's assistant through these proceedings."

"But—" Jesse began, regretting his questions.

"No," Grant waved a hand to silence Jesse, "we needed someone. I was just tryin' to decide who to pick. Thanks for volunteering. Tomorrow mornin' take Private Buck here and whoever else you need and get a tent set up. Make it a big one, a wall tent. Set it up to take testimony. You got legal trainin', so this should be easy for you. Help with the interviews of the savages. I 'spect we'll have sixteen cases for you by noon, counting the ones we already got.

"Now," Grant said, stretching his arms expansively and smiling at the glowing faces encircling the fire, "let's enjoy ourselves. Anybody got a fiddle?"

"Captain Grant." Sarah Wakefield stepped from shadows into the firelight. "Have you arrested Chaska?"

Grant squinted to adjust his eyes and identify Sarah. "Yes, we have," he answered, "and he'll swing with the rest of them." He said this as if Sarah would be overjoyed to hear it.

Sarah's eyes bore deeply into Grant. She spoke slowly and evenly. "If you hang that man, Captain Grant, I will shoot you."

Grant's mouth twisted. "Indian lover!"

"Squaw!" Someone else around the fire said.

Another voice. "Didn't get enough when you lived with him, huh?"

Sarah heard the cries and murmurs and realized that she was not in a position to make threats to an army captain. She felt at that moment that she was at as much risk as when she was in Little Crow's camp. She tried to make a joke of it. "But first, you might have to teach me how to shoot. I'm scared of guns, even unloaded ones."

Her joke fell flat. Sarah retreated back into the shadows with the realization that her words had not helped Chaska. She had to find another way.

๖ 27 ๏

HE NEXT MORNING SIBLEY stood in a tent before a diverse assemblage of his men. Twenty officers, enlisted men, and mixedbloods along with Riggs and Heard sat upon three rows of wooden planks beneath a large, dingy, light-colored canvas canopy.

"Gentlemen, it is time to put our plans into action. Captain Whitney, how many Dakota are assembled in their village?"

"Pushing 2,000, sir. More are coming in each day. Still more are camped in little groups out on the prairie. Just waiting, I guess."

"Mr. Courselle," Sibley addressed a mixed-blood sitting in the back row with five other mostly French-Santee men. "Tell the holdouts that anyone who surrenders will be treated as a prisoner of war. Tell them that we will feed them here or they can starve on the prairie when winter comes. The innocent will not be harmed if they give themselves up. But tell them that, unless these people arrive very soon, I will go in search of them with my troops and treat them as enemies. And if any more murders and depredations are committed upon white settlers, I will destroy every camp I can find, without mercy. Have them show white flags of truce when they come in. Do you have any questions?"

113

Courselle shook his head and mouthed, "No."

"Then take your men now and spread the word."

The six stood and departed the tent.

Whitney cleared his throat. "Sir, if they keep coming in, they'll overcrowd the friendlies' village. There just isn't room."

"Captain, start another village of them nearby if you have to. Just keep a watch on them all."

"How will we feed them?"

"Eventually, Captain, once we have a better handle of how many there are, take about a thousand of the Indians and, under guard, head down to Yellow Medicine. Dig potatoes and gather corn. Camp there. The harvest there should be ready in about a week or so. But today we have more immediate concerns. Major Galbraith, your report, please."

John Galbraith, late the government agent of Yellow Medicine and Redwood agencies, stood to address Sibley. His prominent Adam's apple bobbed as he cleared his throat and straightened his slender frame. "Colonel, seven were arrested yesterday, this morning nine more were taken in to custody. Sixteen in all, ready to go on trial."

"Keep it up. Bring in all the criminals. General Pope does not want us to be lenient. Let me read his latest missive."

Sibley unfolded a brown piece of parchment paper and read, "'I altogether approve of executing the Indians who have been concerned in these outrages. I don't know how you can discriminate now between Indians who say they are and have been the prisoners, and all who are guilty whatever the number should in my judgment be hung. Your task is to achieve a final settlement with all these Indians. Do not allow any false sympathy for the Indians to prevent you from acting with the utmost vigor.

"'Be assured I will sustain you in whatever measures you adopt to effect this objective.'

Sibley looked up. "The message is clear. Reverend Riggs has accepted the task of interviewing the former captives to bring forth more charges. A tent has been set up for him. Lieutenant Buchanen and Mr.

Heard will assist. Former white captives will be brought to you to question and to ascertain which Santee to bring to trial."

Riggs felt the burden of his responsibility as he inquired, "Who is the defense counsel?"

"Reverend," Sibley answered, "these people are not American citizens. They will not have counsel. You are their grand jury."

"I'll question them. But I don't accept your assignation of grand jury."

"Call it what you will. You'll determine whether or not these people shall come before the commission. You'll question the former white captives and mixed-bloods. Try to sort out their accusations and send names to me for arraignment. Begin your task now."

Riggs rose, his shoulders slumped, and exited the tent. Sibley looked at the front row where his five military commissioners sat together. "Gentlemen, those who have committed depredations must be brought to justice. We will begin with the sixteen that have been arrested. Mr. Heard, our lawyer from St. Paul, will record everything that transpires as court reporter. You are dismissed to embark upon this mission. God be with you."

"One moment, sir." A dark-haired captain in the second row stood, his face flushed. "My wife, Colonel, you know they took her at Lake Shetek. They hauled her off, and I don't know what the red devils have done to her. Just promise me one thing."

"Yes, Captain Duley. What do you want?"

"When the time comes to hang the bastards, let me pull the lever."

Sibley's face flashed sympathy and then resolution at Will Duley. "You shall have that honor. I promise you."

❧ 28 ❧

STEPHEN RIGGS, JESSE BUCHANEN, and Isaac Heard walked through a bustling Camp Release toward the single-wall tent erected for the interrogation. Men sat before their A-frame wedge tents frying salt pork and heating coffee. Some marched in formation in a morning drill.

Jesse brushed his blond hair from of his eyes and wondered what he had gotten himself into. "Gotta learn to keep my lawyer mouth shut," he thought. "What would JoAnna think about this?"

His thoughts wandered to that last afternoon with her in her father's cozy parlor. "Don't be foolish," she had admonished. *Well*, Jesse considered, *she probably will approve of this. It isn't very dangerous duty.*

"Thank God she's safe in St. Paul. Thank God she wasn't out here and didn't have to go through what these women did," he muttered to himself as he walked just behind Riggs and Heard. Still, he worried that a great unfairness was happening, and he was part of it.

Several women were gathered near the entrance to the tent, escorted by two blue-uniformed guards who stood on either side of the opening. When the three interrogators approached, one guard saluted and took a step forward.

116

"These here are Margaret Cardinell, Harriet Fallant, Mary Schwandt, and Mattie Williams. They got ev'dence 'bout the accused," the guard reported.

Riggs paused before the women and gazed into their eyes as if seeking a hidden truth within them. "Are you all here with testimony about the same Indians?"

"No, sir. I'm Margaret Cardinell. Me and Harriet here want to tell you about One Who Forbids His House. They call him Te-he-do-ne-cha. Mary and Mattie, they's here about Tazoo, the Juggler."

"I think it's best to handle this case by case. Margaret, Harriet, please enter. Mary and Mattie, wait, please. We'll be with you soon."

Riggs motioned with his arm to the open tent flap. Margaret and Harriet entered, followed by Riggs and the two other men. The sparse furnishings included half a dozen camp stools and a small portable writing desk. The dim translucence of the tent's interior added to the melancholy mood of those within.

"Mr. Heard, you should use the table. You're our record keeper. Let's arrange the other stools into a circle. I think we can communicate better that way. Ladies, I know this will be hard for you," Riggs said gently. "Tell us what happened as best you can."

Margaret Cardinell brushed her red hair from her freckled and sun-burned face and began hesitantly. "It . . . it happened by Beaver Creek, 'cross the river from Redwood. We heard there was killin' at the agency. We thought it was the Yankton from Dakota, so we got in a wagon and headed toward Fort Ridgely. I 'spose there was a dozen of us all tol'. When we got out on the prairie, dozens of them Indians appeared. They seemed to just come up outta the grass like they was spirits. Some of the men, they left us, ran for their lives like the cowards they was. The Indians, they ran 'em down and killed 'em."

"Kilt all the men," Harriet Fallant interjected, "then they took the rest of us. 'Cept the littlest ones. Them they kilt too. Smashed the heads of babies, they did." She bent her head and sobbed, "One was mine."

"What about One Who Forbids His House?" Riggs inquired. "It is he of whom we must ascertain guilt. What did he do? Did he kill anyone?"

"Things hap'ned so fast." Margaret's voice became breathless. "The Indians was killin' all over. He was there. I don't know if he kilt anyone. I think he kilt Martha Classen's pa, her nephew, and husband. I'm not sure. I was so scairt."

"But we do know what he did later, don't we, Margaret," Harriet reminded her, and her eyes became cold.

"Yes, Reverend, after they beat us and dragged us with them, One Who Forbids His House took me the third night and," she choked out the words, "and raped me."

"I was there when he took her," Harriet said between clenched teeth. "He was always ready to fight, went on every war party and then came back to rape the women."

"You are certain it was One Who Forbids His House?"

"There ain't no doubt, Reverend." Tears streamed down Margaret's face as memories flooded back. "I'd go to my grave swearin' it was him that did me."

Riggs turned to the men with him. "Mr. Heard, Lieutenant Buchanen. Unless you think differently, I believe there is evidence to bring this man before the commission."

The two men nodded their silent assent.

Riggs stood and placed his hands on the women's shoulders, then looked into their eyes once again. "Bless you, children. You have suffered far more than I'm sure we can imagine. You will be called for the trial. Stay nearby and may the Almighty take away your suffering and despair. You may leave. Please ask Mary and Mattie to enter."

Moments later Mary Schwandt and Mattie Williams entered the dim tent.

Riggs motioned for them to be seated. He looked earnestly at each and began, "Tell me your story."

⚘ 29 ⚘

wo wall tents were spliced together to accommodate Sibley's Military Commission. Near the end of the back wall, a long table spanned most of the tent's width. Five officers in blue uniform tops sat behind it.

One camp stool for the testifiers had been placed before the commissioners. Planks resting upon cut tree stumps provided seating for those called or required by the commission.

Two enlisted soldiers stood at either side of the tent opening opposite the commission. The tent flaps at either end were open, allowing fresh air to flow though. The musty smell of canvas slowly spread as the noon sun gently warmed the tent.

Colonel Marshall stroked his full, dark beard thoughtfully. A small sigh escaped his lips. *Time to get on with it*, he thought. His hand moved to his almost completely bald head as he scratched a small red mosquito bite atop it. Then he spoke.

"Gentlemen, in moments our proceedings will begin. Mr. Heard will record. You may feel free to ask questions as you wish. Lieutenant Olin will act as judge advocate and begin the questioning. We will be firm and respectful. No demonstrations will be tolerated from any of the onlookers.

"We have sixteen on the docket today. All have been questioned by Reverend Riggs and the arraignments signed by General Sibley. Mr. Heard, who is first?"

"The mulatto Joe Godfrey, or Otakle, as the Sioux call him."

Marshall looked back at the soldiers. "Bring in all concerned with this case," he ordered.

Moments later they filed in. Two solders marched before a sinewy black man, and two kept pace behind. Joe Godfrey's hands were shackled by iron manacles. He shuffled more than walked. His skin had a yellowish tinge, and his short hair curled over his ears. A black mustache drooped to a short beard that framed his chin. His clothing was the rough but clean attire of a white frontiersman, homespun woolen pants and a cotton shirt. Two men and two women followed along with several more soldiers. All took seats on the planks except for Godfrey, who stood before the commission.

Marshall looked at Olin and nodded his head. Olin, from his seat behind the table, looked hard at the man before them.

"Are you Joe Godfrey, the man known to the Sioux as Otakle?" Olin inquired sternly.

"I am," Godfrey replied.

"As duly sworn members of the Military Commission assigned to preside over these proceedings, I have in my hand charges against you signed by Colonel Henry Hastings Sibley. They read as follows:

Charge and specification against Otakle, a colored man connected with the Sioux tribe of Indians. Charge, murder. Specification first. In this, that the said Otakle, or Godfrey, a colored man, did, at or near New Ulm, Minnesota, on or about the 19th day of August, 1862, join a war party of the Sioux tribe of Indians against the citizens of the United States, and did with his own hand murder seven white men, women, and children (more or less), peaceable citizens of the United States. Specification second. In this, that the said Otakle, or Joe Godfrey,

120

a colored man, did, at various times and places between the 19th of August, 1862, and the 28th day of September, 1862, join and participate in the murders and massacre committed by the Sioux Indians on the Minnesota frontier."

Olin paused. His eyes bore into Godfrey like a steel drill. "How say you, guilty or not guilty?"

Without hesitation the black man responded, "I am not guilty."

"Then sit," Olin gestured to the stool before them. "We want to hear your story. Start at the beginning. How did you arrive at becoming an Indian?"

Godfrey sat and looked unafraid at his accusers. He spoke in broken English, but his voice was clear and articulate. "I am twenty-seven years old. I was born at Mendota. My father was a Canadian Frenchman, and my mother a colored woman, who was hired in the family of the late Alexander Bailley. I was raised in Mr. Bailley's family. My father is, I think, living in Wisconsin; his name is Joe Godfrey. My mother is also living at Prairie du Chien. I last saw my father and mother at Prairie du Chien seven years ago.

"I lived with Mr. Bailley at Wabasha, and also at Hastings and Faribault. I had lived at the Lower Agency five years. I was married, four years ago, to a woman of Wabasha's band, daughter of Wakpadoota. At the time of the outbreak, I lived on the reservation on the south side of the Minnesota River, between the Lower Agency and New Ulm, about twenty miles below the agency and eight above New Ulm."

"What does Otakle mean?" Bailey questioned.

"He Who kills Many," Godfrey answered.

"Does your name convict you?" Bailey continued.

"No, I killed no one. To kill in war is an honor. If people are killed in a house, my people give credit to the man who first enters the house. It is a brave thing to do. Even though someone else may have shot them from a ways off, they might be only pretending. It is the same in touching a slain person. The person with first touch is given credit whether the act was done or not. Such was the case with me. I just entered the house first. I did not kill anyone in it."

"So," Crooks interrupted, "what was your part in the fighting?"

"The first I heard of the trouble, I was mowing hay. About noon an Indian was making hay near me. I went to help him, to change work. He was to lend me his oxen. I helped him load some hay, and as we took it to his place, we heard hallooing, and saw a man on horseback, with a gun across his legs before him. When he saw me, he drew his gun up and cocked it. The Indian with me asked him, 'What's the matter?' He looked strange. He wore a new hat, a soft gray hat, and had a new white leather ox or mule whip. He said all the white people had been killed at the agency. The Indian with me asked who did it, and he replied the Indians, and that they would soon be down that way to kill the settlers towards New Ulm.

"He asked which side I would take. He said I would have to go home and take off my clothes and put on a breech-clout. I was afraid. He held his gun as if he would kill me. I went to my house and told my wife to get ready, and we would try to get away. I told my wife about what the Indian had told me. I told her we would try to get down the river. She said we would be killed with the white people. We got something ready to take with us to eat, and started. We got about 200 yards into the woods.

"The old man, my wife's father, said he would fasten the house and follow after. We heard someone halloo. It was the old man. He called to us to come back. I told my wife to go on, but her mother told her to stop. I told them to go ahead, but the old man called so much that they stopped and turned back. I followed them.

"I found my wife's uncle at the house. He scolded my wife and her mother for trying to get away. He said that all the Indians had gone to the agency, and that they must go there. He said we would be killed if we went towards the white folks, that we would only be safe to go and join the Indians. I still had my pants on. I was afraid, and they told me I must take my pants off and put on the breech-clout. I did so. The uncle said we must take a rope and catch a horse.

"I started with him towards New Ulm, and we met a lot of Indians at the creek, about a mile from my house. They were all painted and said I must be painted. They painted me. I was afraid to refuse."

Godfrey paused and gazed plaintively at the commissioners. His face appeared open and honest. He took a breath and continued his testimony. "They asked me why I didn't have a gun, or knife, or some weapon. I told them I had no gun. The old man had taken it away. One Indian had a spear, a gun, and a little hatchet. He told me to take the hatchet, and that I must fight with the Indians and do the same as they did, or I would be killed.

"We started down the road. We saw two wagons with people in them coming towards us. The Indians consulted what to do and decided for half of them to go up to a house off the road on the right-hand side. They started but I stopped, but they called me and told me I must come.

"There was an old man, a boy, and two young women at the house—Dutch people. The family's name was something like Massopust. The boy and two girls stood outside, near the kitchen door. Half of the Indians went to the house. Half remained in the road. The Indians told me to tell the whites that there were Chippewa about, and that they, the Indians, were after them.

"I did not say anything," Godfrey continued his testimony. "The Indians asked for some water. The girls went into the house, and the Indians followed and talked in Sioux. One said to me, 'Here is a gun for you.' Dinner was on the table, and the Indians said, 'After we kill, then we will eat.' They told me to watch the road, and when the teams came up to tell them. I turned to look, and just then I heard the Indians shoot. I looked, and two girls fell just outside the door. I did not go into the house. I started to go round the house. We were on the back side of it when I heard the Indians on the road hallooing and shouting. They called me, and I went to the road and saw them killing white men. My brother-in-law told me that I must take care of a team that he was holding, that it was his.

"I saw two men killed that were with this wagon. I did not see who killed them in the other wagon. I saw one Indian stick his knife in the side of a man that was not yet dead. He cut his side open and then cut him all to pieces. His name was Great Spirit.

"Two of the Indians that killed the people at the house have been charged. Their names are Wakiyani and Mahhwa. There were about ten Indians at the house and about the same number in the road. I got into the wagon, and the Indians all got in.

"We turned and went towards New Ulm. When we got near to a house, the Indians all got out and ran ahead of the wagons, and two or three went to each house, and in that way they killed all the people along the road. I stayed in the wagon and did not see the people killed," Godfrey concluded.

Colonel Marshall looked perplexed as he stared at Godfrey. "Let me get this straight. You only held the horses and had nothing to do with the killings?"

"Yes. They killed the people of six or eight houses—all until we got to the 'Travelers' Home.' There were other Indians killing people all through the settlement. We could see them and hear them all around. I was standing in the wagon and could see three or four or five Indians at each house. When we got near the 'Travelers' Home' they told me to stop. I saw an old woman with two children, one in each hand, run away across the yard. One Indian, Mazabomdoo, shot the old woman and jumped over and kicked the children down with his feet. The old woman fell down as if dead.

"I turned away and did not see whether the children were killed. After that the Indians got in the wagon and told me to start down the road. We started on and got to a house where a man lived named Schling, a German, an old man," Godfrey related.

"The Indians had found a jug in the wagon and were now almost drunk. They told me to jump out. I jumped out and started ahead, and the Indians called to me to come back. They threw out a hatchet and said I must go to the house and kill the people. Mazabomdoo was ahead. He told me that there were three guns there that he had left while he carried out flour, and we must get them. I was afraid.

124

"I went into the house. There was the old man, his wife and son, and a boy and another man. They were at dinner. The door stood open, and the Indians were right behind me and pushed me in. I struck the old man on the shoulder with the flat on the hatchet, and then the Indians rushed in and commenced to shoot them," Godfrey said.

"The old man, woman, and the boy ran into the kitchen. The other man ran out some way, I did not see how, but when we went back to the road, about twenty steps, I saw him in the road dead. He was the man I struck in the house. I heard the Indians shoot back of the house, but did not see what at.

"After we started to go to Redwood, one little Indian who had pox marks on his face, and who was later killed at Wood Lake, said he struck the boy with a knife but didn't say if he killed him. He told this to the other Indians.

"We saw coming up the road two wagons, one with a flag in it. The Indians were afraid, and we started back and went past the 'Travelers' Home.' We got to a bridge and the Indians got out and laid down in the grass about the bridge. I went on up the road.

"The wagons, with white men, came on up and stopped in the road, where there was a dead man, I think. They sounded the bugle and started to cross the bridge, running their horses. The foremost wagon had one horse of a gray color. Three men were in it and had the flag. Just as they came across the bridge, the Indians raised up and shot. The three men fell out, and the team went on. The Indians ran and caught it," Godfrey continued.

"The other wagon had not got across the bridge. I heard them shoot at the men in it, but I did not see them. After the Indians brought the second wagon across the bridge, three Indians got in the wagon. After that all of them talked together and said that it was late, the sun was nearly down, and that they must look after their wives and children that had started to go to Redwood.

"Many of these Indians lived on the lower end of the reservation. The two-horse team that they had just taken was very much frightened, and they could not hold them. They told me I must take hold and drive them. I took the team, and they all got in. We then had four teams. We started from there and went on up. When we got to where the first people were killed, the Indians told me to drive up to the house," Godfrey said.

"The two girls were lying dead. I saw one girl with her head cut off. The head was gone. One Indian, an old man, asked who cut the head off. He said it was too bad. The other Indians said they did not know. The girl's clothes were turned up. The old man put them down. He is now in prison. His name is Wazakoota. He is a good old man. While we stood there, one wagon went to another house, and I heard a gun go off.

"We started up the road and stopped at a creek about a mile further on. We waited for some of the Indians that were behind. While we were, there we saw a house on fire. When the Indians came up, they said that Wakpadoota, my father-in-law, had shot a woman who was on a sick-bed through the window, and that an old man ran upstairs, and the Indians were afraid to go into the house. They thought he had a gun, and they set fire to the house and left it.

"We then started on from that creek and went about seven miles to near a little lake, about a hundred yards from the road. We saw, far away, a wagon coming towards us. When it was only two miles from us, we saw it was a two-horse wagon, but the Indians did not know if it was white people. When it came nearer, they told me to go fast. The Indians whipped the horses and hurried them on," Godfrey said.

"Two Indians were ahead of us on horseback. Pretty soon we came near, and the team that was coming towards us stopped and turned around, and the Indians said it was white men, and they were trying to run away. The two on horseback then shot, and I saw a white man, I think it was Patoille, fall back over his seat. After that I saw three women and one man jump out of the wagon and run.

"Then those in the wagon with men jumped out and ran after the women. We got up to the wagon. Patoille was not dead. The Indians threw him out, and a young Indian stuck his knife between his ribs,

126

under his arm, and another one, who is with Little Crow now, took his gun and beat his head all to pieces.

"The other Indians killed the other white man near the little lake and brought back the three women—Mattie Williams, Mary Anderson, and Mary Schwandt," Godfrey said.

Mary looked to Mattie as tears formed in her clear-blue eyes and slowly rolled down sun-browned cheeks. Mattie reached over and clasped Mary's hand tightly. She whispered softly into her friend's ear, "It's our story now. Let's see how he lies."

"He can fool 'em, Mattie. His face, it looks so honest. He don't speak English that good, but his voice is so soft and nice to hear. They might believe him."

"Patoille's wagon was full of trunks," Godfrey continued. "The Indians broke them open and took the things out. There was some goods in them. Patoille being a trader. They put one woman in the wagon I drove. The other two were put separately in the other wagons.

"The one in my wagon, Mary Schwandt, was caught by Mazabomdoo, Tazoo had Mattie Williams. We then went on and stopped at a creek about a mile ahead to water the horses. Then they called me to ask the woman that was wounded if she was badly hurt.

"She said, 'Yes.' They told me to ask her to show the wound and that they would do something for it. She showed the wound. It was in the back. The ball did not come out. She asked where we were going. I said I did not know but supposed to Redwood.

"I asked what had been done at the agency. She said they did not know, that they'd came around on the prairie past Redwood. I told her that I heard that all the whites at the agency were killed and the stores robbed," Godfrey continued.

"She said she wished they would drive fast so she could have a doctor to do something for her wound. She was afraid she would die. I said I was a prisoner, too. She asked what would be done with them. I said I didn't know; perhaps we would all be killed. I said maybe the doctor was killed if all the white people were.

"After that we started on, and got to the Redwood Agency about nine o'clock. It was dark. The Indians looked around and did not see any people. We went on to Wacouta's house. He came out and told me to tell the girl in my wagon to go into his house. I told the girl, but she was afraid and said she thought the other women were somewhere else.

"I told her that Wacouta said they were in his house and she had better go. Wacouta told her to go with him, and she got out and went with him. I then went on to Little Crow's village, where most all of the Indians had gone. I found my wife there. We stayed there some time, and then started for the fort.

"They asked me to drive a team. After we got there, they commenced to fight. They broke into the stable and told me to go and take all the horses I could. I got a black mare, but an Indian took it away from me. They fought all day and slept at night in the old stable under the hill.

"The next morning they fought only a little. It was raining. We then went back to Redwood. In about six days after, all of the Indians started and said they would go to Mankato. They came down towards the fort on that side of the river and crossed near the 'Travelers' Home.'

"When they got opposite the fort they stopped and talked of trying to get in again, but didn't. About noon they went to New Ulm. I saw no white people on the road. I got to New Ulm about two hours after noon. They burned houses and shot and fought. They slept at New Ulm that night and the next day went back to Little Crow's village."

"Godfrey," Captain Grant asked, "there were two attacks on New Ulm. Was this the first or the second?"

"It was the second, Captain. I was in Little Crow's village during the first."

"Continue," Olin ordered.

"After a few days, we went to Rice Creek, stayed there a few days, and then started again to come to Mankato. After crossing the Redwood River, we went up the hill and saw some wagons on the prairie on the other side of the river. After the Indians had crossed over the Minnesota River to where they saw the wagons, those that stayed back went over early the next morning. I went with them. We got there at sunrise. We heard shooting just before we got there. They were shooting all day. They killed all the horses."

"Stop!" Marshall said abruptly, his expansive forehead tinged red with anger. "Horses. You say they killed horses? This sounds like Birch Coulee to me. Men died there, not just horses."

"Twenty-five of my men," said Grant. "After a cowardly sneak attack on a sleeping camp."

Godfrey was startled but quickly regained his composure and resumed his monologue in a steady voice. "At night the Indians killed some cattle and cooked and ate some meat. Some talked of trying to get into the camp, and some tried it all night. Others talked of watching till they should drive them out for want of water. Three Indians were killed that day, so the Indians said. I saw some wounded, I should think five.

"In the morning some more talk was had about trying to get in. In the meantime, we saw soldiers coming up, and half of the Indians started to try and stop them, and the other half stayed to watch the camp at Birch Coulee. They went down to try and stop the soldiers, and afterwards came back and said it was no use—that they couldn't stop them.

"Some wanted to try and get the whites into Birch Coulee, but others thought they had better go back. They fired some shots, and then started back. The Sisseton got to us while we were there the second day, about two or three hours before the Indians all left. The Indians left a little before sundown. They crossed the river at the old crossing and went up to the site of Reynolds' house, the other side of the Redwood and camped.

"They started about midnight to go to Rice Creek," Godfrey continued, "and got there about sunrise. Stayed there several days. While we were at Birch Coulee, Little Crow was at the Big Woods. He got back to Rice Creek two days after we did. We went from Rice Creek to Yellow Medicine and stayed there about two weeks. While there ten or twenty started every day to see if soldiers were coming.

"When they reported that soldiers were on the way, we moved our camp to where Mr. Riggs lived, then up to Red Iron's village, then to a little way from where the friendly camp was. After scouts reported that soldiers had crossed the Redwood, Little Crow made a speech and said that all must fight, that it would be the last fight and that all must do the best they could. Scouts reported about midnight that soldiers were camped at Rice Creek.

"In the morning we all started down to Yellow Medicine, got there a little before sundown. Some were there earlier. We stayed at Yellow Medicine all night. Some wanted to begin the attack in the night, but others thought it was best to wait until morning. In the morning, the fight began. After the fight, went back to the old camp at Camp Release," Godfrey said.

"Little Crow tried to get all to go with him, but they would not. Little Crow started away in the night. I didn't see him go. I never was out at any of the war parties except once at New Ulm, the last fight, once at the fort, at Birch Coulee, and at Wood Lake. They thought that the Winnebagoes would commence at Mankato and attack the lower settlements."

Colonel Marshall glanced bemusedly to his right and then his left. Incredulous, he commented, "You were at all these major conflicts, and yet you fired no gun and killed no one? I find this hard to believe. You may step down. There are others who wish to testify as to your role in this war."

Olin looked up from a sheet of paper and called, "Mary Woodbury, please come forward."

Godfrey and Mary passed each other as the woman took her place on the chair. She swiftly looked down and avoided his gaze.

"Mrs. Woodbury," Olin began, "what can you tell us of the mulatto Godfrey or Otakle?"

Mary straightened her calico print dress and tried to sit primly on the small stool. For a moment she stared at Godfrey and then turned to face the commissioners. Her blonde hair highlighted her bronzed, creased face. "I seen him two or three days after the outbreak at Little Crow's village with a breech clout on, and his legs and face all painted up fer a war party, and that he started with one fer New Ulm," Mary testified. "He looked very happy with the Indians. He was whoopin' around and yellin', apparently as fierce as any of 'em.

"When they came back, there was a Wahpeton, named Hunka, who told folks that the negro was the bravest of all, that he led them into a house and clubbed people with a hatchet. I was standin' in the prisoners' tent door, and I heard the Indians ask Godfrey how many he had kilt, and he said only seven. I saw him once, when he started off. He had a gun, a knife, and a hatchet. He was proud of his killin'. I know he was."

"Mrs. Woodbury," Crooks asked, "did you actually see him kill anyone?"

"No, sir, but I betcha he did."

Mattie Williams was called forward next. "When the war party took me and Mary Schwandt, Godfrey wasn't armed. But he was as much in favor of what they was doin' as anyone. He never tried to help us. Maybe he couldda helped with Mary Anderson, but he didn't."

Hiram Bailey asked sympathetically, "What did happen to Mary Anderson?"

"Like Godfrey said, they took her into Wacouta's house, where we all was. Mary was in bad shape. The bullet was in her stomach. Wacouta hisself, he tried to dig the bullet out. But he couldn't get it. I think he was afraid a hurtin' her."

Mattie choked back tears and swallowed hard before continuing. "Mary, she took the knife and dug out the bullet herself. But it was too much. Later that night," she sobbed and wiped her eyes with her hands, "she died."

Mattie was dismissed and returned to her seat. Olin looked at Mary Schwandt.

"Miss Schwandt, do you have anything to add?"

Mary slowly rose and walked to the stool as tears welled in her eyes.

"Mary, how old are you,?" Marshall asked gently.

"Fourteen, sir."

"What happened to you?"

"It was like Mattie said. I was raped too. But not by Godfrey. I don't know who they was that did it. One thing I want to say. We was separated from the other captives and taken west. Two other girls was with us. We wouldn't be here today if it wasn't for two men what rescued us."

Olin said, "I know the men. For the record, what were their names?"

Mary sat straight and spoke clearly. "Nathan Cates—he's only got one arm—and Solomon Foot. They was heroes."

"Indeed they were, Miss," Olin concluded. "Do you have anything to add?"

Mary Schwandt looked down and shook her head, then stood and returned to her seat.

"David Faribault," Olin intoned. "Please come forward."

Faribault, a half-breed who had been in the Dakota camp but not gone on any raids, took the seat before the commission.

"What do you know of this man, Joe Godfrey?" Olin inquired.

"I heard Otakle boast that he killed seven with a tomahawk. He said he killed children too but did not count them. Many saw him at Fort Ridgely and at New Ulm. He fought and acted like an Indian. I saw him. He never told me that he was forced into the outbreak."

Faribault returned to his seat as the commissioners leaned toward Marshall.

In a whispered voice, Marshall asked, "I say he's guilty and should hang, especially on the second specification. It's plain he was in a lot of battles. Anybody have an objection."

Olin said with deference. "Sir, let's clear the tent. I have a thought."

Marshall returned his gaze to the people assembled before him. "Major Forbes, keep the prisoner under guard and clear the tent of him and everyone else. We'll let you know when to come back in."

Godfrey and his escort quickly exited through the tent flap, followed by everyone save the commissioners and Heard.

"Mr. Olin?" Marshall questioned.

"Sir, this is my thought. So far we have no eyewitness evidence that Godfrey killed anyone. We have a lot more cases to hear, and it could get confusing. Riggs already tells me that some Sioux claim they weren't at such and such battle or they fell asleep or didn't shoot or whatever. We need someone who was there to help us sort this out. Perhaps a deal might be in order in return for Godfrey's testimony."

"What kind of deal, Lieutenant Olin?" Bailey wondered.

"Let's hold this case open. Don't sentence him now."

"You mean hold it over his head?" Grant asked.

"Exactly, but he'll know that if he cooperates we'll go easy on him when it's over."

"So," Marshall mused, "we get Godfrey to help us sort through the accused so we get the right ones to hang, and we let Godfrey live. Will he do it?"

"He will if he wants to live," Olin replied.

"Then let's do it. Nearly fifty people were killed in the Beaver Creek area across from Redwood. I want to nail the killers. Maybe Godfrey can help. Lieutenant Olin, make him the offer. Get Riggs involved. We'll delay sentencing."

The Marshall called, "Major Forbes, bring in the prisoner and all concerned."

Godfrey was returned to his stool in front of the commissioners. Those who had witnessed or participated in the proceedings filed to their places behind him.

"Will the prisoner, Joe Godfrey, stand," Marshall commanded.

Godfrey rose and gazed at the commissioners with what appeared to be open-face innocence.

Marshall returned the gaze with a firm stare. "We are going to suspend sentencing in your case until a later date. You will hear from Lieutenant Olin. Return him to confinement and bring in the next prisoner."

As Godfrey left the tent, Chaska was led in by a similar escort of four.

❧ 30 ☙

SARAH WAKEFIELD SAT WITH Angus Robertson, a middle-aged man who had escaped the killings at Beaver Creek.

Chaska was led to the stool before the commissioners. He looked back at Sarah before he sat down. The fear in his eyes was as clear as a fire bell in the night. Sarah tried to reassure him with a small smile and nod of her head.

For the second time that day Rollin Olin stood to read charges. He cleared his throat in preparation. "'Charge against Wechankwashtodopee, a Sioux Indian, otherwise known as Chaska—murder. Specification, in this that the said Chaska, Sioux Indian, did, on or about the 18th day of August 1862, kill George H. Gleason, a white citizen of the United States, and has likewise committed sundry hostile acts against the whites between the said 18th day of August 1862, and the 28th day of September 1862. This near the Redwood River, and at other places on the Minnesota frontier. By order of Colonal H.H. Sibley.'"

As Olin sat upon his chair, Marshall asked, "What do you say in answer to the charges against you?"

Chaska stood, his manacles clinking together. "I plead not guilty of murder."

"Then tell us your story. You may sit if you wish."

"I will stand when I talk to you." Fear had left his eyes, and Chaska spoke with a newly found resolution. "The other Indian shot Gleason, and, as he was falling over, I aimed my gun at him but did not fire. I have had a white woman in my charge, but I could not take as good care of her as a white man because I am an Indian. I kept her with the intention of giving her up. Don't know of any other bad act since Gleason was murdered. I moved up here with the Indians. If I had done any bad act, I should have gone off.

"I was present when the white man was killed. It was a war party who killed Gleason. The other Indian was not a relative of mine. The other Indian fired twice. The others said 'Brother-in-law, let's shoot him.' He had already shot him. I aimed at him because I was told I must kill the whites to save myself. I have been in three battles. I have not fired at any other white man.

"I wanted to prevent the other Indian from shooting. I prevented him from killing the women and children with Gleason. I snapped my gun at Gleason, but it failed to go off. Then I shot over Gleason when he fell. This was the third shot. I afterward snapped at him when he was dead on the ground. That is what happened. I am done."

"Take a seat on the bench, Chaska," Olin instructed. "Would Sarah Wakefield sit before us?"

Sarah and Chaska faced each other briefly as they exchanged places. Sarah again tried to reassure him with a smile. She stood and swore an oath to tell the truth and then sat down.

"Mrs. Wakefield, can you add to the account given by Chaska?" Olin inquired.

"Yes, Lieutenant, I will. I was with Mr. Gleason when he was killed. Myself and two children were riding with him. There were two in the party who attacked us. The Indians were coming up from the direction of the Lower Agency. The other man shot Mr. Gleason. Chaska tended the horses. When the shots were fired, the horses ran, and he caught them. The Indian was near the wagon when he fired. He shot both barrels and loaded up while Chaska ran after the horses. When Mr. Gleason was in his death agony, Chaska snapped his gun at him. He afterwards told me that it was to put him out of his misery.

"I saw this Indian endeavor to prevent the other Indian from firing at me. He raised his gun twice to do it. He said he did not go into this thing willingly. John Reynolds, from the school, knows him very well and considers him a fine man. Chaska had on leggings at the time Gleason was shot," Sarah continued.

"When we got in to camp, he took me and my babes from a tipi where it was cold to one where there was a white woman. Since then he has saved my life three times. When Chaska prevented the other Indian from killing me, the others wanted to kill my children, saying 'they were no use,' but Chaska prevented it.

"I've never known him to go away but twice. He went only when he was freed to go and expressed great feeling for the whites. His mother took me in the woods and kept me when my life was threatened. He saved my life once when Shakopee, the chief of his band, tried to kill me.

"Chaska has no plunder in his tent. They are very poor, he and his family. They have had to beg victuals for me, and he's given his coffee and food to my children and gone without himself. He's a very generous man. I've seen him give away his own shirt to Indians. He's guilty of no crime that I know of."

Olin looked at the other commission members. Seeing there were no questions, he announced to Sarah, "If you have nothing else, you may return to your seat. Next witness, Angus Robertson, come forward."

Robertson sat upon the stool and relayed his contact with Chaska. "I heard the prisoner say before Mrs. Wakefield that he fired the second shot. He said his brother-in-law wanted to kill Mrs. Wakefield and her children, but he prevented it. Chaska said he shot but didn't kill Gleason. This Indian is a very good Indian. He was good towards Mrs. Wakefield and her children."

Robertson fell silent and Marshall said, "If you have nothing else, Mr. Robertson, I will ask Major Forbes to clear this enclosure, and we will deliberate."

Forbes directed all to exit the tent, leaving only the five commissioners and Heard.

"Gentlemen," Marshall began, "what say you regarding Chaska?"

"He shot at Gleason," Colonel Crooks responded. "Once he missed, says intentionally, another time his gun didn't fire. Hang 'im."

Bailley seemed uncomfortable and squinted his face as if he had bitten into a sour lemon. "What about Mrs. Wakefield and her children? Apparently he saved them."

Olin retorted, "Captain, there are stories about her relationship with Chaska. Many think she forgot who she was and got a little too friendly with him. She lived in his tipi for nearly six weeks. Her comments might be biased. He fired his gun. Whether he hit Gleason or not, he was there and didn't stop the murder. I agree with Colonel Crooks. Hang him."

"Objections?" Marshall asked. There was no response. "Heard, bring them in."

In moments Chaska stood before the men who held the power to determine his fate.

Olin began to read, "This Military Commission after mature deliberation on the testimony adduced find the prisoner as follows: Guilty of the specification of the first charge. Guilty of the first charge. Guilty of the specification of the second charge. Guilty of the second charge and do, therefore, do sentence him the said Wechankwashtodopee, also known as Chaska, a Sioux Indian to be hung by the neck until he is dead."

"No!" Sarah screamed. "You can't. This is wrong! He did nothing!"

"Major Forbes, silence that woman and remove her," Marshall ordered. "Then return Chaska to confinement."

Soldiers on either side grasped Sarah's upper arms and pulled her toward the exit. Her eyes beseeched forgiveness from Chaska and flashed anger like hot fire at the commission. The Indian shook his head slowly, his face grim and crestfallen.

❧ 31 ☙

MARY SCHWANDT AND MATTIE Williams were escorted into the tent again. Once more they would have to relive August 18 and their attempted escape. They followed Tazoo, the Juggler, into the commission's tent. Now it was Tazoo's turn to stand before the five men who had his life in their hands.

Grant whispered to Crooks, "Riggs is turning 'em out like thread through a spinnin' wheel. He's lining them up faster than we can move 'em through here. Good for him."

Olin intoned for the third time that day, "'This Military Commission duly sworn and Tazoo, alias Ptandooto, a Sioux Indian, is arraigned on the following charges and specifications. Charge and specification against Tazoo, a Sioux Indian, murder. Specification, in this that the said Tazoo, Sioux Indian did, on or about the 18th day of August 1862, kill or by his presence or agency aid abet in the killing of Francis Patoille and Mary Anderson, two white citizens of the United States. This between Fort Ridgely and New Ulm, Minnesota.' How say you? Guilty or not guilty?"

"Not guilty."

"Then proceed with your statement."

138

Tazoo sat upon the stool and began, "I have had sore eyes for two years, and am not able to shoot at anything. I was camped eight miles below the fort this side of the river. I am a professional juggler, and a young girl came to me.

"I am not able to hunt any and on this account had been planting. All the settlers around New Ulm had kept me from starving. Some young Indians came from town there the morning of the outbreak and told me that the Indian traders at the Lower Agency, Redwood, had been killed. I followed them down towards New Ulm. On the way down, I saw two loads of Indians going towards New Ulm and when I went as far as the Travelers' Home I met three wagonloads of Indians coming back. When they met me, they told me to get in, and I got in. I came along with them, and when they got opposite La Framboise's house we met these ladies." Tazoo pointed at Mary and Mattie.

"I heard the Indians say there was a load of white men and women coming down, and I jumped off. I ran towards the others, and I heard a shot and saw them running off. There were three ladies running off and others, and I told them to stop firing. I said if they killed white women, I would kill one of them. They should take them prisoners. I saw two Indians catch hold of Miss Williams and one got hold of Miss Schwandt.

"If it hadn't been for me, these young ladies would have been killed," Tazoo testified. "Mazeebo took Miss Schwandt by the arm. He is here: one of the Indians who had hold of Miss Williams was killed at the last battle. The name of the other is Hapan.

"This is all I know. I was blind, and I didn't go anywheres. I know this woman, Miss Williams. If this woman is living now and is about to see her relatives, I am the cause of it. I ravished her, but she was not willing and I desisted. I tried to sleep with her twice, but she was too young. Godfrey, the negro, was in the middle wagon with my party."

Mattie Williams took the witness stool next. She testified, "The prisoner raped me. He repeated it. He was in the party what killed Mr.

Patoille. He took me and tied my arms when we was taken. He was with the others in their killin'. He brought plunder back to the village."

Mary Schwandt's turn followed. "I was with 'em when Patoille was killed. This Indian was one that attacked us."

Again the tent was cleared and the commission deliberated. Once again the accused was brought back before them.

Olin concluded, "Guilty of all charges we do thereupon sentence the said Tazoo, alias Ptandooto to be hanged by the neck until he is dead."

Next Tehehdonecha or One Who Forbids His House was ushered in. Margaret Cardinell and Harriet Fallant repeated their story of murder and rape near Beaver Creek.

Lieutenant Olin read the sentence again, ". . . to be hanged by the neck until dead."

๛ 32 ๖

Throughout the day and into the evening, Stephen Riggs questioned former captives and other witnesses about the accused Dakota and others whose names he forwarded for arraignment.

Jesse Buchanen asked occasional questions but mostly listened, increasingly grateful that JoAnna had remained in St. Paul. He cringed as he recalled how persistently she had tried to accompany them.

The Military Commission worked well into the night. It was nearly nine o'clock when the last of sixteen cases was decided. Ten were sentenced to be hanged. Six were acquitted.

The last of the observers and witnesses filed out of the tent, leaving behind the commissioners, Heard and Forbes. Stephen Riggs and Jesse Buchanen joined them. The four sat upon the plank bench facing the commissioners, who remained behind their table. Marshall rose and began to pace between the bench and table.

"Gentlemen, we need to develop a way to move this along more quickly. Reverend Riggs, how many did you arraign today?"

"Forty, Colonel."

"Forty! With dozens, maybe hundreds more in the offing."

"And more Sioux coming in from the prairie," Grant added.

Bailley spoke hesitantly. "It does concern me that many of the worst got away."

"Yes," Olin retorted, "but there are still plenty who deserve to die. We just gotta round 'em up."

"All right," Marshall concluded. "For now we'll take our time, let Riggs do his job and round up more Sioux. But when all the arrests are made and the prisoners arraigned, we must find a way to move these trials faster. This could take a year otherwise. We must . . .."

At that moment Sarah Wakefield burst into the tent. She strode toward the commissioners with anger streaming from every pore in her body. "How could you!" she exclaimed. "Chaska did nothing. He killed no one. He saved me and my family. He protected us and kept us safe. You are nothing more than murderers!"

"Mrs. Wakefield," Marshall's voice remained calm, "Chaska did fire at Gleason even if he missed. We also believe that your opinion may be colored due to your relationship with Chaska."

"Close, relationship," Olin said, a leer at the edge of his mouth.

Sarah glared at Olin with indignation. "I resent your implication. Chaska never touched me. Not once! You are sanctimonious, bloodthirsty fools who don't give a damn about justice, only revenge."

"That's enough, madam. Major Forbes, remove this woman," Marshall ordered.

Forbes grabbed her arm. Sarah ripped it away.

"I'll leave," she shouted. "Just let me see Chaska once more."

Marshall sighed, his face flushed. Still, he relented, "Tomorrow you may see him in the prisoners' tent."

An uncomfortable silence gripped the enclosure as Sarah stomped out. But Jesse sensed a smugness that incensed him.

"Sirs," Jesse stood and spoke against his better judgment, "with all due respect. I must disagree with your decision. My legal training tells me that there was no evidence to convict Chaska, let alone to condemn him to death. The only real eye witness you had backed up his claim of innocence."

142

"Lieutenant," Marshall answered sternly, "we appreciate the role you have taken with Reverend Riggs to bring the accused to us. It is not your position to offer opinions of guilt or innocence. The rule of law that you cite does not apply to the Sioux. They are not American citizens. We will do what we feel is just for all concerned."

"But—" Jesse began.

"You've already said enough, Lieutenant. You are dismissed."

Sarah Wakefield made her way through the still, dark night to her family's tent. She and her two children had been given a small tent of their own. No other whites would share one with her. She was shunned by them.

The darkness of the night was a relief to the woman. It allowed escape from averted eyes, scornful stares, and cries of "squaw" and "Indian lover." Only Susan Brown provided any measure of friendship to her.

Lisa and James were small, still lumps under buffalo robes in the blackness of her tent. Sarah slipped under a robe between them and fell into a restless sleep.

Morning dawned crisp and cool at Camp Release under azure blue skies. Sarah stirred the dead ashes of her fire and found a burning ember from last night. She slipped wood chips onto it and gently blew. After several deep breaths, she was rewarded with smoke and then a small blue flame. Soon she would have a fire big enough to cook breakfast for her children.

Sarah had determined to leave Camp Release and rejoin her husband in St. Paul. But first she had to see Chaska. She had to make him understand. By the time she had fried salt pork and fed her children, the sun's rays felt warm upon her back.

"The day will be bright."

Sarah turned to see Susan Brown standing behind her. "It's still a dark day for Chaska, Susan."

"Yes, I know, Sarah, but you tried. The people know you tried to help him."

"And for that my people condemn me."

"They don't understand," said Susan. "Many whites have died, some are friends and relatives of those here. For six weeks we have been dragged across the prairie by the Santee. You know that many white women were abused in that time. They won't forgive, even over time most will remember, and hate will grow. Only revenge will cool their blood. It is true that you were protected and treated better than many. The whites resent you for it. They will believe what they want to believe about you, and nothing will change that."

"I'm going, Susan. After I talk to Chaska and his mother. My children and I must leave this place. My husband's waiting."

"You belong in your world. Go back to it. May God be with you, Sarah Wakefield."

Susan Brown turned and walked back into the village. Sarah exhaled and determined that the time had come to try to explain and make amends.

Her first destination was the lodge of Chaska's mother. Sarah approached with trepidation. As she reached the tipi, Sarah looked at the ground in front of the entry flap. Crossed sticks on the ground would mean that the occupant was not at home or did not wish to be disturbed. There were no sticks, and Sarah ducked her head and entered.

It took a moment for her eyes to adjust to the dimness of the dwelling. A smoky smog drifted through an opening up above. Chaska's mother sat on her heels, her back to Sarah, poking at the fire.

"Mother," Sarah began, "I'm so sorry."

The old woman stood and faced her former captive. Then she burst into tears that streamed down the weathered brown seams of her cheeks.

"You said you would save his life!" she wailed. "Chaska saved you and your children many times. You have forgotten the Indians now that your white friends have come."

The Indian woman bent her head, gray hair falling over her face as her shoulders wracked with sobs.

144

"No. I never forgot. I tried. At his trial and afterward. I tried to get them to see the truth. I'll keep trying to save him, even from St. Paul."

"You are leaving?"

"Today. But first I must see Chaska."

Chaska's mother tottered to Sarah and wrapped her arms around her. She continued to sob, then whispered in the white woman's ear. "Please, save my son."

"I will try, Mother. I will keep trying."

Minutes later, her eyes still filled with tears and her shoulder wet from those of Chaska's mother, Sarah strode to two guards positioned before a wall tent holding Indian prisoners.

"Colonel Marshall gave me permission to see Chaska," she said.

"Are you Sarah Wakefield?" a soldier asked.

"Yes, I am."

"We've been told to take ya into the tent iff'n ya came here. Follow me."

The young, blue-uniformed soldier led the way into the tent. The flaps on both ends of the tent were open, providing good light and ventilation. About twenty Indians were chained together and sitting upon the ground, some in breechclouts, others in pants. They looked up at her with a mixture of dismay, hate, and scorn.

Chaska sat in the middle of the long chain. Sarah knelt before him. Her face reflected the pain and sorrow of the tragic conditions that had befallen her friend. Sarah held out her hand to grasp Chaska's.

The Indian looked away and refused to take the woman's hand.

"I believed you." Chaska spit out the word like the rapid fire bullets of a gatling gun. "You said the whites would be fair. You must have lied to them about me."

The tears that Sarah had held back now overflowed. She looked down and wept deeply as Chaska continued. "You know that I saved you when Hapa killed Gleason, that I did not let your children be killed and that when Hapa tried to make you his woman I stopped him. Now I will die. I did nothing for this to happen."

"I know, Chaska," Sarah sobbed. "You heard me yesterday. Do you think this has been easy for me? I have no friends. The whites call me a traitor and worse. They have planted seeds of doubt about me with my husband. I must get to him. Indians believe I have betrayed you. I have no people."

"But you are not to be killed."

"Chaska, I had nothing to do with you being brought to trial. I told Reverend Riggs exactly what I said at your trial. I will keep trying to help you, with Sibley, Ramsey, even President Lincoln. Now please, take my hand." She held it out to him again. "I know that I owe you my life. I want to shake your hand and say goodbye in friendship."

Chaska looked hard at the tanned, long-fingered hand held out to him. Then he reached out and grasped it. He said nothing, just held Sarah's hand firmly for a moment as he looked into her tear-filled blue eyes.

Then Chaska released her and turned his head away. His own eyes had misted over.

Sarah stood and sadly, softly cried, "Good-bye, Chaska, good-bye, my friend."

ঙ 33 ৎ

SARAH WAKEFIELD, HER CHILDREN, and all those former captives whose testimony was no longer needed for the trials were informed that later that day they would begin the trip downriver to Fort Snelling.

Sarah trundled the meager belongings she had into a bundle and hoisted it into a wagon. Jesse Buchanen approached her and asked, "Do you need any help, Mrs. Wakefield?"

She wheeled around with blazing eyes as she recognized the man in uniform. "Not from the likes of you! Are you looking for more innocent men to kill?"

"Ma'am," Jesse replied calmly, "we just ask questions, Reverend Riggs and me. Our job is just to pass the accused on to the commission. If I had a vote, it would have been to spare Chaska."

"He's innocent, Lieutenant. I was there. I know."

"I believe you, and I hope the truth comes out before it's too late. But . . . if you may, what I wanted to ask is if you'd do me a favor."

Sarah, at first furious, now became wary. "What do you need?"

"My fiancée is JoAnna Miller, daughter of Colonel Miller. She lives up on Summit in St. Paul. Would you please see that she gets this?"

147

Jesse handed Sarah an envelope. "And would you talk to her? She has this idea in her head that she should come out here as soon as it's safe, whenever that is. JoAnna just doesn't understand how dangerous it really is. Explain to her what I'm doing and how it's best if she stays in St. Paul. She might listen to you."

Sarah's eyes softened as she took the envelope from Jesse. "After all the horrors I've seen, maybe helping young lovers will make things a littler better." A small smile played at her lips. "I'll see your girl, Lieutenant, and I'll do what I can. In return, I also ask a favor. Do what you can about Chaska. He deserves to live."

Jesse hesitated, knowing he had very little influence. Then he realized that Sarah needed some reassurance, and he nodded. "Do you need any help right now?" Jesse asked again.

Sarah looked at her small bundle. "No, I really haven't much to take with me. What I need help with, repairing my reputation and maybe my marriage, I'm afraid you wouldn't be of much use. And one more thing, Lieutenant, there have been so many terrible things done by both sides in this war. This is really a time for fairness. It's time to heal."

"Mrs. Wakefield, the wounds are deep. Healing won't come easy. It might take lifetimes."

≈ 34 ≪

HAT SAME AFTERNOON another of the prisoners was unchained and brought to the tent where the trials were being conducted. As Joe Godfrey was led into the empty enclosure, one man rose to greet him, Lieutenant Rollin Olin. He gestured for Joe to sit upon the plank bench and then plopped down beside him.

Olin glanced up at the escort and ordered, "Wait outside. I want to speak with the prisoner alone."

Godfrey was dressed in his non-Indian clothing, long woolen pants and a cotton shirt. He sat calmly, hands folded in his lap, and stared at the ground.

"I suppose you're wondering why I had you brought here. Do you want some coffee?" A steaming tin cup rested upon a nearby bench.

Godfrey shook his head and replied, "I am here for whatever you wish. I have no choice."

"But you do, Joe. I'm going to make you an offer."

Interest flickered in the mulatto's dark eyes as he turned his gaze to Olin.

"I'm sure you're wondering why no verdict was given in your case yesterday. We have delayed it. We believe that there is enough evidence to hang you. But maybe your death is not the best way for you to serve our interests."

Godfrey's eyes narrowed. Then he asked incredulously, "How do you think I could best serve you?"

"Joe, these cases are confusing. Reverend Riggs has dozens to question. Indians look alike to whites, many have similar sounding names, we don't know who's telling the truth. You were there. No one has pinned a killing on you yet. But you know a lot about who did what and how they did it. We want you to help us sort things through. If you help us, your sentence will be commuted, and you will not hang."

"You want me to betray my people."

"We want you to help us find the truth. Officially, we'll call you an interpreter."

"How long will I be in prison if I do this?"

"Ten years, maybe less. Part of the time confined on a reservation. Otherwise you'll be dead before spring."

Godfrey smiled slowly, showing bright white teeth. His soft voice was almost musical. "I told you I did nothing wrong yesterday. That I was against the war. Now I'll prove it by helping you make it right by naming the bad Indians who murdered whites."

"I remind you that several white women dispute your innocence," Olin said. "But we will let that go. You will be rewarded with your life. For now you will be given your own tent. It won't be safe for you around the other prisoners once we put you to work."

"When do I start?"

"Soon, Joe. We're going to slow things down just a little. Reverend Riggs will continue to question former white captives. We will soon need to erect another camp because of the large numbers of Indians coming off the prairies, hundreds of them, and we are still arresting more men as we determine evidence."

The camp became more chaotic in the days ahead. The friendlies' village overflowed and another camp was established. On October 10, Sibley called his officers together in his headquarters tent to review and plan.

"Men, first a bit of personal news. You recall that I asked to be relieved of this command. I believed that my job was done, the war was concluded, and the captives freed. My request to return to St. Paul and civilian life was turned down. President Lincoln has promoted me to general and ordered me to remain in command."

"Hear, hear!" Major Welch shouted as he leaped to his feet in applause.

The other two dozen officers in the room rose simultaneously and clapped vociferously. Sibley smiled broadly and then held his hands palms down before him, urging silence.

"Thank you, thank you. I'm gratified at the faith our president has placed in me, and I will do as asked. First off, I want patrols sent out to hunt for food, bury bodies and search for survivors. I've heard that there are still people hiding out there who think the war is still going on."

"There've been a bunch of prairie fires on both sides of the river," Welch commented. "There're folks we'll never find or count. But we'll try."

"Are we goin' west after the red devils?" Will Duley asked. "The worst of 'em got away."

"Not yet, Captain, we have work to finish here first. How many Sioux are in the two camps, Major Forbes?"

"Just over 2,000, Colonel . . . er, General. There were about 150 lodges in the Indian camp when we got here. Now we've got 243."

"Courselle, Other Day, and their men have rounded up more than I thought possible. How is Riggs doing?"

"Sir," Jesse Buchanen stood, "each day we continue to interview the former hostages about crimes committed by the Sioux. The number of accused keeps growing. Since the sixteen trials on the first day, there have only been thirteen more. The waiting list for trial is growing daily."

"I've seen the lists. It's time to start rounding them up and placing all accused in our custody. I've delayed ordering mass arrests because word would spread and prevent other Indians from surrendering. It's time. Captain Duley, tomorrow reinforce the guard at the second camp. Lieutenant Buchanen, how many names do you have on your list to be arrested?"

"About eighty, sir."

"Captain, get the list from Riggs and bring them in."

"Sir," Lieutenant Buchanen added, "this is just from the list we think are in the second camp. We have another 260-plus to be arraigned."

"It'll be a hell of a job bringin' in all of 'em without startin' a riot!" Duley exclaimed.

"Food is gettin' short, General," Welch informed him. "For both our men and the Indians, we gotta git more food. We've had 'bout a thousand of the reds diggin' potatoes and pickin' corn at Yellow Medicine Agency for a week, but that'll only go so far. We've sent many of the Indian women and children ahead to camp near Redwood, but we are still low on food."

Sibley stroked his beardless chin thoughtfully. "There may be a way," he mused, "to combine two tasks. Yes, yes, there is. First, Duley, make arrests of those on Riggs' list in the second camp. Then we'll go after the rest at Yellow Medicine."

Welch wondered, "How many soldiers should we bring up there?"

"Enough to handle the twelve hundred or so Indians. Now, I know they aren't all men. You've got women and older children working up there, don't you. We got to arrest those who are on the arraignment list. The log jail in the center of camp is now complete and ready for guests. Agent Galbraith, Yellow Medicine was your home. You'll be in charge."

"Fine," Galbraith retorted, "but like Welch said, how do we do this without things gettin' all riled up?"

"Gentlemen," Sibley's look of self-satisfaction resembled a Cheshire cat, "we trick them. Greed is a great motivator, and we'll use it. Major Galbraith, stay behind with your officers. Welch, get me young Sam Brown, the agent's son, he's a quarter Sioux and they trust him. I have a plan."

∽ 35 ∾

ON THE TWELFTH OF OCTOBER, 1,250 Santee were herded by Sibley's infantry around the gardens and fields of the Upper Agency at Yellow Medicine. The agency was dominated by the burned ruins of the warehouse, a large two-story building, fifty feet long.

The Santee had set it afire August 19 shortly after John Other Day had left the building with the sixty whites who had sought sanctuary there. Now the building was a shell with only the stone walls standing.

Throughout the day Santee men, women and children dug potatoes and picked corn, stacking it all near the warehouse. The soldiers pitched their tents about a hundred yards from the ruined building, while the Santee camped at the base of a hill along the Yellow Medicine Creek, roughly half a mile away.

Sam Brown put Sibley's plan for mass arrests into motion that night. The former hostage and son of Joseph and Susan Brown proceeded to the Indian camp. There he came upon Baptiste Campbell and Henry Milford, two mixed-bloods who had fought together and raided on the north of the Minnesota River. Milford was intelligent and had lived for a time with Henry Sibley.

Brown spoke as Sibley had instructed. "Baptiste, Henry, I am sent to tell you that the annuity has come. The roll is to be prepared tomorrow morning. Tell all to come at an early hour and present themselves at the warehouse to the agent, Galbraith, to be counted."

"We will finally get the money due us months ago? It is late, much late. But needed," Campbell proclaimed.

Milford shook his head sadly. "If it came when it should have instead of being delayed in Washington, the war never would have happened. But we will be there in the morning."

The next morning was chilly as Santee flocked to the warehouse around eight o'clock to be counted. At one end of the building a long table had been set up. Seated behind the table were Major Galbraith, Captain Whitney, and two clerks. The clerks worked industriously taking pen to stacks of paper and checking off names on the roll of Santee.

Whitney whispered to Galbraith, "How many do we expect to nab today?"

"I've been told 269. The clerks have the names. Got 'em from Riggs. It should work slick as grass through a goose." Then he called to a clerk, "Johnson, call the first name."

The clerk tried to look official. With a flourish he called loudly, "Catanna!"

An athletic man in his thirties strode forward accompanied by his family, two women and five children. The clerk made a show of counting each with grandeur. "Eight of you. Okay, follow the soldier to the far end of the warehouse."

The armed soldier escorted the Indian family to the opposite end of the building and turned a corner at the warehouse's ruined doorway. They were met by Sam Brown, who stood with other soldiers near large wooden stave barrels.

"You," he said to Catanna, "drop your gun and any other weapons in the barrel. They will be returned to you shortly when you leave. Step inside the building. Women and children, you are to return to your camp"

Catanna looked confused and alarmed. "Why must I do this?"

"Men, as heads of families, must be counted separately. The government wants to pay you extra."

As soon as Catanna and the other Indian men who came later stepped through the doorway, they were stopped, shackled and led away to be confined at Camp Release.

That afternoon Galbraith reported to Sibley in his tent. "Worked like a charm, General. We bagged 234 of 'em. Some weren't there, and a few smelled a skunk and left during the night. But we got most of 'em."

"How many all told?"

"This puts us at 403."

"As far as I'm concerned the guilty, at least those in the camps and surrounding countryside, have been arrested. It's time to move this along quickly. Is Godfrey ready?"

"Yes, sir. He's primed and set to go. I think you'll be surprised at how helpful he'll be."

"The actions of someone like him, whose life hangs by a thread, never surprise me. Let the trials continue in earnest."

Sibley turned and entered his tent. He sat on his camp stool behind a small desk. A sheet of paper and quill pen rested upon it. The general began writing to his wife. "This power of life and death is an awful thing to exercise. When I think that more than 300 human beings are subject to that power, lodged in my hands, it makes me shudder. I shall do full justice but no more. I do not propose to murder any man, even a savage, who is shown to be innocent."

✺ 36 ❧

T HE SMALL STONE CHURCH at the Redwood Agency had been spared destruction during the uprising. Amid ruins and burned-out buildings, it stood as a sentinel of civilization on the prairie. The crisp brownness of the tall grass contrasted starkly with the yellows and fiery reds of the leaves in the valley below.

It was a Sunday, but no congregation sat in the wooden pews and no songs drifted through an open door into the valley. The sun shone through a stained-glass window and cast a bluish light onto the floor. Three men sat in the front pew in earnest conversation. They were Stephen Riggs, Thomas Williamson, and a tall, well-built man, Henry Whipple.

Whipple stood and faced the other two. Just forty years of age, he had been named Minnesota's first bishop of the Protestant Episcopal Church. Known as a gracious but not patronizing man with iron will, he was respected by both the whites and the Indians, who called him "Straight Tongue."

Bishop Whipple wore a dark suit with a high white collar. He ran a hand back through his dark hair, longish in back and receding in front.

157

"I felt it important that we meet before I have to go East. You have a hard task, Stephen. I don't envy you. Heard has called you 'the Grand Jury.'"

"I can't accept that, Bishop. I'm just trying to sort things out. There are certain Indians who are guilty of crimes for which they deserve punishment and which cannot be condoned as acts of war."

"Stephen, there is a broad distinction between the guilt of men who went through the country committing fiendish violence, massacring women and babies with the spirit of demons, and the guilt of timid men who received a share of the plunder or who under threat of death engaged in some one battle where hundreds were engaged."

"That may be, my friends," Riggs replied, "but I am satisfied that the commissioners will do God's bidding."

Williamson shook his head and pursed his lips. "Twenty-nine have been tried so far. I'm satisfied in my own mind from the slight evidence on which these are condemned that there are many others in that prison house who ought not to be there, and that the honor of our government and the welfare of the people of Minnesota as well as that of the Indians requires a new trial before unprejudiced judges. I doubt whether the whole state of Minnesota can furnish twelve men competent to sit as jurors in their trials.

"From our governor down to the lowest rabble, there is a general belief that all the prisoners are guilty, and demand that whether guilty or not, they be put to death as a sacrifice to the souls of our murdered fellow citizens."

Riggs thoughtfully looked down and scratched the top of his curly, mostly-white hair. "Thomas, I have a very high regard for all the gentlemen who compose the military commission. I count them individually among my personal friends. But they are trying Indians, and my sense of right would lead me to give Indians as fair and full a trial as white men. This is the difference between us."

"And now," Whipple interjected, "Colonel Marshall has resigned from the commission."

158

"Transferred," Riggs answered. "They want him leading soldiers again. He's been sent west to round up more Indian prisoners. But George Bradley has been named to replace him. He'll do fine. He's got one of the best legal minds in Minnesota."

"But, Stephen," Whipple rejoined, "this isn't about correct legal rulings. Major Bradley fought at Wood Lake. He was at Birch Coulee. He will carry his own prejudices with him."

"Stephen, Henry," Williamson wondered, "do you think we should share the blame?"

"Why, Thomas?" Whipple inquired.

"In our mission churches, the first sign of a man's conversion to Christ was to give up braids and Indian clothing. When the breech clout and buckskins were replaced by European-American clothing and when hair was cut short, we thought they were on the way to Christ.

"Were we really trying to bring them salvation or just to bring them to a white lifestyle and did this lead us to war?"

Whipple was resolute. "Christianity leads to civilization. The Dakota were savage. I'm committed to bring them to terms with modern civilization. I've written President Lincoln that the glaring defect in our Indian system is that it places no seal of condemnation on savage life.

"I also communicated that there was corruption in the Indian system. I warned that an uprising was inevitable. But we must work toward detribalization and assimilation of the red man. "

"I hope we were right." Williamson seemed perplexed. "We imposed our social model and generated a disintegration of the societal structures of Indian civilization. I believe this war was fought at least in part because of what we did."

"Thomas," Riggs interjected, "that may be so, but the government's treatment of the Santee, their failure to pay treaty obligations, the greed of the traders, these ignited the war."

"I'm afraid the roots go much deeper, my friends."

"I'm leaving for an Episcopal convention in New York," Whipple said. "While I'm in the East, I'll try to meet with the president.

You know that my cousin is General Henry Halleck. Sibley wants me to seek more military aid through him."

"Please seek fairness for the Dakota. More than anyone, you understand what has happened here," Riggs pleaded.

Whipple briefly considered Riggs' admonition and then responded, "While we three may not agree on everything. I believe that we do agree on most, especially that we must treat the Dakota fairly and not mimic their savagery. I prefer that other and abler hands plead for the poor race. To me, it is grievous to be placed in antagonism to others. I love peace, not strife. But God led me to those poor wretched souls. I hear their cries for help. I see the dark record of crime heaped upon them. I dare not be silent.

"Some day people will tell in hushed whispers our shame. They will marvel that their fathers dared to trifle with truth and righteousness and, with such foolhardiness, trifle with God."

"Good luck to you, Bishop." Riggs' voice was firm and sincere.

"And good luck to you, Stephen. Your task is littered with pitfalls. May God guide you each day."

✠ 37 ❧

A WEEK AFTER LEAVING CAMP RELEASE, Sarah Wakefield rode by carriage up a St. Paul street to Summit. The sign read "Avenue," but calling the dirt path such seemed presumptuous. A prankster had drawn a line through the word.

Still, Sarah thought, *the street shows promise*. Some fine large houses were already going up. Money had been made off land, lumber, and flour, and the new homes reflected the potential of future grandeur.

The driver mouthed a couple of clicking sounds, and his horse picked up its pace. A few houses more, and he tightened the reins and commanded, "Whoa, boy, whoa. This is it, ma'am. The Miller house. Should I wait?"

"Yes, I shouldn't be long," Sarah replied.

She walked up a brick pathway and reached the stoop. As Sarah prepared to knock, the door was flung open.

"Mrs. Wakefield!" JoAnna proclaimed. "I received your card that you were coming today, and I could hardly wait! Come in. I'm eager to hear news from the frontier and from Jesse."

The older woman followed JoAnna into the house, down a hallway and into the same room where Jesse had last sat with his fiancée.

161

"Please sit." JoAnna gestured to a chair alongside the small round table and then sat next to Sarah. She poured coffee from a porcelain pot into two cups that rested upon the table top.

"I'm sorry that you had to leave the carriage on the street, Mrs. Wakefield. As you can see, the house is unfinished. The carriage entrance to the front won't be done for weeks, and I believe a brick facade will be added to the house when Father gets back. Now, Mrs. Wakefield, please tell me, what is it like?"

"First, Miss Miller, here." Sarah handed JoAnna an envelope. "This is from Jesse."

JoAnna gleefully ripped it open, smiled as she read and then frowned. "Mrs. Wakefield, he says some nice things, but then he says I shouldn't come to him."

"It's because he cares for you and doesn't believe it's safe. I've been there, I've lived through horrors that I wouldn't wish upon my worst enemy. Jesse and your father are both right to be concerned and wish you to stay here."

"I'm sure it'll be safe soon. Was it really so bad? It must have been horrible."

"JoAnna, I was a captive nearly six weeks. My children and I saw people murdered right before our eyes. My life was saved by an Indian man who protected me in his own lodge."

"Strange," JoAnna commented, "I thought all the Indians were savages. Did they reward the man who saved you?"

Sarah took a deep breath and spoke matter-of-factly. "They've sentenced Chaska, an innocent man, to die."

"Does Jesse know all about this?"

"Along with Reverend Riggs, he questioned Chaska before the trial. I believe Jesse opposed and spoke against the verdict. He said he did, anyway. I think Jesse is a fine young man. He has a dirty business to do . . . but he's trying to do it with honor. You are a lucky young woman. Stay here and wait for your man to come back. This is the best you can do. For him and for yourself."

"Like I said, Mrs. Wakefield, I'll know when it's safe. And, anyway, I'll be surrounded by soldiers when I go. More coffee?"

"No, thank you, I have my own man to tend to. Dr. Wakefield is at Fort Snelling, and I need to return. Good luck to you. Stay here and wait for your fiance. I'm sure it will all be over soon."

The two women stood and briefly embraced. Then JoAnna escorted Sarah out the front door. She smiled and waved happily at her departing guest, who held her hand up in reply.

As Sarah settled into the waiting carriage seat, she thought, *Well, I tried. JoAnna is a beautiful and pleasant young lady. But she just doesn't understand. Blinded by love, maybe. May God give her guidance.*

163

❧ 38 ❧

THE TRIALS COMMENCED AGAIN in mid-October. The wall tent was arranged as before with plank benches for seating, a table for the commissioners, and a stool for the witness. Two major additions were made to the court personnel. Taking Marshall's place in the center of the table was Colonel Bill Crooks. Sitting on the front plank in the middle was Joe Godfrey.

Rollin Olin read the specifications charging Washeshoon, or Frenchman, with murder. He asked "Washeshoon, how say you, guilty or not guilty?"

Washeshoon, who spoke English, replied, "Not guilty. I had a lame arm at New Ulm and could not fire a gun. My gun was bad and would not fire even if I wanted it to."

Godfrey slumped his head upon his breast and began to chuckle. Soon his shoulders shook as he erupted in a fit of musical laughter.

"Godfrey!" Crooks exclaimed. "Do you have something to say to this prisoner?"

The mulatto smiled and ambled near the stool where Washeshoon was seated. "You say you could not fire and had a bad gun," said Godfrey. "Why don't you tell the court the truth? I saw you go and take the gun off an Indian who was killed, and fire two shots. Then you made me reload it, and then you fired again."

From that point on, any protestation Washeshoon made was discounted by the commission. The Indian was sentenced to be hanged.

Another prisoner was brought before the court. This one denied that he had been at Fort Ridgely and said that he had killed no one. The interpreter, Antoine Frenier, translated the questions and answers. Godfrey watched and listened intently like a cat about to spring. Then he again convulsed in laughter.

Once again, Crooks commanded, "Godfrey, talk to him."

Joe straightened up and with a calm countenance approached the accused. His voice became soft and deliberate as he said in the Dakota language, "Toonkanechahtagmane, don't you remember? I was with you when you prepared your sons for battle. You painted the face on one red, and drew a streak of green over his eyes. Then you led them to the fort. I was with you."

The accused was sentenced to death.

Next was Hdahinday. Olin intoned, "You are charged with killing two children. How say you?"

"Not guilty," Hdahinday cried.

Godfrey almost fell off his seat as his body shook with laughter.

"Godfrey, talk to him."

"Hdahinday." Godfrey tried to regain composure as he approached the Indian. "Don't you remember showing me the spear was broken, and saying that you had broken it in striking the child?"

"Godfrey lies!" the accused exclaimed.

"What, don't you recollect you said it when you had your hand upon my wagon and your foot resting on the wheel?"

The avenging angel's words resulted in another death sentence.

And so it went through the day. If Joe Godfrey had first-hand knowledge, he was called upon and often delivered damning testimony or, through his questions, caused the accused to damn themselves. This made many trials move quickly to a verdict.

Often the Indians offered bewildering testimony. A young man of nineteen said that he always attended divine worship at Little Crow's village. He said that he never did anything bad in his life except to run after a chicken at Mendota a long time ago and that he didn't even catch it.

Godfrey disclosed that he had been an active participant in some of the worst massacres on Beaver Creek.

One fiery-looking warrior claimed that he was so upset to see Indians fire on the whites at Fort Ridgely that he immediately lay down and fell asleep on the battlefield. Men with gray hair said they were too old and couldn't fight.

A young man, Red Hawk, was charged with robbery.

Olin asked him, "What goods, if any, did you take from Forbes' store?"

"Some blankets."

"Anything else?"

"Yes, some calico and cloth."

Olin hesitated. "Okay, Red Hawk, anything else?"

"Yes, some powder and some lead and some paint and some beads."

"Anything else?"

"Some flour and some pork and some coffee and some rice, sugar, and some beans and some tin cups . . . and some raisins and twine and some fish-hooks and needles and some thread."

"Were you going to set up a grocery store on your own account?"

Red Hawk sheepishly hung his head. He was given ten years in prison.

Occasionally a Santee was found not guilty. Tahampuhida was charged with murdering whites between New Ulm and Yellow Medicine. He pleaded not guilty, stating, "I have not been at New Ulm, Yellow Medicine, or the fort. I have been the whole time with Red Iron. At the last battle, Little Crow gave notice that all Indians who did not go would be killed. I stayed at a distance on a mound and did not even bring a weapon."

No witnesses appeared against Tahampuhida, and he was found to be not guilty.

But even those found not guilty remained as prisoners.

Late in the day Bill Crooks spoke to the court. "We have heard around two dozen cases. We will recess for the day and begin again tomorrow morning."

As observers and participants filed through the tent exit, Crooks leaned back in his chair, raised his arms and stretched. "Gentlemen, we had a productive day."

✂ 39 ✃

BISHOP HENRY WHIPPLE STOOD TALL, his hands resting upon a lectern. Seated before him were delegates to the General Convention of the Episcopal Church. He had journeyed to New York for one major purpose. He had written a paper that he proposed to submit to President Lincoln, and he wanted the assembled bishops to sign it.

"I come from Minnesota where blood has stained the prairie and runs red in the rivers of my state. I shall submit the following to President Lincoln, let me read it to you:

'We respectfully call your attention to the recent Indian outbreak, which has devastated one of the fairest portions of our country as demanding the careful investigation of the government.

'The history of our relations with the Indian tribes of North America shows that after they enter into treaty stipulations with the United States, a rapid deterioration always takes place. They become degraded, are liable to savage outbreaks and are often incited to war.

168

'The Indian Department has been corrupt and must be reorganized before relations between Indians and whites can be improved.'

Whipple outlined in detail what he thought was necessary to reform the department.

'We feel that these results cannot be obtained without careful thought, and we, therefore, request you to take such steps as may be necessary to appoint a commission of men of high character, who have no political ends to serve, to whom may be referred this whole question, in order that they may devise a more perfect system for the administration of Indian affairs, which will repair these wrongs, preserve the honor of the government, and call upon us the blessings of God.'"

Whipple's presentation was met by silence. An elderly bishop from New Jersey pushed himself to his feet.

"Bishop Whipple," he called, "this is a political issue. Our role is spiritual, not secular. This is not a position we should take."

"Amen, amen," many others shouted.

Whipple strode vigorously before the lectern. Angrily, his face flushed, he responded, "My diocese is desolated by an Indian war, 800 of our own people are dead. I have just come from a hospital where more are dying. I have drawn up a paper to present to President Lincoln, and all I want is your signatures, yet many of you dare to call this politics."

Bishop Alonzo Potter of New York rose to support the young bishop from Minnesota. "Bishop Whipple is right. We cannot ignore what has happened in Minnesota and we cannot ignore why it happened. Give me the paper, Bishop Whipple. I will get signatures for you."

Late that afternoon when Whipple boarded a train bound for Washington, D.C., the paper was in his satchel. Affixed upon it were the signatures of nineteen bishops and twenty deputies.

Whipple's cousin was Henry—"Harry" to family members—Halleck, newly appointed general-in-chief of the Union army. The next morning, after the bishop spent most of the night riding the rails, his cousin escorted him to meet President Lincoln in the White House.

Halleck's head resembled a dome, with the open spaces growing from the middle of his head. His eyes were large, goggle-like circles. Respect for his intellect resulted in a nickname, "Old Brains."

"Harry, thank you for arranging this for me, I know how busy you must be."

"This Indian business is serious, Henry," his cousin told the bishop. "We are all concerned. The president has never been to Minnesota. He wants to know firsthand what's happening there."

"I'm glad that the president has recognized your organizational ability, Harry. I hear the army is in great need of a firm hand."

Moments later, John Hay escorted the two men into the White House's Oval Office. President Lincoln walked briskly from his desk, extending his long right arm. His large hand and long fingers swallowed that of his white-collared visitor.

"Bishop, a pleasure to meet you. I've been getting regular dispatches about the horrors transpiring in Minnesota. I want to learn more. Sit, please."

The president gestured to the chairs set around a small table in front of his desk. The three men sat down, and Lincoln unfolded a sheet of paper from his pocket.

"This is from General Pope. It seems the Sioux are under control and trials against war criminals are underway. How do you assess what is transpiring?"

"Yes, Mr. President," Whipple began, "the fighting is over. But much remains to repair our state."

"I have read your letters about Minnesota and the Sioux. What do you think caused this to happen?"

Whipple sighed deeply and looked into Lincoln's sad, concerned eyes. "There is much to tell. I'll try to be brief. As you know, the Dakota

170

people once had almost all of Minnesota. Then the Chippewa, with guns from the whites, invaded from the north. The Dakota were pushed south and west. The Teton went to the Missouri River region. They divided into seven bands: Brules, Oglalas, Miniconjous, Sans Arc, Two Kettles, Hunkpapas, and Blackfeet. The Yankton moved to areas between the Missouri and Minnesota and the four bands of the Santee remained in southern and western Minnesota.

"Then followed a series of treaties that by 1858 had reduced Santee land to a strip along the Minnesota River 150 miles long and ten miles wide. We took these woodland hunters and tried to turn them into prairie farmers.

"It's my belief that change was the right thing, but it came hard and with a price. Once the Civil War began, the government fell behind on payments to the Santee. Crop failures and delayed payments led to starvation."

Lincoln listened intently. Halleck rocked slightly and, out of habit, rubbed both elbows simultaneously. Detractors insisted that "Old Brains'" brains were really located there.

The president inquired, "The government provided no food?"

"Oh, there was food, Mr. President. We had warehouses on the agency filled with food. Just no money."

"Why didn't they release the food?"

"Because it is the policy of the agents to release them, food and money, at the same time."

"Again, why, Bishop?"

"Traders feared they would not be paid. You see, Indians buy on credit. The traders on the agency keep their charge accounts. When the money arrives, the Indians go to the pay tables, and the accounts are settled. Basically the traders claim all the money and then the provisions in the warehouses are released to the Indians."

"The traders get all the money," Lincoln said incredulously. "It doesn't seem right."

"Mr. President, the traders keep the books. They say what is due on the account. Many have become rich dealing with the Santee, including the American Fur Company and their chief Minnesota agent, General Sibley. Your agents always back the traders. Some of them have become rich, too. The Santee have been lied to and cheated for decades.

"When the Indians protested at the agency and begged that food be released without the long-delayed money, one of the traders, Andrew Myrick, said, 'If you are so hungry, eat grass or your own dung.' About a week later the killing started."

"How many have died?"

"It's hard to say. Estimates range as high as 800. Less than a hundred were soldiers. Most were unsuspecting men, women, and children."

"I've been receiving reports on the trials of the Sioux. It seems that several hundred are under arrest. Are there genuine war criminals or are they just soldiers involved in battles?"

"There were genuine atrocities, sir. Cases of babies being nailed to trees, live women having their stomachs slit open and fetuses ripped out and nailed to wagon wheels. Children have been swung into trees until their brains were exposed. Rapes were commonplace, treachery abounded. But there were also instances when the lives of whites were saved by friendly Santee."

"It will take the wisdom of Solomon to sort through all of this." Lincoln's voice was soft. "So many dead that this government might have prevented. They murdered babies?" The president's hazel eyes moistened, and he momentarily looked away.

The room became still. The steady tick of a clock on the wall was the only sound in the strained silence. Then, as he so often did, Lincoln relieved strain with story. "Bishop, a man once thought that monkeys could pick cotton better than Negroes because their fingers were smaller. He turned a lot of them into his cotton field. Then he found it took two overseers to watch one monkey. I guess we have the same problem. We need two honest men to watch the Indian agent. This Indian service must be reformed. If I get through this war, I am going to see that it is done."

"Here, Mr. President." Whipple proffered the paper signed by the bishops. "Read it, please."

Lincoln took a pair of reading spectacles from his vest pocket and set them upon the end of his nose. He read silently for a moment, took a card from another vest pocket, and wrote a brief note upon it. He handed the card to Whipple.

The bishop glanced at the note. It read, "Give Bishop Whipple any information he wants about Indian affairs. A. Lincoln."

"Give this to Caleb Smith, my Interior Secretary."

"Thank you, Mr. President," Whipple concluded. "One more thing. General Sibley asked that I inquire of you and Harry about the availability of more troops."

"General Halleck, there never seem to be enough troops for my generals no matter where they are. I've informed Governor Ramsey that his quota of troops that Minnesota is due to send us has been suspended. That is the best we can do for now. Thank you, Bishop Whipple. You've been informative. Correspond with me as you wish."

Halleck and Whipple exited the Oval Office, and John Hay entered.

"Was the meeting productive, Mr. President?" asked Hay.

"Bishop Whipple talked with me about the rascality of this Indian business until I felt it down to my boots."

∞ 40 ∞

THE DAY AFTER WHIPPLE LEFT Washington to return to Minnesota, President Lincoln met in the White House library with his cabinet advisors. Seven men sat around a large table covered by a green cloth chatting amongst themselves as they waited for Lincoln to enter the room. A massive bookshelf entirely filled the wall behind them.

A door opened, and the president stepped in, followed by Hay. Lincoln sat in the open chair at the head of the table, unfolded a sheet of paper and smoothed it upon the table top. "Gentlemen, we have many war concerns to discuss, but first I'd like to talk about Minnesota. We have a letter here from General Pope. Secretary Stanton, you have read it. Please summarize the contents."

The secretary of war coughed softly and began, "This missive is dated October ninth. As of that day, Pope declares that the hostilities are over. The Indians are now under guard in camps on the reservation. The west and south of Minnesota are largely depopulated as the white population has mostly either been killed or fled. Seven to eight hundred are likely dead. Patrols are still out seeking survivors and counting the dead.

"Trials are now ongoing regarding war criminals there. Around 400 are to be tried, and Pope wants to, in his words 'exterminate them all.' Dozens have already been sentenced to die but no one has been executed yet."

Lincoln's "God of War" looked directly at his president. "It seems that even though Pope, Governor Ramsey, and General Sibley wish to proceed immediately with the hangings, there remains some questions about authority. They seem to be awaiting final word from you, sir."

Welles had listened with his eyes shut, almost as if he were sleeping. His eyes snapped open. "This is disgusting! The tone and opinions of the dispatch are discreditable. I have no doubt that the outrages committed by the Sioux were horrible. But what was the provocation?"

"I share your concern, Gideon," Lincoln said. "I have informed Pope to stand by, yet he seems eager to begin the hangings. Pope writes that General Sibley wants to execute those already convicted immediately and then send the rest to Fort Snelling.

"Secretary Smith, tomorrow you will send your assistant secretary, John Usher, to Minnesota. He is to inform General Pope that there will be no hangings of Indians without permission from me. I had a visitor recently, and I now question more that ever the validity of these executions. Now, Secretary Stanton, tell me where General Lee is today."

﹂ 41 ﹁

JOANNA MILLER SAT IN the sunny parlor of the Summit house and paged through the *St. Paul Pioneer Press* looking for news of the war and trials. A flame in the fireplace took the chill out of the morning air as the smell of burning cedar filled the room.

Then she saw what she had been looking for. "TROOPS TO RESUPPLY," the headline read. JoAnna skimmed the story. Tomorrow morning a company of soldiers with wagons would start on the river road to Camp Release. Food and supplies for the winter were the cargo.

"Our brave men have smashed the Uprising," the account read, "but the trials are taking longer than anticipated. In the event that they must remain on the frontier into the winter supplies will be taken under escort from Fort Snelling."

JoAnna paced to the mantle above the fire and took down a small black box. She removed the cover and took out a folded piece of paper. It was the letter from her father granting her safe passage into the frontier.

This is it, she thought. *My chance for a safe journey under guard to Jesse. It might be my only chance until spring. I'll take it!*

JoAnna journeyed the few miles to Fort Snelling that afternoon. The limestone walls gleamed brightly in the afternoon sun. The three-story round tower dominated the main entrance. From the tower sentries oversaw the confluence of the Minnesota and Mississippi rivers and all approaches to the fort. It was from there that JoAnna had bid goodbye to Jesse.

Guards at the gate questioned JoAnna and granted her request to meet with Adjutant-General Malmos in the commander's quarters at the opposite end of the fort. She and an escort passed along the barracks, blacksmith shop, and bakery. Soldiers were busily occupied with drill and menial tasks.

In a few minutes JoAnna was sitting across the desk from the camp commander.

"Welcome, Miss Miller," Malmos greeted her. "The daughter of Colonel Miller is always welcome here. How can I be of service?"

"How goes the war against the savages?" JoAnna asked coyly.

"It's over!" Malmos proclaimed. "We're just cleaning up now. Of course there's work to be done. The trials must be finished, executions carried out, and the disposition of thousands of the Santee decided. Many will be sent here. But the real fighting is over."

JoAnna smiled brightly, "But you still supply our soldiers on the frontier?"

"Of course, Miss. Why just tomorrow morning a company is leaving for Lower Sioux."

Now was her chance. JoAnna widened her deep-blue eyes and smiled shyly. "Since the fighting's over, I want to go with them tomorrow to see my father and Jesse Buchanen. Look at this, please." She handed Colonel Miller's note to Malmos.

Malmos was taken aback by the request and hesitantly took the note. He affixed a pair of spectacles and read it. "But, Miss Miller, this still isn't the right time. We still have safety concerns."

"General Malmos," JoAnna implored as tears welled in her eyes, "you yourself said the fighting was over. My father says it's all right if I have an escort and the fighting is over. Tomorrow I'll have an escort, and you say there's no fighting. You have to let me go."

Malmos sadly shook his head. "You've got me. Against my better judgment I will authorize your journey. Do you need assistance getting your necessities from your house?"

JoAnna brightened and smiled broadly. "No, sir. I anticipated that you would be reasonable. I brought what I need, and I will be ready to leave in the morning."

"Captain Folsum leaves at precisely five tomorrow morning. Be ready, they won't wait for you." Malmos silently hoped she would oversleep.

Early the next morning, fifty men and ten wagons headed down the river road to the west. In the midst of them, one wagon carried JoAnna Miller.

ಏ 42 ಲ

BACK AT CAMP RELEASE the trials continued. Joe Godfrey continued his assistance to the commission. Now past the middle of October, the coolness of the morning stretched into the afternoon. Coats and shawls became common attire for both participants and observers.

Two Indian men, one young and one old, sat on stools before the commissioners. The room hushed as two young boys, aged eight and ten, were led to the front of the tent. The older boy glared at the Indians with the fierceness of a hawk. Olin looked at them sympathetically, "Boys, what are your names?"

The older answered, his accent heavily German, "I am Bernard Heidgerken. Dis is my brudder, Charlie."

"Where did you live."

"Ve lived by Beaver Creek."

Softly, Olin inquired, "Where are your parents?"

"Dead," Charlie sobbed, "dem kilt 'em. Dat old one, he kilt my mudder."

"Dat one," Bernard pointed at the younger, "I sawed him kill two. One vas our fadder."

"You're sure?" Bradley asked. "Tell us what happened."

"Der vas lots of us. Ve come from above Beaver Creek and vas goin' to da fort. Ve vas gittin' close by der, ven Indians stopped us."

"Dey said dey wouldn't hurt no one," the smaller boy cried.

Bernard patted his brother gently upon his shoulder and continued. "Dey said iffn' ve vent back vhere ve come from and gived up our teams they'd let us be."

"But?" Olin questioned.

"Dey started shootin' inta us. One man, he dropped dead right off. Den some vomen. Dey took all da resta us."

"Who led them?" Bradley wondered. "Stand," he ordered the two Indians.

For a long moment the two boys and two Indians stood a few feet apart. The accused were impassive. The older boy's eyes were afire.

Bernard pointed at Tinkling Water. "I sawed dat Indian shoot a man vhile he vas on his knees at prayer."

With tears streaming down his cheeks, Charlie shouted as he pointed at Round Wind. "And I sawed him shoot my mudder!"

"You are sure about this?" Bradley said sternly.

"I svear to God in Heaven," Charlie answered.

"Return them to their seat," Olin ordered a guard. Then he spoke to the younger Indian man. "Tinkling Water, what do you have to say in defense?"

The Indian stood and faced the commissioners. "The boys lie. I was not there at all on that day."

"Round Wind, what say you?"

The older Santee rose to his feet like an old accordion stretching out, then spoke in a voice low and croaky like an old bull frog. "I was on the other side of the river that day. I was not at Beaver Creek."

Hiram Bailey peered intently at Round Wing and then questioned, "I've seen you before. Aren't you related to Joe Renville, the former agent?"

"I am married to his sister."

"Didn't you have something to do with Little Crow?"

"I was his crier. I told the people what he wanted told."

"Little Crow has escaped to the west. Why didn't you go with him?

Round Wing stood silent an instant before looking Bailey directly in the eyes and responding. "I have done nothing wrong. I killed no white. There was no reason to flee. These boys are children. They are mistaken."

Tinkling Water and Round Wing were sentenced to be hanged.

Next to come before the commission was Makataemajin, or One Who Stands on the Earth, and Black Wing. They were both elderly, with streaked, dingy white hair. Crevasses seamed their faces like worn rivers on a brown prairie. Their physiques were opposite. Makataemajin's face was dominated by a large nose that terminated sharply, making his whole head seem pointed. The other's face was perfectly flat and seemed to be two feet across.

As the two men sat, Black Wing closed his eyes and promptly fell asleep. His mouth dropped open, and a soft snoring emanated like the purring of a kitten.

Neither could speak English. Antoine Frenier, the interpreter, stood near by. George Bradley led the questioning.

"Makataemajin, you were at New Ulm. One hundred fifty-some died in that vicinity. How many did you kill?"

"None, I have not fired a gun in many years. I was at New Ulm but killed no one. My two sons died there. I am too old to fight."

"That's what all you with white hair claim," Bradley rejoined. "But people say different.

"Black Wing," Bradley continued, "you were there. How many did you kill?" Frenier repeated the question but received no response from the old Santee.

"He seems to be sleeping, sir," the interpreter responded.

"Then poke him! Wake him up! I want to look him in the eyes when I question him!"

Frenier jabbed Black Wing sharply in the ribs. The Indian's eyes popped open, and Bradley began again. "You are accused of murder at New Ulm. The following evidence has been compiled against you."

As Bradley read, the old Indian's eyes closed, and his jaw dropped open. The colonel looked up from the charges. Aghast, he ordered, "Wake him up! Stir him up!" Frenier poked him again.

This proceeding continued for some time. The old man would fall asleep every time he was left alone or someone began to speak. When jabbed or poked, his eyes would snap open, and his jaw would clamp shut. If some simply shouted at Black Wing, his eyelids would slowly peel back like an overstuffed bird and then shut again before they were completely open.

"Major Bradley," Bill Crooks interjected, "I've gone over the charges on this fellow. We have no witnesses against him. I don't see how he could have stayed awake long enough to kill anyone. Nothing has been proved against him."

"I agree, Colonel," Bradley replied and then commanded loudly, "Lead him out!"

Black Wing's eyes jerked open at the sudden shout. Then they shut again, his jaw dropped, and he began to snore. The guards led him away in a deep slumber. Makataemajin was sentenced to hang.

The next morning, wind swept like a hurricane through the camp. A prairie fire turned the sky black with smoke and sprinkled it with crimson embers. Trees were torn from their roots and tents blown away. In their log prison the Santee huddled together, convinced that even the Great Spirit had forsaken them.

Through the maelstrom and into the camp rode Colonel Marshall at the head of 200 men. The soldiers encircled thirty-nine Santee men and about one hundred women and children, captured in Marshall's foray into the Dakotas.

❧ 43 ❧

LATE THE NEXT DAY, a smoky glaze hung over Camp Release in the chill of the gathering twilight. Destruction wrought by the windstorm was still evident in scattered debris and broken tent poles. Henry Hastings Sibley gathered selected officers, his military commission and other personnel into his wall tent. Planks provided seating.

"Gentlemen," the general announced, "we have several critical issues to address. First of all, we are running low on food for both our men and the Indians. The foraging at Yellow Medicine has bought us some time, but now that's about gone.

"Winter's almost upon us, and forage for the horses is about used up as well. If we stay here much longer, snow will come, and the roads will be impassable. I won't let this army become marooned and starve."

"What's the plan, sir?" Will Duley asked.

"We'll strike the camp here and move to the Redwood Agency. Many women and children have already been sent near there. I've asked that supplies from Snelling be sent there. We'll be farther down the river and close to Fort Ridgely. Load the prisoners into wagons and guide the other Indians along. There are still some prisoners held at Yellow Medicine, plus the ones that Marshall just brought us."

He turned. "Colonel Crooks, what is the progress on the trials?"

"So far we've tried 120. One hundred have been sentenced to death. We have about 300 more chained up and waiting to appear before the commission."

In exasperation, Duley exclaimed, "So when do we start hangin' 'em?"

Sibley shook his head. "Not yet, word has come from Washington that no hangings are to take place without the president's go-ahead."

"How long?" Duley wondered.

"No word on that. We wait."

"Sir," Rollin Olin interjected, "speaking of time. These cases are really moving slowly. We could spend all winter on this."

"They're guilty of murder," Duley shot back. "Indians ain't American citizens, and they ain't entitled to our rights. These're war criminals. Hang 'em now!"

Sibley frowned. "Captain Duley, you are right to a point. The Sioux have not been provided defense attorneys. We need to provide a semblance of fairness, however. Still, how can we speed this up?"

Hiram Grant stood to respond. "Look, we spend a lot of time trying to establish that the accused actually killed someone. We question witnesses, Reverend Riggs tries to establish direct links. We try to find eyewitnesses. Is this all necessary?"

"What do you mean?" Sibley asked.

"Just this, General. We should ask the question: 'Were you there?' Were they at the Redwood Agency, the ferry, Fort Ridgely, Birch Coulee, Hutchinson, Acton, Wood Lake, Beaver Creek, New Ulm. If they were there, if they shot at all, they participated in the killing, whether it can be proved they actually killed anyone or not."

"In other words," Sibley summerized, "if they were there, they're guilty."

"Yes," Major Forbes agreed, "and they'll readily confess to being at the battles. They're proud of it. These savages think of themselves as soldiers, warriors even. They're proud of having fought in these battles."

"The fact that they mostly killed women and children doesn't seem to matter to them," Sibley concluded. "They feel cheated and justified."

Olin looked up from his notes and added, "In at least two-thirds of the cases so far, the prisoners admitted that they fired. But most of them say it was only one or two shots and that no one was killed. Some say that they just wanted something. One Sioux stole a horse and gave as his excuse that it was just a little one. Another took a pair of oxen and said it was a gift for his wife. We've had many young men, aged eighteen to twenty-five, insist that they were too young to fight and their hearts were too weak to face fire."

"What about the band that said they all crept under a stone durin' a battle and ate corn and beef?" Duley snorted derisively. "Brave warriors! Bull! Cowards is what they are!"

"I like Grant's idea." Sibley turned the discussion back to the trial. "I don't care how innocent they proclaim themselves to be. If they were at a battle, they are guilty as sin and deserve to die."

Jesse Buchanen frowned and shook his head. Justice was being ill-served, he thought.

Stephen Riggs had been silent. Wearily he rose and faced the assembled officers, "I took this task with trepidation. I knew that there were those who deserved to die. I also know that there are those who are innocent, who even saved the lives of white refugees. I have written President Lincoln that most of the condemned should be executed to meet the demands of public justice.

"But I'm concerned about the fairness of these proceedings. Instead of taking individuals to trial, against whom some specific charge can be brought, we subject all grown men, with a few exceptions, to an investigation of the commission, trusting that Indians are considered guilty by the military commission until proven innocent. Most will be condemned on general principles without any specific charges being proved. Proof of innocence must be established by the accused themselves. The opposite of our system of law. But we've already established that these men are not entitled to the protections afforded Americans, haven't we?"

185

"Thank you, Reverend Riggs," Sibley replied. "I don't think we need your services any longer in this regard. I know that you have spent much of your life working among the Sioux. Stay with us. Your services may be required again before this is over."

Wondering how Riggs' reassignment would affect him, Jesse asked Sibley, "What am I to do, sir?"

"We are still searching for survivors and burying victims. Once we get settled at Redwood, I want you to take out a patrol addressing this. You may be assigned to the reverend again as events dictate. Gentlemen, we strike camp tomorrow. I want to be at Redwood in two days. There the trials will resume reflecting our change in philosophy."

Jesse was discouraged as he pushed the flaps aside and entered his tent. He couldn't shake from his mind the nagging question, "Are we trying the right Indians?" His mood brightened considerably when he saw an envelope on his camp stool. He impatiently ripped it open knowing it was from JoAnna. He read:

Dearest Jesse,

Mrs. Wakefield came to visit me. What hardships she must have endured. She cautioned me about going to see you and father but don't worry. I'll go under escort with soldiers all around to protect me. General Sibley has sent for supplies and wagons and soldiers will soon leave to deliver them. I plan to show my father's note and go with them. I'm told that the fighting is over and that the bad Indians are either all captured or have gone to the Dakotas. I want so much to see you and be with you. I'm so proud of the work you're doing. My father tells me how important it is. The savages must be punished. I'm so glad that you are in a position to see that the right ones face their maker.

I miss you and I long for the day when all war will be over. I want life to be normal again so that we can be together and become man and wife.

With love,
JoAnna

Jesse quickly penned a reply.

JoAnna, my dearest love,

I wish it were all as simple as your letter makes it seem. But it is complicated here and my service with the Military Commission troubles me at times. All of the Dakota are not criminals, contrary to what you might read in the newspapers we have to sort it all out. I too wish that this were over. Perhaps some day there will be no wars to fight. JoAnna, I long to see you too but you must not come here. No matter what you hear, it is not safe. There still is danger all around. You would be in much peril. I pray that soon we will be together but this is not the time.

Jesse

⁊ 44 ⱶ

OR A WEEK THE SUPPLY WAGONS from Fort Snelling ground and rocked over the uneven trail on the north side of the Minnesota River. At first there were few signs of the rampage in the valley. But as they neared New Ulm, burned out homes and desolate countryside became commonplace.

After a brief stop at Fort Ridgely, the detail moved back onto the trail above the river flats and resumed their trek to the west. Occasionally, they would come upon a dead, badly decomposed body and stop to bury it. JoAnna, who had been bubbly and talkative as the journey began, became more subdued and sober.

"It's horrible," she said to Sam, the teamster on her wagon. "Why did they do such terrible things?"

"Well, Miss, seems that they wanted ta wipe us all out. Seein' as we was tryin' ta do the same ta them. This here is the result."

"The governor wants to exterminate them. The Sioux, they'll all be killed or driven out of Minnesota, won't they?"

"Seems like that's the goal, Missy. It's why we still got men out here, why we're bringin' supplies to 'em."

More corpses were found in the Beaver Creek area across from Redwood Ferry. JoAnna grew less talkative and averted her eyes as they passed mutilated bodies of men, women, and children.

"Thought they wudda got 'em all buried by now," Sam observed. "I know they bin tryin'."

Six-foot-tall grass waved on either side of the trail. JoAnna admired how pretty the purplish stalks seemed in the gentle wind. The tranquility was shattered in a heartbeat. The swish of an arrow in flight ended in a thud as it entered Sam's neck. Blood splattered in small flecks on JoAnna's dress and face.

The young woman froze in startled shock as Sam slumped forward and fell off the wagon. Her scream was drowned out by war cries from all around as the tranquil sea of grass became alive with Santee warriors firing bullets and arrows at the soldiers.

Captain Folsum galloped to the rear, imploring his men to action. "Form up, men," he yelled. "Get into ranks and fire back! Give it to 'em!"

The team of horses hitched to JoAnna's wagon panicked in the confusion of gunshots and screams. They bolted, racing through defenders and attackers alike. JoAnna reached desperately for the reins, but they were dragging on the ground between the wagon and the team.

After tumbling backward into the wagon box atop bundles of winter blankets, JoAnna grabbed a railing alongside the wagon bed and held on. The horses, lathered and snorting, ferociously continued to gallop over the plain.

Eventually they hit a dry creek bed and raced down the bank. A back wheel rolled over a boulder, bouncing the wagon into the air. When it came down, only the two right side wheels touched the ground. The wagon skidded on its side, snapping the yoke that connected the horses. JoAnna was flung head over heels as the wagon skittered to a halt and the team of horses thundered away.

Dazed, she struggled to her feet. The prairie was strangely silent. The gunfire miles away faded into the distance as the Santee pushed the soldiers down into the river flats.

JoAnna Miller stood alone on the grass-blown prairie, bruised, dirty and shaken by the tumble from the wagon. She was wracked by sobs as despair overcame her.

"Why didn't I listen?" she cried to the prairie wind. "I don't know what to do, where to go, where the soldiers are!"

She walked to the wagon. It was tipped on its side, cracked and splintered. The cargo, blue woolen blankets, was strewn upon the ground. She collapsed face first upon a bundle of blankets and beat her fists into it as tears streamed down her cheeks.

Then realization settled upon JoAnna that, if she were to survive, she must compose herself and formulate a plan.

"Find the river," she mumbled to herself. "That'll bring me to white people, a town maybe, or the fort or maybe even Camp Release. She stood and then reached down by her feet to take a blanket. JoAnna knew the nights were cool.

Shining silver and cool under the blanket was a pistol. "Sam's gun," JoAnna whispered. "It was loose by the wagon seat." She picked it up, not knowing how to use it. But she wrapped the blanket around it convinced that it would become a necessity. Then she began to walk in a direction she hoped would take her to the Minnesota River.

ᔥ 45 ᕀ

HE NEXT MORNING, OCTOBER 23, Camp Release was struck and 1,600 soldiers escorted 2,000 disheveled Santee down the Minnesota River toward the ruined Redwood Agency. Four hundred of the Santee were in chains and crammed into open wooden wagons for the bone-jarring journey.

The wind once again began to howl like a distant pack of wolves. It blackened the clouds and drove dust like tiny missiles across the prairie. The soldiers wrapped scarves or pieces of cloth or clothing around their faces. But dirt and dust still covered their faces and caked into their ears, eyes, and noses.

The army, prisoners, and civilians spent a miserable night on the cold, windy, treeless expanse. Morning brought relief as the winds calmed, and the sun shone brightly through clear autumn air.

Great flocks of geese in chevron flight honked and clattered high above Sibley. The general gestured at them and remarked to Olin, "At least they have sense enough to get out of here in the winter. We, on the other hand, hole up and freeze."

"Funny, isn't it, sir, soon we'll be in the river valley. That's where the Sioux have always wintered. Less wind, more protection down in the valley. We're bringing them home. It's good we've already sent many of the women and children that were at Yellow Medicine there."

"Yes, Lieutenant, but this will only be a temporary home for them. We've got about 400 to send to Hades."

"General," Olin squinted and pointed east down the trail, "look. There's a rider comin'. Looks he's in a big hurry to get somewhere."

"I fear it's to us," Sibley replied. "I hope it's good news."

Minutes later Corporal Willie Sturgis from Fort Ridgeley jerked his exhausted horse to a halt before Sibley and leaped from the saddle. "Genr'l," Willie panted as the horse behind him snorted and blew, "the Sioux . . . they hit the supply wagons that was comin' to ya yestaday. 'Bout twenty got kilt, the rest made it to Ridgely!"

"What Sioux?" Sibley demanded. "We either have them or they've gone to Dakota."

"Some musta come back," Willie gasped. "Least ways they was there, wherever they come from. And Genr'l, they's one more thing."

"Yes, Corporal, what?"

"There was a woman, Colonel Miller's daughter. She was with the troop. The horses took off with the wagon she was in. She went one way, and the Sioux pushed our men t'other. We don't know what happened to her."

"God in heaven! How? Why?" Sibley exclaimed. He turned to an aide at his side. "Go get Colonel Miller and Lieutenant Buchanen. Hurry!"

Within minutes Miller and Jesse were before General Sibley.

"Bad news," Sibley said, looking at the ground and averting the questioning looks of the other two men. "Your daughter, Stephen, I don't know what she was doing out here, but the Sioux hit the supply wagons she was with. She's missing."

Miller stood in stunned silence. Then he remembered the note she had cajoled him into signing. He covered his eyes with his hands as he slowly shook his head with enormous regret and disbelief.

"Where!" Jesse demanded.

"Apparently about halfway between Camp Release and Redwood. They must not have heard we were coming to Redwood. Lieutenant, I told you that your next assignment would be to search for survivors and to bury bodies. You will immediately form a company and search for Miss Miller. I pray to God you find her safe."

"General," Miller said firmly, "let me go, too."

"Stephen, take a troop and go east from here. Lieutenant, go to the west. God be with you both."

Jesse placed his hand upon Miller's shoulder. "We'll find her, sir, I can feel it. It'll be all right. She's a strong-willed woman."

"That's what got her into this," Miller replied. "That and my weakness. Damn the note she had me sign!"

Within the hour both men were leading a company of soldiers on a frantic search for JoAnna.

Sibley ordered the rest of his army to resume their march down the river. As the sun began to set, the procession reached sight of the Indian camp near Redwood. Women and children rushed out to see their fathers, brothers, and uncles. A great collective wail rose from them when they realized the broken condition of their chained, dispirited men.

Sibley called to his interpreter, "Frenier, shut them up!"

The Frenchman rode into the midst of a cacophony of anguish. In Dakota he shouted, "Quiet now! Across the Minnesota forty-five white men, women, and children lie unburied. They were murdered by these men that you cry for. They shed no tears. Remember this and be quiet!"

The Santee grew silent and returned to their camp. The next morning they joined Sibley's army and the prisoners as they marched the remaining few miles to the deserted Redwood Agency.

Sibley walked through the little town and sadly shook his head. Olin, Bradley, and Provost Marshall Forbes, a former trader at the Agency, trailed just behind. The soldiers camp was bivouacked nearby. They called it Camp Sibley.

"Forbes," the general ordered, "get another stockade built to hold prisoners right away. Where can we hold the trials?"

193

"Well, most of the buildings were burned or damaged, but LaBathe's trading post seems untouched. It's not a big cabin, but big enough."

"Good. Get started again. You've a lot to get through. Who's first?"

"Cut Nose."

"See that he gets what he deserves. What about Henry Milord. I raised him, you know. He's a smart young man."

"Riggs says that he shot *at* a woman. Others shot, too. Henry says he missed, somebody didn't."

"It's a shame," Sibley said sadly. "It was inevitable that young men like Henry would be drawn into this war, next to impossible to remain on the sidelines be they half-breeds like Henry or full-bloods. They must take responsibility and be held accountable, but I pity them. I pity Henry."

Francois LaBathe had been a trader at the Redwood Agency. On the morning of August 18, he had been one of the first killed by the Santee, even though he had resisted cutting off their credit.

Now his former trading post would become the seat of justice for his killers. The one-room log cabin had three small windows and was smaller than the double wall tent used previously. But not so much space was needed. The commissioners, a few court personnel, the accused and a witness or two were all that was needed. The new plan of establishing guilt by mere presence at a battle would shorten trials considerably, and fewer witnesses were necessary.

When the trials resumed, Cut Nose was the first to stand before the commission. Olin read the charges and stipulations of murder.

Bradley asked, "In the stipulation you are referred to as Mahpeokenejin, or Who Stands on the Cloud. You are also called Cut Nose. How did this come to be?"

Cut Nose touched his nose, momentarily covering the open space where his right nostril had been. His hair was unkempt, framing a sallow face and sunken cheeks. But hate flamed in his black eyes.

"I fought Other Day." Cut Nose spat on the wooden floor boards. "The traitor bit my nose."

"You are charged with killings at the agency and Beaver Creek. How say you?"

"I killed no one. When Little Crow said to kill the traders, I went along. I am accused of killing a carpenter, but I did not do it. I just fired my gun in a store. My nephew died at Fort Ridgely. I was at Hutchinson when my son was killed. But I saved the family of Agent Brown."

Olin commented, "By his own admission he fired during a fight. By our standards that should be enough."

"Yes, Lieutenant," Bradley mused, "but the charges against this Indian are particularly egregious. There are claims that he killed twenty-seven people. In fairness to all, particularly his victims, I want to hear more. Samuel Brown, sit up here, please."

The young man rose from a seat along a back cabin wall and strode to a place in front of the five commissioners.

Bailey asked, "On the 19th of August what contact did you have with the Indian known as Cut Nose?"

"On the 18th we heard of killing on Beaver Creek," Brown answered. "We feared that the Upper Agency would be attacked, too. George Gleason left with Sarah Wakefield and her children. But we waited. My father was away on a trip, and my mother wasn't sure what to do. At four in the morning of the nineteenth, shouts from outside woke us up. A man was yelling that 400 Yankton had come to the agency and were killing everybody.

"We loaded our wagon, hitched oxen to it and headed for Ridgely. Our neighbors and five men who caught up joined us. We had three wagons. After about five miles an Indian stepped on the trail in front of us. It was Cut Nose. Before we knew it we were surrounded. Shakopee was with them, too.

"My mother told them who she was, a Sisseton, and that she was related to Akepa and Little Crow and a friend of Standing Buffalo and Red Iron. Dewanea said that we must follow them and that we were as good as dead. He told the other Indians, they were all Santee, that whites had taken him prisoner many times. Dewanea said now it was his turn and that they should kill us all.

"They took our horses, and Dewanea took my sister's bonnet and put it on. He started to laugh and sing war songs. He said, 'Indians will now have a good time. If we get killed it is all right. The whites wanted to kill us all, and they are delaying the payment so they can starve us. I'd rather be shot.'

"One Indian said that my mother had saved his life by taking him into our house when he was freezing and that they should not kill us. Then the leaders talked to each other."

"What did they decide? Was Cut Nose part of it?" Bradley inquired.

Brown hesitated, then answered, "I don't know what Cut Nose said. Other Indians said that my family would be spared but not the others. They would kill the men. My mother told them that these were her friends and that the Sisseton would hunt down their murderers. The leaders met on a little knoll off by themselves. When they came back, they let the men go. The women and children were taken to Little Crow.

"He did go to a wagon and tell a Scotch girl there that he wanted her for his wife. She should get out and follow him. She refused, and Cut Nose took his knife and held it over her. He grabbed her hair and threatened to scalp the girl. She left with him."

"Did you see Cut Nose kill anyone?" Olin asked.

"No, sir. But on the trail to Little Crow's village, we came across three men and a woman. They had been cutting grain. Scythes and pitchforks were nearby. Their bodies were all hacked up.

"Cut Nose laughed and held up his thumb. A piece had been bitten out near the nail. He said one of the men had bit him when he was working the knife in the man's chest. He said the man was hard to kill and that he thought he would never die. Cut Nose had rubbed blood from his thumb and the whites all over his body. He was the ugliest man I've ever seen. That is all I know about Cut Nose."

In the stillness of the room Olin cleared his throat. "You're excused, Samuel. There is one other who wants to tell about Cut Nose. Justina Krieger, come forward."

As Samuel Brown retreated to the shadows of the back wall, a woman in her late twenties took his place. She was slender and worn. Strain showed in her deeply tanned face.

Rollin Olin began the questioning. "Mrs. Krieger, where was your homestead?"

The woman began in a soft, low, German-accented voice. "Flora Township, western Renville County."

"Louder, please," Olin requested, "Was it a German settlement?"

"Mostly, yes, sir."

"How did you come into contact with Cut Nose?"

"We heard the Indians was makin' trouble. We got together at Kitzmans' cabin and decided ta go ta Fort Ridgely."

"How many of you were there?" Crook wondered.

"Fifty, maybe, we was in eleven wagons. We went all night 'til two or three in the morning of the 19th when we started out ta Beaver Creek. We planned ta head 'round the stream toward the fort. The sun had been up 'bout two hours, and we thought we'd made 'bout fourteen miles. We figgured we was nearly half way ta Ridgely when eight Indians on horseback overtook us.

"There was eleven men in our train. They wanted ta fight and set the wagons fer defense. But the Indians put down their guns and made friendly signs. One was a friend of my brother, Paul Kitzman. He walked toward us, and Paul stepped from behind the wagons. They shook hands, and the Indian kissed Paul like a Judas. He said it was Chippewa that was killin' whites, not Sioux. That Chippewa were 'tween us and the fort and that ta go on meant death. They told us ta go back home and said they would help us get there," Justina testified.

"The Indian walked through all the men and women shakin' hands and tellin' them that he was friendly and would protect them from the Chippewa. The children, who were scairt of Indians got quiet and we felt safe. The Indians put their guns away, and our men put their guns in the wagons. Then we turned 'round the wagons and went back where we come from.

"For the first five or six miles the Indians rode with us. We stopped ta eat, and the savages ate away from us. We started back down the road alone. Then the Indians rode up from behind and rode all around us, in front, back and alongside. This made us nervous, and the men began ta call ta each odder in German. Some thought we should shoot, but the guns were in the wagons and some said gittin' them would cause suspicion, and maybe the Indians would start shootin' at us.

"Paul said, 'All our guns are in the wagons, while each Indian has his in his hand ready ta fire in an instant and every white man would be kilt at the first shot, before a gun could be got outta the wagons.'

"We saw two men lying dead alongside the road. A change came over the Indians. They seemed angry and frantic. They formed a battle line. All but one of them had a double-barreled shotgun. Cut Nose said, 'Give us your money!'

"One savage came to us and took what we had. I had a pocket-book and my husband came for the money. I gave him five dollars. He handed me his pocket-knife and said, 'They're goin' ta kill me. Keep this to remember me.'

"The Indians left us, then but we were sure they'd be back. When we got 'bout a mile from our house we saw two more dead 'long the road. The men took their guns from the wagons, and we hoped ta reach a house where we could be safe. We got 'bout a hundred yards from our house, when suddenly the Indians came outta nowhere all 'round us and opened up on us."

After a painful pause, Justina continued. "All but three of the men fell in the first fire. I think some did fire back but it happened so fast I'm not sure. Fross, Zable, and my husband were the only men left. The Indians told the women that if they left with them they would be spared. Some went, others refused. I said I'd rather stay and die with my husband and children.

"My husband told me ta go. He said they prob'ly wouldn't kill me and that maybe later I could get away. One of the women who started off with some of the Indians turned around and yelled at me ta come with them. She took a few steps, and they shot her dead. They kept shootin' till six women and two more men dropped dead. They had kilt some children but most were hidin' in the wagons. Then the fiends moved ta the wagons. They beat the children with the butts of their guns. It was terrible, horrible." Justina choked as tears streamed down her cheeks. She sobbed softly.

"Take your time, Mrs. Krieger," Olin said sympathetically. "Compose yourself."

She dabbed her eyes with a handkerchief and took a deep breath. "Children got beat bad. Then some of 'em got off the ground. Blood was streamin' down their faces. Then they beat them again until they was dead.

"Cut Nose, him, the butcher," Justina said, pointing at the accused, "he jumped inta a wagon filled with about a dozen children. He tomahawked them all. I can still hear it, the thuds, breaking bones, the screams. The little ones, they was so scairt, they couldn't move. They just waited their turn ta die." The woman covered her ears as if still hearing the screaming and shook her head, then continued.

"There was a woman, holdin' a baby. They . . . they took 'im from her and nailed the baby to a fence. When the mother screamed, they chopped off her arms and legs and left her to bleed to death on the road.

"My husband was the only man left. I was still in our wagon. He stood by it and begged me ta go. Two Indians were aimin' their guns at him, and he knew death was near. They shot at the same time. He fell ta the ground, and they shot him twice more to make sure he was dead." Justina lowered her head and trembled as she mustered strength to finish her gruesome testimony.

"I stood up from the wagon seat ta join him. They blasted me with buckshot, and I fell back inta the wagon box. My children and stepchildren were back there, nine of 'em, one in a shawl. Some Indian dragged me out of the wagon onto the ground. I lost my senses then. It was about four in the afternoon.

"I woke up late on the night of August 19th. The northern lights lit up the sky. I wish it hadn't. I could see the dead, could see what they done ta us. I heard two men talkin'. They were Sioux. They were lookin' over dead bodies and robbin' 'em. I pretended I was dead, held my breath.

"One of 'em took a knife and cut off my dress. My chest was cut a little but at my stomach the blade went in deep and bared my guts. They took my arms outta my clothing and pulled my hair as they threw me ta the ground.

"When I woke up, everyone was gone, 'cept the dead."

"How did you survive then, Mrs. Krieger?" Crooks asked softly.

"First, I followed the light from the sky and went ta my cabin. I put on some clothes and then I wandered, ate plums, drank from streams. I even ate grass and drank from a slough. It got hot, and my tongue swelled up from thirst. In the early morning I sucked dew from the grass and when my clothes got wet I sucked the dew from them.

"I was alone from August 19th to September first, that's when soldiers found me. I had come ta a creek. It musta been close ta the Minnesota. My clothes were 'bout ripped off me again. I was weak and wore out. I laid down thinkin' I'd never get up. It rained all day. I pushed myself up ta look around one more time. That's when I saw the soldiers. They was part of the burial party sent out from Ridgely. They took me ta their camp at Birch Coulee and put me inna wagon.

"Then the battle started. They tipped all the wagons they had fer protection but they left mine upright. It was shot ta pieces in the battle. Spokes on the wheels got shot off. The cover was shot to pieces. During the fight, I put a cup ta my lips ta take medicine. It was shot from my hand. I got five little scratches ta go with the seventeen wounds from before."

"What happened to the others, the women, the children?" Bailley inquired.

"Some got away. Two of my sons and a Gest boy escaped. Some got took by the Indians. Anna Zable, they didn't get her. They left her fer dead with a slashed shoulder and stabbed side. But she recovered.

"My daughter, the thirteen-year-old, Lizzie, when the shootin' was happenin,' she yelled at the children ta throw themselves down on the ground and not move 'til she called 'em. When the Indians left, some of the children and Anna got the others and brought them ta my house, 'bout a quarter mile away. Eighteen children were with her. Most was hurt bad. They stayed in my house that night, Wednesday, the twenti-eth, I think, and stayed there 'til morning. Then Anna decided to take the oldest girls onto the prairie. Lizzie woke my two stepdaughters and another boy, August Urban. Minnie, my six-year-old girl, took my baby along."

"Where were you, Mrs. Krieger?" Crooks asked.

"They thought I was dead after the shootin.' When I woke up it was dark, and only the dead were there. That's when my belly was cut open and I lost my senses again. My children told me that my baby had been layin' just a few yards from me. My thirteen-year-old daughter, the oldest child left, took the baby to Anna Zable, thinkin' me dead too.

"When I came to, I found the clothes and headed east. I think I was 'bout six miles away by daylight. When Anna took the children out to the prairie they left the little ones in the cabin. I was told that most had died, some were sleepin.' Anna was right to be scairt that the Indians were comin' back. They did but she shouldda kept all the children with her."

Justina paused, overcome with emotion, her voice low and bro-ken, then continued. "The fiends burned the cabin in the morning. The children were still in it.

"Later, I guess, the third day, them that was left was in the Tille house. The baby was sleepin' on the bed. Anna and the girls thought they heard Indians and went out ta the woods ta hide. That was the last anybody ever saw of my baby. It was a miracle that any made it out alive. Anna brought five to Fort Ridgely. Eight of my children got there one way or 'nother. I praise God. But twenty-four, they killed twenty-four o' my friends, and my husband." Justina bowed her head and sobbed softly. In her hands she turned over and over a small pocketknife.

Silence bathed the room. The five commissioners stared at Justina and then at Cut Nose. A minute later the Indian was sentenced to die.

❧ 46 ☙

N THE AFTERNOON OF OCTOBER 25, the patrol led by Jesse Buchanen came upon a small cabin near Beaver Creek. The young lieutenant pushed open a stubborn door and entered the house.

Lying on some rags in a corner appeared to be a skeleton covered with a yellow parchment. Jesse knelt down at the form's side. On its breast lay another form, much smaller but with more flesh. Jesse was both sickened and relieved. While the condition was sad beyond description, it couldn't be JoAnna. To his astonishment the tiny form moved. Then the skeleton-like object's eyes flickered open.

The mouth moved and a whisper soft as rustling grass implored, "Kill me."

Jesse leaned close and whispered in her ear, "We're here to help you, miss."

Her reply was barely understandable. "I can hardly see. You're white? Thank God." Her hand fumbled out and clasped the soldier's. Jesse grasped the bony appendage gingerly like thin porcelain, fearing it would break.

"Sergeant Coles," Jesse said softly as if in a funeral home, emotion choking his voice, "this woman is badly malnourished. Probably hasn't eaten anything of substance for weeks. Take some salt pork and hardtack and cook it into a broth. Maybe she can take it and get some strength back. I'll leave you here with ten men. I have to keep looking for Miss Miller. When this woman is able, bring her to Sibley." He didn't share his true thoughts, "If she somehow manages to live."

Jesse and the rest of the company remounted and resumed the search for JoAnna.

For two days Sergeant Cole and his men cared for the mother and her child. Finally the woman was more clearheaded and able to speak coherently. Her vision had returned.

Cole asked, "Who are you? What happened?"

"I'm Justina Boelter. We lived near here, by Beaver Creek, me, my husband, and three little ones. On the eighteenth . . ." She paused. "What's the date today?"

"October 27, Mrs. Boelter," Cole answered.

The woman was silent, painfully thinking, then groaned, "Nine weeks. It's been nine weeks. We was eatin' breakfast. It was a beautiful mornin'. The cabin windows and doors was open. Then an Indian squaw broke through the door with an axe in her hands. She looked 'round quick and ran out ta join other squaws outside. I went ta the door ta see and heard gunshots comin' from Reef's house, our neighbor. My husband got worried about our cattle and said he was goin' out ta see about them.

"Michael Boelter, my brother-in-law, come running in yellin' that the Indians was killin' people. He lived just down the road and ran out ta the field lookin' fer his father. I took my children and started to follow him. Michael come back and took my baby. Screams came from the Reef place. They was killin' Mrs. Reef and her children. Michael ran off holdin' the baby. I tried ta keep up holdin' on ta my two- and six-year-olds, but we couldn't keep up, and I soon lost sight of Michael."

Justina was silent a moment and mumbled, "I never saw or heard of my husband after he left ta see ta the cattle."

She continued in a stronger voice. "They din't find us, and we hid in the woods. We din't go far. I found some raw potatoes in a cellar. We ate them. On Friday, four days later, I went ta my in-laws' house. It was horrible."

Justina struggled to cover her eyes with an almost-translucent hand before continuing. "My mother-in-law was lyin' on the floor, they cut off her head. Outside five children were dead."

"Mrs. Boelter," Cole comforted, "you don't have to tell us this now. Wait. Get stronger."

"No, I can do it. I've kept this inside me fer nine weeks. I've gotta tell what happened. What if I don't make it? No one will know.

"For the next five weeks or so we wandered and hid. We found potatoes, cucumbers, drank rain water. My baby was gone, so I nursed my two-year-old. My older daughter, the one that was six, got sicker and sicker. She was starvin'. The night she died it was rainin'. We just had thin dresses, and they was all ripped. I was too weak ta bury my dead child or ta move away from it. Then my milk stopped. The dead body started ta stinking, and I managed ta crawl about ten feet away from her where there was a grapevine. My little one and me ate grape leaves to live. It rained four days, and we were wet, cold and starvin'.

"Then the sun came out and things heated up. Flies covered my poor dead, dear one. I managed to crawl another fifty yards. We lived there on grape leaves and rain water for another two weeks.

"Then things got worse," Justina continued. "An early hard frost kilt the leaves, and our food was gone. I was almost dead, but I gathered all the strength I had ta search for food agin. I left my child in the woods, and I found a field where I come across a small pumpkin and a few potatoes. I wasn't strong enough to carry 'em all back to the woods so I had ta make two trips.

"We sat down ta eat but suddenly a family of snakes, big and small, came outta the ground all around us. They crawled over me and I screamed, but they din't hurt us. After a time, I wus glad they wuz there. I was so lonely.

"The weather turned colder and I knowed we had ta find shelter. I decided to come back here, to my own home. This is where we laid down ta die. Then you come. You were sent from God. I don't think we coulda lasted 'nother day."

A day later Sergeant Cole brought Justina Boelter and her child to Sibley at his camp at the Redwood Agency. Her ordeal was over.

47

OLE BROUGHT JUSTINA TO THE CARE of Dr. Alfred Mueller, post surgeon at Fort Ridgely, who was sent to the Lower Agency to care for the sick and injured there. Mueller also tended to the hundreds of Santee who were camped under guard near the agency.

The speed of the trials before the commission continued at a rapid pace. Baptiste Campbell and Henry Milford, both mixed-bloods, were brought before the five men. Olin read the charge of murder, then asked Milford, who had lived in Sibley's home, for a statement. Joe Godfrey sat nearby watching intently, but the quick process reduced his need to contribute. He had offered testimony in fifty-five cases.

"I went over the Minnesota with Baptiste," Milford answered. "We were forced to go by Little Crow. I shot near a woman but did not hit her. Others shot too. They killed her."

"Campbell," Olin charged, "it's your turn. Keep it short."

"I crossed the river, too. We were told to get cattle and kill every white man. If we didn't the Soldiers' Lodge would punish us. There was a farm between Birch Coulee and Beaver Creek, and we found many cattle. When we tried to drive the cattle, they ran off. The owner tried to stop us, and I shot at him but I did not hit him.

"I am a good shot, and if I had tried to kill him I would have. I only shot because I believed Little Crow wanted me to. My brother Joe, Little Crow's wagon driver, and me were sent by our chief to Hutchinson. He told us if we didn't kill white men, we would be killed. But I killed no one there."

"You both fought in battle? You both shot at whites?" Bradley asked.

The two prisoners nodded affirmatively. After a brief discussion between the commissioners, both were sentenced to death.

On November third, forty-two trials were conducted. Isaac Heard recorded the complete records of each one.

In one trial typical of the day, Olin intoned, "The Military Commission duly sworn and Napayshne, a Sioux Indian was arraigned on the following charges and specifications. Charge and specification against Napayshne, a Sioux Indian. Charge: Participation in the murders, outrages and robberies committed by the Sioux Tribe of Indians on the Minnesota Frontier.

"Specification: In this that the said Napayshne did join with and participate in the murders, outrages and robberies committed on the Minnesota Frontier by the Sioux Tribe of Indians between the 18th day of August 1862 and the 28th day of September 1862 and particularly in the Battles at Fort Ridgely, Birch Coulee, New Ulm, and Wood Lake. He was wounded at New Ulm and is accused of killing nineteen persons. How say you?"

The prisoner rose and stated, "I was not at the fort. I was not at New Ulm. I had a sore knee and couldn't go."

Thomas Robertson was called to the witness chair. "I heard the prisoner say the morning after the first massacre that he had an old gun but had killed nineteen with it. This was in front of John Moore's house."

A Santee, Wakinya was sworn in and stated, "I never knew anything about the prisoner."

Napayshne restated, "I never fired my gun. I was forced to go to Wood Lake."

The commission sentenced him to hang.

The charges and specifications for each case were virtually the same with only slight variations. The trials began to last less than five minutes.

After the charges against him were read, Tahohpewakan stated, "I went with a party to pick up things the whites left behind."

Louis LaBelle testified, "The prisoner was among those who were on horseback in the battle referred to in case 236."

Bradley, in monotone read, "We find you guilty and sentence you to be hanged by the neck until dead."

Next, Paypaysin was led to the chair before the commission. "I was at Fort Ridgely and stood near the stable. I fired three shots."

"Guilty, sentenced to be hanged."

Amaytoahakshedo testified, "I was at the fort. I went with the others to die. I was at Birch Coulee. I fired two shots, maybe three."

Bradley made the familiar reply, "Guilty, sentenced to be hanged."

By the final cases, the need to hear from the defendants was dispensed. Simple testimony that someone was at Fort Ridgely, Birch Coulee, New Ulm, or Wood Lake was enough to hang that person. In one case a witness stated, "I saw the accused fire a shot at Fort Ridgely." The accused did not testify and was sentenced to death.

At the end of the day the commissioners reported to Sibley in his tent. "General," Bill Crooks was somber, "we have completed your directive to us. The last of the prisoners was tried today."

"What are the totals, Colonel?"

"We conducted 393 trials. Three hundred twenty-three were convicted. Three hundred and three sentenced to die. Since we arrived at Redwood ten days ago, we disposed of 272 cases."

"Good, good," Sibley replied. "You have completed an enormous, thankless task. What of John Other Day's brother?"

"Sentenced to die, sir." Crooks answered.

"I will parole him. John made an impassioned plea on his brother's behalf. He led sixty-two to safety, and God knows how many other lives John's saved in this war. It's the least I can do for him to save his brother."

"Should we began building gallows?" Olin wondered.

"No." Sibley shook his head. "I would like the executions carried out as soon as possible and so would General Pope and Governor Ramsey. But our president is somewhat reticent. He has his doubts and we can't proceed without authorization. We've got to wait."

"Doubts!" Olin exclaimed. "How can he have doubts? We did the questioning, arraignments, trials. We know what happened here and who did it. There should be no delay. Besides, how can we continue to feed this hoard of redskins?"

"He is the president, Lieutenant Olin. He will do as he wishes. But I wouldn't worry. Mr. Lincoln was raised on the frontier. He knows what we've been up against. He'll do the right thing.

"But you raise a point. We can't stay here. I don't want to spend the winter on this prairie. By my count, we have about 1,600 Indians here who are, umm," he cleared his throat, "let's call them detainees, not prisoners. I'll have Colonel Marshall and his men escort them to Fort Snelling. It will be easier for the government to feed them there.

"I'll follow a couple of days later with the rest of our troops and the prisoners. We'll bring them to South Bend on the river near Mankato. I've ordered a stockade built there for the condemned. Ironically, the place has been named Camp Lincoln."

∾ 48 ∾

HILE SERGEANT COLE NURSED Justina Boelter and Jesse combed the prairie for JoAnna, the object of the search wandered lost on the prairie. JoAnna surprised herself at her own resourcefulness. She drank from streams when she came upon them or licked the dew from the long stems of grass in the morning.

At night she rolled the blanket around herself like a cocoon and found whatever shelter there was, usually prairie grass.

Occasional clumps of woody growth provided nuts and berries for sustenance. Otherwise she resorted to roots. But JoAnna knew it was just a matter of time. If she didn't find help soon, she would succumb to the elements, starve or be found by Indians.

She had studied the pistol and fired it once at a rabbit. Although she had missed badly, she gained knowledge of how the weapon worked.

Toward evening, JoAnna came upon a hillside. "Strange," she observed, "there's a door in the hill."

She cautiously approached it, opened the door, and peered into the darkness as a cool, musty smell wafted over her. "A dugout," she remembered, "this is what people on the prairie lived in until they built something better of wood or sod."

It was just a small, dank hole cut into the hillside, but it was shelter for a night. JoAnna smiled in spite of herself. "I live in a big house on Summit, and yet this little hole in a hillside brings me joy." She smiled in spite of herself. "I feel like a big rabbit. Things are different. Small pleasures, I guess."

Her reflections came to an abrupt halt. With a start JoAnna snapped her head in the direction of the sound of pounding hooves muffled by the thick grass. Six Indians were galloping toward her. Gunshots thudded into the door of the dugout and a splinter of wood sliced into JoAnna's cheek. She stepped into the darkness and shut the door behind her.

There was an opening in the door at eye level covered by a removable piece of wood. JoAnna removed the square of wood and watched with wide eyes as the Sioux, whooping and firing, swept closer.

Fumbling in her bundled blanket, she managed to find Sam's pistol. JoAnna pointed the gun barrel through the opening, then picked out the rider leading the others. She closed her eyes and squeezed the triger.

The sound of the gun shot exploded in the little room. Acrid smoke stung her eyes. JoAnna rubbed them in amazement as she peered from the opening. Five warriors had reined in their horses. The sixth horse ran loose, for its rider had tumbled to the sod with a bullet in his forehead.

With newfound respect, the remaining five Santee kept their distance as they poured shot into the old door. Occasionally a bullet splintered through, allowing narrow rays of light to filter into the room. One piece of furniture had been left behind, a wooden table. JoAnna pushed it onto its side and huddled behind it.

She didn't dare stand in front of the door, but JoAnna knew she must shoot back. *Five of them left*, she thought, *and I've got four bullets. Things don't add up very well.*

She stood to the side of the door along an earthen wall and extended her arm to shoot from the opening. "Have to let them know I'm still here," she reasoned as she fired. Three shots left.

✄ 49 ✄

THE PRESIDENT OF THE United States stood behind his desk and gazed thoughtfully at a letter in his hand. Seated around a table before his desk in the Oval Office were his secretary, John Hay, and Secretary of War Edwin Stanton.

The tall man turned to face the others. "Pope wants to start hanging them now. Three hundred three of them. They say the trials are all over. The verdicts are in. You probably don't know that my grandfather was killed by Indians back in 1784.

I myself volunteered for the Black Hawk War back home. Didn't fight though. My bloody struggle was with mosquitoes. I had a musket that somebody told me to take care of but I broke it. Did you know that an old Indian man wandered into our camp? The boys were ready to make short work of him. I intervened," Lincoln smiled ruefully and held up a fist, "if you know what I mean."

He walked to the table and sat down with the two men. "What I'm trying to say is that I don't really have any animosity toward the red people. They are a primitive people trying to exist while an advancing culture is sweeping away their world. I suppose I'd fight back too."

"I have a letter from Governor Ramsey." Stanton reached into his vest pocket and unfolded a sheet of paper. "He's talked with Pope and writes: 'I hope the execution of every Sioux Indian condemned by the military court will be at once ordered. It would be wrong upon principle and policy to refuse this lest private revenge would on all this border take the place of official judgment on these Indians.'"

"Mr. Secretary," Lincoln replied, "those who committed rapes and murders should be executed, not soldiers who fought in a war. I've sent this message to Pope: 'Please forward, as soon as possible, the full and complete record of these convictions.' I asked for information to help me determine the most guilty parties and a careful statement about the results of the trials. I want Pope to send the names of the condemned to us. Get Whiting and Ruggles from the attorney general's office to review them. Then I'll go over them."

"Mr. President," Hay produced a letter, "this is from Pope. I don't think you've convinced him."

"Read it, John."

"I'll get to the heart of it. He writes: 'The only distinction between the culprits is as to which of them murdered most people or violated the most young girls. The people of Minnesota are exasperated to the last degree and if the guilty are not all executed I think it nearly impossible to prevent the indiscriminate massacre of all the Indians, old men, women, and children. My troops are entirely new and raw. They share the sentiments of the citizens toward the prisoners. I will do the best I can, but fear a terrible result.'"

"Gentlemen, I will not be stampeded."

"There's more, sir," Hay continued. "Here's an editorial from the Stillwater, Minnesota, newspaper: 'We tell you, Abraham Lincoln, that the remaining twenty thousand men of Minnesota will never submit to such ingratitude and wrong. We tell you plainly and soberly, if these convicted murderers are dealt with more leniently than other murderers, the people of the state will take law and vengeance in their own hands, and woe to any member of the hated race that shall be found within our borders.'"

"There are political implications, Mr. President," Stanton added, "the Democrats just scored major gains in many states. We only control the House by twenty-five votes. Your re-election campaign could be a tough one. Maybe you should give Minnesota what they want?"

"I will not hang men for votes. I will do what is right. That is my response to Minnesota."

ও 50 ଔ

An icy gloom swept through the morning air as Jesse and his men continued riding along the north side of the Minnesota River searching for survivors and bodies. Occasionally they came upon a badly decomposed corpse and buried it. Jesse held his breath and prayed to God each time a body was sighted, but finding Justina Boelter had renewed his hope.

"Corporal Wall," Jesse called, "there's a hill and ridge up ahead. I'll take half the men onto the prairie. You take the others onto the river flats."

"Sir," Wall asked, "what's the date?"

"November first, I believe."

"Lieutenant, we better find Miss Miller soon. It's cold enough that we could get a snow. Without shelter, she'd really be in a fix. If'n the Sioux haven't . . ."

"I know, Corporal," Jesse finished. "Time is against us. But we can't stop looking, not while there's any chance left. We'll meet up on the other side of the ridge."

JOANNA SHIVERED AS SHE PEERED through the opening in the dugout door. Were the goose bumps from fright or chill? She didn't know. The Sioux horses remained tethered near the oak savannah where the men had camped.

They were coming toward her. On foot, through the tall grass, they were coming, JoAnna was sure of it. She steeled her resolve, cocked back the hammer of the pistol and waited.

Funny, she thought, *a couple of weeks ago I would have gone to pieces in a moment like this*. How deeply she longed to see Jesse once more. But she was fatalistic. "What will be, will be," she muttered.

Then, directly in front some thirty yards out, JoAnna saw grass stir. "Did it move, or was it a sudden breeze?" she murmured. "No," she determined, "it moved."

This time the young woman rested the pistol barrel on the bottom ledge of the opening in the door. Slowly she squeezed the trigger. Through the explosion and black smoke, JoAnna saw a Santee brave stand erect, throw his hands into the air and fall backward.

Instantly JoAnna stepped behind the dirt wall alongside the door as shots riddled through it. She checked the pistol's cylinder. Two bullets left and at least four Indians. The odds were hopeless. One bullet for them, she thought, and maybe one for me. *They won't take me alive*, she resolved.

She peeked through a hole in the door. "This is it," she exclaimed. Four men raced toward the dugout, firing as they ran. They had spread out and knew that they would overwhelm the woman inside. JoAnna aimed and shot again. This time the bullet sliced through grass and missed.

"One bullet," JoAnn sighed. She closed her eyes and held the gun to her temple. One tear rolled down her cheek. A tear for the memory of the love she would never see again.

She pulled the hammer back. Gunfire, she heard gunfire again. But this was more than the four Indian men who were within steps of the door. This was many more. JoAnna peeked through the opening.

Blue-clad soldiers were galloping over the prairie toward her, blasting carbine shots as they rode. The Santee had turned and were returning fire. One soldier fell from his horse and tumbled hard onto the prairie. But within moments the Indians were overwhelmed. Three fell mortally wounded yards from the dugout. The fourth made a run for it through the grass. A lone cavalryman rode him down from behind and slit his back with a curved sword.

The brave somersaulted as he fell and struggled to his feet. The rider drew his revolver and snapped off one shot. The Santee collapsed face forward, dead.

Jesse Buchanen reined in his horse in front of the dugout. JoAnna pushed the door from inside. The hinges snapped and the door fell forward with a pancake plop.

Jesse stared down incredulously from astride his horse. The woman in front of him was scrawny, filthy, and streaked with blood. Her clothing was tattered and her hair a matted, tangled mop. But she was the most beautiful woman Jesse had ever seen.

He leaped from his horse and into JoAnna's wide open arms. "Thank God, we were in time! JoAnna, I love you so much!"

JoAnna clung tightly to Jesse, her rescuer, the man she loved, as she buried her head against his comforting chest and sobbed in relief. "I just knew you'd be here. But in another moment. . ." She stopped, the rest of the story better left untold.

"I had to see you again, Jesse. That's what kept me alive." Then their embrace tightened as their lips met in blissful reunion.

❧ 51 ❧

T HAT EVENING JESSE LED HIS COMPANY back to Sibley's camp at the Redwood Agency. JoAnna Miller rode at his side. The soldiers lined the roadway into the ruined little town with cheers and cries of "Huzzah! Huzzah!"

The flap of Sibley's headquarters tent opened. Stephen Miller stepped out, followed by Sibley. JoAnna raced into her father's arms and his deep embrace. Tears flowed freely from the eyes of both daughter and father.

"I don't care what the men think," Miller muttered as he wiped his eyes, "my baby has come home to me."

He needn't have been concerned. Several veteran soldiers were wiping tears from their eyes as they watched.

On November 7, Colonel Marshall and three companies of soldiers began a weeklong march down the Minnesota River to Fort Snelling. The four-mile-long procession herded over 1,600 Santee, many crammed into open wagons, many others trudging alongside.

Samuel Brown rode on horseback alongside a wagon carrying his uncle, Charles Crawford. Charles had been tried for two separate crimes by the commission and acquitted each time. Samuel's father Joseph

219

Brown, besides being an agent, had been a general of militia. When his house at the Yellow Medicine Agency was plundered and ransacked, Crawford took Joseph Brown's uniform and wore it on the journey down the river.

They were four days out from Redwood and approaching the little river town of Henderson.

"When will your father join us?" Crawford asked Brown.

"I'm sure they've left the Redwood. My father will stay with Sibley. He has been made superintendent in charge of the Indian prisoners."

"The husband of a Sisseton will oversee the condemned. Life is strange."

"But, uncle, they won't join us. We go on to Fort Snelling. They'll stop near Mankato."

"Too many will die needlessly. Some should. Cut Nose, Hapan, Dowansa were bad to the whites. But many killed no one and didn't even shoot. Round Wind should not hang. He was with Red Iron. There was no counsel for any of us."

"Only one asked for a lawyer. It was refused."

"Nephew, many did not understand the charges. They thought it was good to fight in battle and freely admitted they were there. There was no one to tell them that by their words, the commission would sentence them to die. Murderers and rapists were treated the same as soldiers."

Colonel William Marshall rode into Henderson at the head of his column. The street was soon lined on both sides by sullen townspeople. Hate stained their faces.

Lieutenant James Gorman trotted beside Marshall. "They're so quiet. It's eerie. Look at their faces. If looks could kill, we wouldn't need bullets. Ship 'em all east and let them stare at rebs."

"Lieutenant, they don't hate rebs the way they hate Sioux. Keep an eye on them. We should've gone around this place. Alert the men to keep the people back."

Suddenly the silence broke and anger boiled over like an unwatched pot of water. Men, women, and children began to shout and cry at the Santee.

"Damn you to Satan!" screamed an elderly man.

A young woman's face twisted in anguish. "You should all die! Murderers! Murderers!"

A shower of rocks and stones poured from the sky like a rainstorm as the populace flung them at the procession.

A woman edged toward the wagons and then screamed, "You killed my husband!" She raced to a wagon holding a young woman with a baby at her breast. Enraged, the white woman tore the child from her mother's arms held the baby above her head and dashed it violently to the ground. Soldiers dragged the woman away and picked up the crippled infant from the hard earth and returned it to its stunned mother.

The assault by the white woman sparked the mass of townspeople to rush the wagons. Men, women, and children with guns, knives, clubs, and stones overwhelmed the wagons as soldiers desperately tried to stand their ground and push them back.

Townspeople grabbed old Indian men, women, and children by the hair and pulled them from the wagons. They beat the helpless, miserable victims until soldiers stopped them.

A few wagons back, Charles Crawford tucked his head down and covered it with his hands. Samuel Brown held on tight as his horse reared and pawed the air in fright.

"Look there!" a man screamed, a pistol in one hand and a whiskey bottle in the other. "That savage has a uniform on. Who'd he kill ta git it?"

The man rushed the wagon and pointed his pistol point blank at Crawford's chest. Marshall galloped into the melee with saber drawn. A swift downward motion with the flat of the blade knocked the gun to the earth.

"He saved whites, you fool!" Marshall shouted. "Now get back! All of you get back!"

221

Marshall raised his pistol above his head and fired into the air. "Gorman, have the men fire above them and push them back. Then hold the line until we get these wagons through town!"

The soldiers fired a ragged volley and then formed ranks to drive the people off the street. Then they held their position as the procession hurried through Henderson.

The injured baby died in her mother's arms. Their wagon stopped just long enough to place the child in the crotch of a tree, "buried" in traditional Santee ritual.

Sibley and his men left Redwood two days after Marshall. Major Brown had made sure that his prisoners had little chance of escape. They were crowded into small carts, four apiece and chained together. Their journey resembled a herd of animals on the way to market.

JoAnna rode in an uncovered supply wagon with two armed soldiers on the front seat.

The line of march brought them by the devastated German town of New Ulm, which had been twice attacked in the war. Many buildings had been burned and the townspeople driven away. One hundred and forty whites had died within miles of New Ulm. By November 9 the citizenry had returned and were busily recovering bodies and burying friends and relatives who had been killed months before.

Jesse saw the danger potential and flanked JoAnna's wagon.

"Keep your head down," he instructed her. "Things could get kinda rough up ahead."

"Indians?" JoAnna wondered.

"No, white people," Jesse answered as he spurred his horse forward.

As the procession drew near, the townspeople spotted it. "It's dem!" a man shouted as he tossed a spade aside. "Da murderers are comin'!"

"Kill da fiends!" yelled another man.

Crazed with hate and consumed with revenge, the people of New Ulm went berserk. They charged the caravan with pitchforks, hoes, clubs and rocks. Jesse Buchanen galloped up the line to Sibley. "General!" he shouted. "They're overrunning us! They're beating the prisoners! Some women are the worst of them. Should we fight back?"

"No, Lieutenant. Now they're just attacking the Indians. If we fire, even into the air, they'll turn on us!"

A skinny German spied JoAnna and ran along the wagon beside her.

"You one o' dem dat got friendly wit da reds?" he proclaimed accusingly. "Maybe ya need a white man again." He grabbed the wagon rail and hefted himself up as JoAnna tried to push him back. The man had one foot into the wagon bed when Jesse galloped up sword in hand. He leaned from his horse and belted the intruder over the head with the hilt of his sword. The man tumbled heavily off the wagon to the ground.

"Stay down," Jesse shouted at JoAnna. "Don't let them see you."

JoAnna lay back in the wagon bed and pulled a blanket over herself as Jesse rode off.

Sibley watched in amazement as a white woman slugged a manacled Santee man repeatedly in the face. His jaw was obviously broken as he toppled from his wagon.

A soldier stood his ground and tried to push the attackers away from the wagon. He was clubbed over the head and folded to the ground.

"That's it!" Sibley yelled. "These Dutch she-devils are like tigresses. Brown, Buchanen, order the men to fix bayonets and push these people back. We must maintain order!"

The soldiers formed into two lines. Bayonets affixed to the Springfield muskets gleamed in the cool sunshine.

"Advance!" commanded Brown, and the soldiers moved forward.

At first the mob tried to hold its ground. They hurled rocks and insults at the blue-clad men. Then, in the face of a determined, assembled force, they broke and ran back to town. Fifteen Santee and one soldier were badly hurt.

The next day the beleaguered procession reached South Bend, where the Minnesota River twisted sharply northeast to join the Mississippi at Fort Snelling.

A large wooden stockade had been constructed to hold the captives. Mankato was nearby, but Sibley wanted to camp apart from it.

As the prisoners were secured in their new holding pen, Sibley met with his officers in the tent camp established for his soldiers. He stood with them on a bluff overlooking the river as the sun set majestically.

"Major Brown, I trust all the prisoners got here," said Sibley.

"Yes, General, some got beat up pretty bad at New Ulm, but we've got 323 here. All the condemned and those sentenced to prison are being secured in the stockade."

"Colonel Miller," Sibley turned to the tall officer with a neat salt-and-pepper beard, "you are in command of Camp Lincoln. I need to go to St. Paul. You have two tasks: keep 303 ready for the hangman and maintain order. Your main concern with the latter lies down that road."

Sibley gestured toward the flickering lights of the frontier town. "There's been trouble from New Ulm and Henderson. Mankato is bigger than both. Keep a close eye on things. I don't want any more trouble from civilians."

"Don't worry, General. I'll keep order," Miller responded confidently.

Sibley softened his tone and spoke confidentially to Miller. "How's your daughter doing?"

"She's recovering, General. Funny, she seems stronger now."

"Crisis can bring out qualities buried deep inside. Keep her in Mankato. Let's not take another risk with her, not yet."

"Remember your promise, General," Will Duley interjected. "Those heathens still have my wife and children somewhere, or else they murdered 'em. I get to pull the lever."

"My promise to you is not forgotten. But how many hang and when is not up to me. We still wait on Lincoln That's all that's left for us to do. Wait."

℅ 52 ℃

JOANNA TOOK UP QUARTERS in the Mankato Hotel. Colonel Miller thought it more fitting than housing his daughter in a prison camp. Escorted by four soldiers, he rode over the rough dirt main street of the growing river town to pay her a visit.

He dismounted before the two-story white frame building and entered the hotel. JoAnna awaited him in the women's parlor. She arose from a lustrous, black horsehair chair when her father appeared in the doorway.

"Father, welcome to my humble abode," she said jokingly.

Miller smiled and led her to the dining room, where they were seated at a small table. "JoAnna, every day I thank God that you survived your ordeal."

"Providence might have had something to do with it," she agreed.

"I couldn't bear to have lost you, and I still fear for you. Mankato is a rough town filled with new immigrants and refugees. It's no place for a young, single woman, and the prison camp certainly isn't any better. A troop is going back to St. Paul tomorrow. I want you to return home with them."

A look of disappointment and then resolution washed over JoAnna's face.

"No, Father. I'm going to stay here. It's where you are and where Jesse is. Besides, I've taken a job."

"A . . . a what?" her startled father sputtered.

"A job. Dr. Weiser was in here last night. He says that there is sickness at Camp Lincoln and that he needs a nurse."

"He asked you! Joe Weiser and I will have to have a little talk. He won't put my daughter in danger!"

"Father, Dr. Weiser simply made a statement that he had a need. He didn't ask me. I asked him if I could help. Then the doctor told me to talk to you first. That's why I asked that you come by today."

"Well, JoAnna, you can't. It's simply out of the question."

"Why?"

"I don't want you around rough men and sick Indians. Besides, there is the danger of contagion."

"Father, women have served as nurses to armies since men first fought each other. I can do this. Anyway, I came here with people from Camp Release where measles first appeared. I've already been exposed. I want to do something, and this seems to fit."

"Well, I will not allow it. You're going home."

JoAnna slowly shook her head, her dark curls swaying before her face. "Father, I love you dearly and I don't want to go against your wishes. But I feel this is my duty to do what I can to help these men. Please?"

Stephen Miller sighed in resignation. Then he asked, "What about Jesse? I thought you were getting married soon."

"The war is still on, Father. Jesse will understand."

ఴ 53 ಞ

ONE HUNDRED MILES UP the Missouri River from Two Kettles's village and Fort Pierre, a long flat-bottomed boat slid through the muddy, frigid water of the river. It was November, and winter was coming early on the plains.

Charles Galpin turned up his coat collar and stood as he looked back from the prow of the boat. Four men churned their oars. Bundles were stacked in the middle of the deck. A woman sat in the back near one of the bundles. It was his wife, Matilda. The bundle contained the body of their son.

They were gold miners returning from an expedition to Montana. Their son had sickened and died, and Matilda refused leave his body in the desolate wilderness. She was Yankton Dakota and determined to ensure that Johnny would be given a proper funeral with her people.

A brisk wind bit Galpin's back, gripping him like dozens of icy fingers. He was about to sit down as they rounded a river bend when shouts from the near bank greeted them.

"Come to shore! Come or we will shoot!"

The bank was lined with Indians, their guns and bows trained on the boat.

"Whatcha make of it, Major?" one of the oarsman yelled. "Should we make a run fer it?"

"They've got us covered and we're within range. Matilda," Galpin called to his wife, "whaddya think?"

The stocky buckskin-clad woman walked unsteadily to the prow. "They are Dakota, my people. Go to shore."

"Head in to 'em!" Galpin cried. The boat swung toward the Indians on the riverbank.

As the vessel drew near, Indians splashed into the water and pulled it ashore. One slipped a rope around the gunwale and tied the other end to a cottonwood off the river's edge. Sleepy Eyes of the Sisseton Santee stepped forward. "We are peaceful hunters, but we can find no game. Give us food," he demanded.

"We're just comin' back from Montana," Galpin explained. "We ain't got much food, and we sure ain't got any to give away."

"Give us whatever you have, or we will take it. These people," Sleepy Eyes gestured to the band around him, "have traveled from Minnesota in three moons. We have found barely enough to keep alive. Women and children are with us."

"That's 'bout 800 miles in three months. Amazin' that you could do that with women and children. But it doesn't change the fact that we don't have no food to spare."

Matilda rose up. "I know you. I know your parents. You are Santee. Here I have my dead son." She pointed to the covered bundle in the back of the boat. "We bring him home to be buried with my people. Will you stop us?"

The woman looked intently at the Santee and then whispered in alarm to her husband, "Charles, they've got old men with them. Dakota don't take old men to hunt. Something is wrong. There is danger!"

With that Matilda produced a hatchet from the deck and slashed the rope constraining the boat. The river current immediately grabbed the craft and sucked it downstream. The five men and Matilda dived to the boat deck as a torrent of shots rang over them like angry hornets.

Julia Wright, her hair grimy and snarled, dress in tatters, jerked her head up with a start. She stood shivering knee deep in the river filling a container with water downstream from the Santee warriors and the boat. Sudden visions of rescue loomed as the flat bottom appeared.

"Help!" she shrieked. "White woman! Help!"

Galpin, now out of range from the Santee rifles, shouted back, "We can't stop. They'll be on us in no time! Who are you?"

Dismayed, the woman cried, "Julia Wright from Shetek in Minnesota! Laura Duley is here too! Six children left. Find a way to help! Please help!"

"We'll tell! We'll send help! Hold on!"

With heartless cruelty the river pulled the boat and the prayed-for salvation away. A trace of hope flickered in Julia Wright's face. White people had seen her. They knew that eight survivors from Lake Shetek were still alive. Too late for her son George, and too late for baby Frances Duley, who had succumbed to the effects of torture, but just maybe there was hope for the rest.

✥ 54 ✥

HARGER, KILLS GAME, AND Swift Bird had waited patiently. They counseled together about the meaning of the visions and what they should do. On a brisk November morning, they rode slowly along the river to Primeau's trading post.

"I feel the time is near," Charger said. "The captives are not far away."

Kills Game considered Charger's thoughts. "If you are right, then there are others who want to share our quest. What will we tell them?"

"We will form a lodge, a society of warriors. Societies come from dreams, and we have had a dream vision. Ours will be different. We will rescue these captives, and we will help those in need. We will cross clan lines and lines of tribes. If a hunter is hurt and cannot provide for his family, we will do it for him. Our dream is to do things to better all people. It is a dream of peace."

"You are Naca," Swift Bird proclaimed to Charger, "the thinker of thinkers."

A flurry of activity greeted the three young Teton as they neared the trading post. A flatbed boat was anchored along shore, and several strange white men stood in front of Primeau's.

230

"Leesen to thees!" the proprietor exclaimed as he saw Charger, "eet ees like you say! Tell him, Galpin."

"You Charger? Primeau told me about ya. Says ya had a dream. Well, I guess it's comin' true. 'Bout a hundred miles upriver, near where the Grand River enters the Missouri, we ran inta a bunch of Indians, Santee from Minnesota they was. Well, they tried to take our food but we got away.

"Just downriver a woman yelled at us, sad lookin' wretch. She said there was another woman and six children from Shetek held by the Indians. I guess them's yer captives."

"It is my dream," Charger looked at his two friends, "now we must act. We will go to rescue the white captives."

Primeau couldn't stifle a laugh. "It'll take more than just three boys to take those people back. Do you think that the Santee will just give them to you?"

"They'll fight'cha," Galpin agreed. "They looked in pretty rough shape. I think they've been runnin' ever since they left Minnesota."

"There are more young men who think like us," Charger countered. "We will find them, and they will help us. There are many young Teton who want to do a brave deed."

"You'll need things. I admire your grit. Come back when you are ready to go. I'll supply you, " Primeau offered,

The three thrashed their horses and galloped back into Two Kettles's village. They screamed "Hoka Hey!" as they rode pell mell through the camp. People scrambled to escape the pounding hooves of the wild-eyed, snorting animals. Cries of alarm and warning were shouted.

Once Charger and his friends had reached the far end of the camp, they jerked their horses' heads around into a sharp rearing turn. Then they raced back to the center of the village and reined in to an abrupt halt.

As the animals stood sweating, foaming and snorting, some people cheered in admiration of the display of horsemanship. Others cried that they were abusing horses and needlessly alarming the Sans Arc.

The horses pawed and danced as Charger exclaimed, "Brothers, it is time to show that you are brave Teton warriors! Join us! We go to rescue white captives from the Santee. Our vision is upon us!"

An older man shouted, "Wacintonsni, fools!" and turned his back on the three. Many others simply shook their heads in bewilderment or disgust and walked away. But here and there a young man strode toward Charger and the others to stand alongside of them, crying, "I will go!"

Eight joined the three: Comes Back, Mad Bear, Pretty Bear, One Rib, Strikes Fire, Charging Dog, Four Bear, and Red Dog. The eleven ranged between sixteen and twenty-one years of age.

Charger looked at the ten young men before him and raised his arms. "We will be soldiers against the Santee!" he cried.

An elder spat disgustedly upon the ground. "*Akicita wacinton-sni!*" he yelled. "You will be Fool Soldiers!"

The crowd of Dakota picked up the chant of "Fool Soldier, Fool Soldier!" as the eleven sought a quiet spot by the river to plan their future. Charger stood in the midst of his converts, who sat in a circle upon the ground. He paced slowly and explained what lay before them.

"Ignore the ridicule of the elders. We are young, we have not counted coup. We don't know about war or battles other than the stories our grandfathers and uncles have told to us. Now we have a quest. Wakan Tonka wishes us to find the captives taken by the Santee. Our journey may be long and cold. The north wind has already brought snow to us.

"The Santee will not give us their captives easily. We must be wise in our dealing with them. We do not seek them to fight and kill Santee. The captives might be harmed. Yet, if we must fight, we must be brave and be prepared to die!"

Swift Bird shouted, "We will fight to save the white women and children. We will die if we must."

"Han! Ho!" the others cried.

"In the village," Charger continued, "they called us fools and crazy. Some will think we are traitors because we challenge our brother

232

Santee for the whites. We will be ridiculed and maybe sent away from the Sans Arc. Are you strong enough?"

"We are strong!" the ten cried.

"Then go to your lodges and prepare yourselves. Bring food, blankets, whatever you have for the journey. Then we will gather at Primeau's."

When the small band congregated at the trading post, Charger was hoisting a bag of coffee onto a pack horse. The proprietor stood alongside him.

"Primeau was good," Charger grinned. "He gave more than the robes were worth. We have much coffee, sugar, and bread."

"Eef you find the Santee," Primeau explained, "you must have a feast for them before they will even talk to you about the captives. After you rescue them," he paused and smiled ruefully, "bring them here to me. We will find a way to get them to Fort Randall. Good luck to you. May God be with you."

"Wakan Tonka sends us," Charger proclaimed as he swung onto his horse's back, wheeled him toward the village and galloped away followed by his young band. They rode through the village to taunts of "Fool Soldiers!" Then they pushed down the river bank and swam across the Missouri. They scrambled up the opposite bank, paused and looked back at their village.

Charger reached into a leather bag and removed a small mirror. He held it up and flashed it into the sun above the village.

"Now they will know that the 'Fool Soldiers' have made it across. If it is the work of fools to save women and children, protect the weak and give to those who need help, then fools we will be. Let us ride to find the Santee."

∽ 55 ∼

I N MID-NOVEMBER, WHILE the camp of the condemned was established near Mankato, the remaining sixteen hundred Indians, mostly women and children, were interned at Fort Snelling.

In the commander's house, several officers gathered around a table in the ground floor sitting room. A crackling blaze in the fireplace warmed the room. Tin coffee cups sat before the men. Colonel William Marshall, Colonel Bill Crooks, Lieutenant Will McKusick, army doctor Alfred Mueller, and Reverend Stephen Riggs engaged in fervent conversation.

"All right," Crooks exclaimed to Marshall, "you got them all here. Now what do we do with them?"

"Hold them, Colonel, until President Lincoln tells us what to do."

"And when will that be? Ramsey, Pope, and Sibley keep asking for some sort of disposition, but we hear nothing. We both served on the commission that sentenced them to die. The condemned sit in Mankato awaiting the noose, all 300 I hope, and we sit here having to feed . . . how many, Lieutenant?"

"Sir," the lieutenant replied, "we left Redwood with 1,658 and arrived here with 1,601. Forty-five are men, mostly old. The rest are women and children."

"You lost fifty-seven? How?" Crooks demanded.

"Hard to tell, sir. There was measles at Redwood. Some mighta died from it. Some mebbe got away, and there was soldiers and folks out there just itchin' to git back at them Indians. Some mighta got shot."

"So," Crooks continued, "we've got the rest to care for. As I understand it, Colonel Marshall, you have command over the camp and the 300 men who came here with you."

"Lieutenant McKusick will be my camp superintendent," Marshall said. "Since you're the new commander of Fort Snelling, Colonel, we take direction from you. I think your decision to move the camp off the bluffs and onto the flats by the ferry was wise."

"Too cold up here. Besides, I like being able to look down into their compound."

"I'm concerned with what'll happen in the camp." Riggs spoke for the first time. "Idle hands are the devil's workshop."

"That's why we asked you to meet with us," Marshall explained as he rubbed his bald head. "Reverend Riggs, this should be an excellent opportunity for you and your brethren to convert and teach these savages."

"I'll certainly do what I can. But General Sibley still has need of me in Mankato as well. I must minister to the condemned with Father Ravoux. I'll have to divide my time between here and Mankato."

Crooks thought a moment and then asked, "What other men of the cloth are here?"

"Several," the missionary answered. "Samuel and Gideon Pond, the Williamsons, Thomas and his son John, Samuel Hinman from the Redwood Agency. There's a nice teacher from Redwood, too, with her new husband, a one-armed trader who used to be a soldier, Emily and Nathan Cates. I think you know him."

"Yes," Marshall replied, "I heard he fought bravely at Fort Ridgely. I was with him at Wood Lake. A little mystery about him, as I recall. Apparently his employer was hanged as a traitor. But his actions indicated strong loyalty to the Union, and that's good enough for me."

235

"And Sibley, too," Crooks commented. "Seems that General George Thomas himself vouched for Cates."

"Work with these people," Marshall instructed Riggs. "There's an empty warehouse between the stockade and the fort. Use it as a school and meeting house."

"I will when we have enough Santee interested to make it worthwhile. For now, it will be tipi-to-tipi. Do you think the stockade is sufficient to hold them? What if they try to escape?"

Marshall laughed aloud just as he took a sip of coffee, spraying a light-brown mist. "It's not so much to keep them in as to keep molesters away from them. The guards outside the walls have orders to shoot either way, people trying to get in or out."

"What about food?" Riggs wondered.

"Standard fare for soldiers," Crooks answered. "Meat, bread, beans, sugar, vinegar, salt, and coffee."

"The Santee like meat."

"Well, Reverend, they won't get buffalo," the Colonel rejoined, "but the government has seen fit to allow us to procure beef. But here's a little fact for you. An ox weighs about 1,500 pounds. It'd be nice if that's what we had to feed them. But dressed out, the ox is 450 pounds, and when the meat is dried, only about 112 pounds. So you see, we have to be judicious in our rations."

"Dr. Mueller," Marshall observed, "you've been silent. Your reputation for saving lives at Fort Ridgely precedes you. Any concerns?"

The Swiss immigrant, a hero along with his wife, Eliza, at the battle and siege at Fort Ridgely, shook his head. "Whenever this many people are crammed into tight quarters, disease is sure to follow. It'll affect the fort as well."

Riggs expounded. "We had cases of measles at Camp Release, and the first death was in Mankato on November 11."

"The good doctor never lost a man to the Sioux, but measles is something else," Marshall noted.

"We still have a great many sick men. It takes about eight to fifteen days after exposure for measles to appear," Mueller said. "In a couple of weeks, it could run rampant throughout the camp. Given statistics I've studied, it is my belief that all but about fifteen percent of the Sioux will become infected."

Riggs considered Mueller's comments. "In all my years with the Santee, this was a very rare disease. If they haven't been exposed to it before, then I agree, a measles epidemic will be deadly among the Dakota."

"No one said this would be easy," Crooks concluded, "but we all have our jobs to do. Colonel Marshall, see to security, Reverend Riggs tend to their souls, and Dr. Mueller, try to keep them healthy. Hopefully, Lincoln will decide what to do with them soon."

56

ANOTHER MEETING WAS TAKING PLACE within the hovel of dwellings in the stockade campground. Wabasha, Wacouta, Red Iron, and Little Paul sat in a circle around a fire. The blaze snapped merrily and spread warmth within the canvas tipi. But no cheer from a fire could melt the icy mood of the four men who stared intently into the flickering flames.

"We should have gone with Crow," Wacouta mumbled.

Wabasha poked a stick into the fire, causing sparks to fly upward. "It would have gone bad for us, for anyone who stood against Little Crow at the end. We would have been blamed. We could not fight, we could not run. Now we sit here, most of the warriors have gone west to the Teton, some are waiting to die at Mankato while we await our fate with women and children."

"What will happen to us?" Red Iron asked. "Do they forget that the Sisseton and Wahpeton stood against the Mdewakanton, and we would not let them pass to the north with the captives?"

Wabasha responded, "All the whites care about is that our skin is red and that some Sisseton fought as warriors with Little Crow. Even the Winnebago who are not Dakota are being driven from their land.

Chaska killed no one, and Mrs. Wakefield told how he saved her life. But Chaska waits to die in Mankato."

"They will move us," Little Paul said. "All of us will be driven from the valley and from Minnesota. We will sit here in these cold lodges made of white man's cloth. We use the thin blankets because we don't have enough warm buffalo robes for all the people."

Wabasha slowly shook his head. "It is sad. The young men said that they would sweep down the river valley until they knocked at the gates of Fort Snelling. We came down the valley, it is true, and now we sit before the gates of the fort, but as prisoners, not warriors."

"Many are growing sick," said Little Paul. "The red spots are showing on the faces and bodies of many. Our medicine is no good for this."

"The doctor from the fort has been here. Maybe he will help," Wacouta replied with hope.

"If it is good for the whites, we will be helped," Red Iron said, "otherwise they will let us all die."

The missionaries were determined to do whatever possible for the spiritual and physical needs of the interned. They aided Dr. Mueller with the sick as they gradually made headway with their heavenly mission.

Many of the Santee had been part of the missions on the reservation. Now great numbers of them were desperate and looking for rays of hope. The Ponds, Williamsons, Hinman, and Riggs offered eternal salvation. At first John Williamson held meetings within the confines of the tipis. His father, Thomas, returned to Mankato.

When Riggs and Ravoux brought letters from the prisoners at Mankato proclaiming a mass conversion to Christianity, a larger room was needed. The upstairs loft of the warehouse outside the stockade walls became a place for church services as well as a school classroom.

Reverend Riggs stood at a makeshift pulpit before his new congregation. Hundreds were crouched down beneath the rafters, sitting cross-legged. Only the glistening of their eyes revealed some in the darkness. There was no fire. Only body heat warmed the upper level, and the frozen breath hung in the air.

239

Riggs bowed his head in prayer and waited. There was no sound save the ragged breathing of an old man.

"In times of great distress," the pastor began, "God provides hope and opportunity. Many of you and your brothers in Mankato have made confessions and professions. Through Jesus Christ there is new life for all, for you and the condemned. I know that many of you hold medicine bags. These are just idols. I know that these have been treasured for generations, but they represent the past. You must cast away these false idols as you come to the Son of God. Lay onto Christ as your only hope.

"I have here hundreds of letters from those waiting to die in Mankato." Riggs opened a box filled with letters. "I will read one to you. Listen to this. 'Brother Santee, soon I will die. But I have chosen to follow Christ. Even if they hang me, I will live forever through Him. I have been baptized, and hope all Santee will too.' It is signed, 'Hapan.'"

Over the next few weeks Santee threw away idols by the score as hundreds were baptized and confirmed. John Williamson presided over a bonfire of hundreds of charms and medicine bundles.

School work also progressed as the teacher from Redwood, Emily Cates, and her husband, Nathan, scrounged books, mostly Bibles, and devoted their time to teaching reading. Adults and children filed into the warehouse daily to learn how to interpret the strange marks on the pages.

Williamson helped as well. He paused from working with a middle-aged Indian man and turned to Nathan. "It's strange, Mr. Cates, for years we have striven to change how these people live.

"We had twin goals, conversion to Christ and a cultural adjustment. In fact, we unofficially decided that changing how they lived, bringing them to the white culture, needed to be done before we brought them to Christ. Certainly we did both, but if they didn't accept the white man's way of life, bringing them to Christ seemed pointless.

"Now this war has made both possible. Hundreds are learning to read and coming to Christ. In twenty-five years we converted only about sixty souls. Now we are converting that many in a single afternoon. Strange, isn't it? God works in mysterious ways."

"What do you think changed?" Nathan asked.

Williamson thought pensively, then replied, "In this place there is only fear of the unknown to occupy their minds. We missionaries offer hope and kindness. Their gods could not prevent the disaster that has befallen them. Maybe they hope Jesus Christ will save them."

"This life is harder than leading an army."

"You were a soldier, Mr. Cates. Do you miss it?"

"The Civil War brought a strange turn for me. I don't just mean the loss of my arm. It brought me here, and it brought me to Emily. I've lost my taste for war, both in the South and in Minnesota."

As Williamson turned back to his students, Emily stood near Nathan and whispered, "What do you suppose the pastor would think if he knew that Jefferson Davis had sent you to Minnesota to start the uprising and that you had had a change of heart?"

Nathan smiled and lovingly touched Emily's cheek. "God works in mysterious ways."

౫ 57 ౭

S NOW HAD DUSTED THE PRAIRIE, and Charger's band of Fool Soldiers trotted over frozen ground up the Missouri River. The gray sky and snow-covered land melded together into an endless, dreary whiteness.

After several days, they came upon the camp of a Yanktonai chief, Bone Necklace. The visitors were welcomed into the village as guests and were soon warming themselves in Bone Necklace's lodge.

They sat, ate and smoked before Charger explained their mission to the chief. "We seek the white captives from Minnesota. We will free them and bring them to their people. Have you seen them?"

"Several warriors on a hunt," Bone Necklace responded, "came across the Santee band. They are led by White Lodge and have eighty tipis. They are moving up the great river seeking help from the Teton."

"The miner, Galpin, said whites were with them and that he was attacked by the Santee," Pretty Bear commented.

"No one spoke of whites with the Santee. There are many crying children in the camp. They are hungry and cold. That is why they tried to capture Galpin's boat. They wanted the provisions in the boat, not to kill the whites, I think."

"Where are they?" Charger asked.

"Close, young one. They are near."

The next morning the Fool Soldiers resumed their journey. Fifteen miles up the river brought them to the camp of the Santee on a bend of the frozen Missouri. With the sun's rays were dimming in the west, Charger instructed his band to make camp apart from the Santee. They erected their single tent and then approached White Lodge's camp.

A lone watchman sentinel met Charger. "Who are you and why do you come here?" he asked.

"I am Charger of the Sans Arc Teton, and I want to meet with White Lodge."

Wordlessly the watchman motioned for the young men to follow, and they rode into the Santee village.

White Lodge limped from his tipi and encountered Charger, who dismounted from his pony and strode toward the chief.

"*Hau koda*," greeted White Lodge.

Charger respectfully returned, "*Hau koda*."

"Who are you and why do you come to my camp?"

"My friends and I have come upon you and your band of people in a good way. We want to have a meeting with you. *Us wolakota wicasa pi*, good-hearted red men, want to talk serious with an open mind. We have coffee, sugar, and bread for you."

White Lodge observed the eleven young men with caution. But it was not the way of the Dakota to leave guests out in the cold. Besides, they hadn't had sweetened coffee since they left Minnesota three months earlier.

"Join us in my lodge where the air is warm and we can talk. We will eat."

The other ten Sans Arc dismounted and followed White Lodge into his home. They unwrapped the blankets that had protected them from the cold and sat upon buffalo robes.

White Lodge's tipi was the largest in the camp and was soon crowded with Sans Arc and Santee. Word of the visitors quickly spread through the camp, and all but the old or very sick huddled around White Lodge's dwelling.

The Indians drank the sugary coffee and wolfed down chunks of bread. Some slipped their portion into leather bags to give to their children.

"Thank you, White Lodge, for sharing the warmth of your lodge with us," Charger began.

"Why do you wish to meet with me?"

Charger looked around the tipi before speaking. A fire burned in the center, and the space was filled with a light smoky fog. Smells of bodies and smoke filled his nostrils. Charger and his friends sat on one side while White Lodge, his son, Black Hawk, Pawn, and other leaders sat on robes opposite. Crowded behind both groups were Santee men and women from the camp.

"You see us here," Charger explained. "We are only young men. Our people call us crazy and fools, but we want to do something good. We have come here to buy the white captives and give them back to their friends."

White Lodge looked scornfully over the fire at Charger. "I do not bargain with boys. You were not in Minnesota. You did not fight the whites. These captives I have taken after killing many of their people. I will not again be a friend to the whites. I have already done a bad thing, and now I will keep on doing bad things. I will not give up the captives. I will fight until I drop dead."

Silence hung in the air like the soundless snowflakes that drifted to the prairie outside. White Lodge had been resolute. He would not bargain.

"You are right. We have not counted coup or seen battle. But we are pledged to do a good thing. We have horses and food to trade," Charger countered. "Will you sit as a council and listen to us?"

White Lodge looked indecisively at his companions. Then Red Dog reached into a pouch and took out a long-stemmed red stone pipe.

"I will fill this pipe," he announced. "Let us all smoke so there will be no lies between us."

As Red Dog slowly filled the pipe, he began a pipe song. White Lodge produced a hand drum to assist the singer while other young men joined in the chant. When the pipe was full of tobacco, Red Dog puffed it, and then passed it to his left.

"Let our prayers go up to Wakan Tonka with the smoke," he said.

The pipe was passed until all had smoked, and the tobacco in the pipe was used up.

Then Charger spoke again. "We welcome our cousins, the Santee to our land. Our hearts are glad that you are here. You know we are good men. When a man has a possession he must be paid. We will buy these hostages."

"We have adopted them," White Lodge answered. "They are Santee now."

The young man stared into White Lodge's eyes. "As you can see, we are young. Still but this doesn't make us fools. We know what we are doing and have good reasons in doing so. Our people call us crazy. They call us *Heyoka Akicita Tiwahe*, the Fool Soldiers Band because we want to help the whites. This came to me in a vision. We are only here for the betterment of our people, for we fear for their lives. The great white father is only looking for reasons to get rid of us. And now he has one."

White Lodge stared intently in turn into the eyes of each of the Fool Soldiers as he tried to read their emotions. He wiped a strand of gray hair from his eyes and replied, "The great white father has many promises that he is not loyal to. This I know is true for all of us. The white man has never helped us. He has only taken what is important to us. This white man has taken the buffalo off of their homesteads and forced us to live like a pack of coyotes. The buffalo is sacred. We use every part for our tools, food, weapons, clothing, and shelter. We even use his dung to warm us. We are forced to take from the whites what we don't have to keep our people well. Until the great white father fulfills his promises, I will not return these white women and children."

Charger considered the elder chief's words and answered, "The buffalo were the heart of our life. They are the reason we are here to talk. I am thankful for that, but right now we need to make moves like the buffalo once did. What we decide today will be with us in the days to come. We must stay together and make decisions together, or we will be gone like the buffalo."

White Lodge looked at Pawn, drew a deep breath and spoke. "The buffalo are gone because of this white man. He is the reason why we sit here. I have some of his people, and with his people in my hands my people will survive. I am unwilling to give up his people. This is the only way that I feel that I am going to be able to feed my people."

Once again the silence of a standstill cast a pall in the lodge. Then Four Bear spoke. "I can see the pain that you and your people feel, but keeping these whites will not make anything better."

Calmly and evenly he continued, "The white man, he is a trickster and has many legs. This I know. But for the survival of all our people, we need to trick the white man himself."

"White Lodge," Charger resumed, "we all need to walk as one Red Nation. If we do not, we will not last the long ride. We cannot live our lives like we are different from each other. We are two different men, but, at the same time, we both are actually brothers. We have to treat each other with the respect and love for one another that brothers have amongst them. I have a younger brother who is not any bigger than a baby. I know that there are babies within this camp. Those sacred lives they hold do not belong to us. We can make decisions now that will only help them live their lives, and they are the reason I do this."

One Rib had been silent. Now he confidently exclaimed, "White Lodge, I know that you are a man whose word can be trusted, but please let us take these whites from you. If you keep these whites, they will cause nothing more than trouble for all of our people. You know the soldiers will come and hunt you down. There will be trouble for all Lakota. We are willing to buy them."

For a long moment White Lodge considered. His son, Black Hawk, leaned over and whispered into his father's ear. Then hesitantly

White Lodge asked, "What will you give for them?"

Charger knew that the Santee chief was wavering and quickly replied, "We have sugar and coffee, and we have our own good horses. These are the best ponies of Two Kettles's herd. They are the best of all the Teton horses. We will trade them for the captives."

White Lodge slowly drank from his coffee cup while Charger and his friends waited in anticipation. Then the Santee leader rose slowly to his feet with Black Hawk's help. He arranged his blanket around his body and stood before the fire.

"We come from the east," he began, "where the sky is red with the blood of whites the Santee have killed. We took the captives after killing many people. But," White Lodge's eyes flashed flame as he shouted in anger, "the whites have done more bad to us than we have done to them! They took the land of our fathers and did not pay us as they promised. Now we will never be able to return to the valley of the Minnesota. It is all gone," he said fiercely. "Now we will fight until we are all dead!"

While the old chief sat, Santee voices rose as they argued among themselves. Then Charger motioned for Kills Game to speak.

"Our horses are the fastest. They will carry you with speed and safety into battle."

Swift Bear echoed his friend's comments. "Our horses are strong, too. They will carry you far without tiring. Trade the captives for them."

Once again White Lodge struggled to his feet. His eyes glared like lightning bolts and silenced his noisy council. "No!" he shouted. "The captives must stay with us!"

Silence gripped the dwelling once again. Charger stood and faced the Santee leaders.

"Three times," he said menacingly, "we have offered our horses for the captives. You have refused. Now, we will take the captives. We will put them on our horses. If you make trouble for us, the soldiers with guns will come against you from the east."

Charger strode toward White Lodge and cried as he pointed to the west. "And the Teton will come against you from across the river.

Then we shall see if you are brave!"

The Fool Soldiers whooped war cries as they leaped to their feet. The older Santee, council members, signaled their warriors for protection. Tensely each group handled their weapons in preparation.

"Father," Black Hawk spoke, "I ask that you reconsider. I have love and respect for you and the elders. But I also respect these young men who have shown much courage to come here and speak to you as they did."

He turned to the young Teton. "Charger, you have done right. We ate your food, and you have been straight with us. Father, we are starving. We need these horses from the Teton if we are to go and live in Canada. I have one white child in my lodge which I will give up even though my wife will grieve."

Black Hawk faced the other Santee. "All of you do as I have done and give up your captives."

White Lodge stared at his son and answered, "Let us meet in council."

The Santee huddled, the young ones arguing for the horses offered by the Sans Arc Teton. Reluctantly White Lodge faced Charger once again.

"We will exchange the captives for the horses and other supplies you have. But we must talk with those who have adopted. Three of the white girls replaced Santee children who have died. It will be like a death in the lodge if those are taken away. You must bargain for each."

Charger was relieved but now realized that this would not be one deal for the hostages. They would have to negotiate for each captive separately.

The Fool Soldiers returned to their lodge and waited patiently for White Lodge to announce that the negotiations would begin.

Charger was worried. "They take so long. Is something wrong in the Santee camp?"

Kills Game reassured his friend, "White Lodge has probably changed his mind again, but do not worry. The warriors want our horses. They will make White Lodge trade."

Just at dawn a messenger from White Lodge appeared at the Sans Arc camp. White Lodge was ready to bargain. The young men caught their hobbled horses and rode back to the bend in the Missouri and the Santee. The exchange would be made in the center of camp.

The Fool Soldiers tethered their horses and left Strikes Fire to watch them as the rest gathered in White Lodge's tipi. A fire burned in the center. White Lodge sat on robes directly across from the entrance. He motioned for the Sans Arc to sit on his left. On the other side of the tipi sat a white woman with six children huddled around her.

Charger viewed the captives with dismay. They were nearly naked except for tattered cotton garments. They mostly wore the clothes they had on when they left Minnesota.

Laura Duley stared dumbly into the fire. The children clung to her and whimpered, but Laura made no effort to acknowledge them, let alone offer comfort. Black Hawk stood and pointed at her. "This is the woman Laura Duley, one of these girls and the boy are hers. The woman is mad, she was weak and her mind left her. The other three girls have no mother and were adopted by Santee women."

Black Hawk paused and gazed at a face-blackened Santee woman with ragged strands of hair hanging over her face. The hard lines of his face softened briefly. Charger speculated it was Black Hawk's wife.

Then the chief's son continued, "The other girl belongs to the Wright woman and lives in the lodge of my father."

"I do not see the other white woman," Charger said.

Black Hawk shook his head. "My father has changed his mind. He will not part with Julia Wright. But he will let her girl go for one horse and a blanket."

"This is how it will be," Charger thought once more in dismay. Each captive would be bargained for individually.

"Bring the girl to us," Charger agreed.

Black Hawk looked to his wife to escort little Eldora Wright to

Charger. The child was nearly asleep and leaning against Emma Duley.

Eldora was startled awake when the Indian woman took her arm and shouted, "Mama?"

Emma leaned down and whispered in the little girl's ear. Eldora was led to Charger, who wrapped a blanket around her shoulders.

Charger gently took her hand and greeted softly, "*Hau, hoksila.*"

Then, thinking he should have spoken in English, he was surprised to hear, "*Hau,* Waanatan."

Black Hawk smiled at them. "The girl was treated like a daughter in my father's lodge. She knows the life of a Dakota girl, and she has been told your name."

Throughout the day the bargaining continued. Starting with the youngest child, each of the captives was traded for a horse and then a blanket, or coffee and sugar. As each exchange was made, the captive rose like a player chosen in a game and walked to Charger on the opposite side of the tipi. Finally Laura Duley was exchanged.

Her daughter, Emma, in broken Dakota spoke to Charger. "Waanatan, my mother is lame and will need my help to walk across the tipi."

"Let the Santee woman assist her," Charger said. Then in a low voice to Emma, "If you go back over there, they might keep you."

Black Hawk announced, "My woman does not want to touch the madwoman. Let the girl help her mother."

Charger looked down at Emma. "Cannot your mother walk alone?"

"No, her foot is hurt and she doesn't have a crutch. And she must be led because . . ." Tears pooled in the girl's eyes.

Charger comforted her by placing his hand on her shoulder. "Go to her," he said.

Emma tapped her mother's shoulder, and the woman struggled to her feet. Leaning heavily on the little girl, she limped across the tipi.

Charger looked around. Six white children and a crippled white woman were now in the hands of his Fool Soldiers. But one was still missing.

White Lodge rose to his feet holding a war club. He looked with disdain at the Tetons. "Go now," he commanded. "You have the captives."

Charger stood steadfast. "No, you still have the Wright woman."

Sparks flew in the old man's eyes as he snapped back, "You will not get her. She is my wife. I am old. My first wife is old. I need the white woman in my lodge. She is a good cook and speaks Dakota. She takes care of me. I will not let her go!"

Furious, Charger leaped to his feet. "The Santee are liars! They promised to exchange all of the captives for the horses. You have taken much more and now White Lodge breaks his word by refusing us the last captive!"

Pandemonium broke loose as White Lodge raised his war club and rushed toward the captives. "I will kill them all," he stormed.

Children screamed, Santee shouted, and the Fool Soldiers blocked White Lodge's attack by forming a human shield around the captives. White Lodge swung wildly and brought his arm back to strike again.

Black Hawk caught his father's arm in a steel grip and held tight. He forced White Lodge to sit and brought him wincing to the ground. Breath came in short bursts as the chief glared at Charger.

"I warned you," Charger reminded, "if you harm us, the soldiers will come with guns and chase you like rabbits across the prairie. The Teton will avenge us, too. You will all be run into the ground and killed."

The Santee gathered around their leader in earnest conversation.

Pawn implored, "Listen to the young Teton. It is foolish to keep this white woman."

Swift Bird leaned over and whispered in his friend's ear, "Waanatan, the soldiers don't even know that these people live, and the Teton think we are fools."

"They don't know that," Charger gestured at the Santee and

smiled grimly.

Shortly Black Hawk motioned to his wife, who ran from the tipi and returned in minutes with Julia Wright.

"Give me a horse, a gun, and two blankets for the woman," White Lodge demanded.

"No," Charger responded. "We will give you one horse and two blankets. Nothing more!"

Once again the fiery chief reached for his club and sought to rise in anger. But Black Hawk placed a strong hand upon his shoulder and held him down.

"The deal is made. Take the whites and go."

The children scrambled out of the tipi with the Fool Soldiers while Emma helped her mother exit. Charger took Julia's arm. He looked with pity into the woman's battered and bruised face.

"What happened to you?"

"Four days ago I cried out to white men in a boat. This was my punishment."

"Come, you are free."

It was November 20, 1862. The captives were exactly three months and 800 miles from Lake Shetek.

↭ 58 ↮

WAR WEIGHED HEAVILY UPON the president of the United States. One observer commented that he was literally bending under the weight of his burdens. Lincoln was consumed by his pledge to save the Union, and the recent "half a loaf" victory at Antietam sustained him. But the president was troubled by the events in Minnesota.

He had delayed a decision regarding executions and demanded an accounting of the condemned and the trials from General Pope. Bishop Whipple's words of needed reform stuck to him, and he couldn't release them.

Lincoln leaned back in the chair at his desk. He looked down at the stack of letters he was reviewing about the Minnesota conflict. In his mind echoed the words of Minnesotans who came to lobby him personally.

Senator Henry Rice had read a letter from Whipple. "We cannot hang men by the hundreds. Upon our own premises we have no right to do so. We claim that they are an independent nation and as such they are prisoners of war. The leaders must be punished, but we cannot afford by a wanton cruelty to purchase a long Indian war—nor by injustice in other matters purchase the anger of God."

Congressman William Windom had introduced a bill in Congress to require that all Indians be moved from Minnesota. A letter signed by Windom claimed, "The outraged people of Minnesota will dispose of the wretches without law. These two peoples cannot live together." He implied that Lincoln's delay would push Minnesotans into mob violence and that the president would be to blame.

Senator Morton Wilkinson added, "Either the Indians must be punished according to law, or they will be murdered without law."

Lincoln picked up Pope's reply to his request for an accounting and reread it. "The only distinction between the culprits is as to which of them murdered most people or violated most young girls. The people of Minnesota are exasperated to the last degree, and if the guilty are not all executed, I think it nearly impossible to prevent the indiscriminate massacre of all the Indians—old men, women, and children."

Dr. Thaddeus Williams' letter was next. The doctor demanded executions as he depicted, "Four hundred human beings butchered, their entrails torn out and their heads cut off and put between their lifeless thighs or hoisted on a pole, their bodies gashed and cut to strips and nailed or hung to trees; mothers with sharp fence rails passed through them and their unborn babies; children with hooks struck through their backs and hung to limbs of trees—these are the shadows which flit in the backgrounds of the picture, and cry, not only for justice, but for vengeance."

Even Stephen Riggs was unmoved. He wrote: "But knowing the excited state of this part of the country, the indignation which is felt against the whole Indian people in consequence of these murders and outrages, the indignation being often unreasonable and wicked, venting itself upon the innocent as well as the guilty, knowing this I feel that a great necessity is upon us to execute the great majority of those who have been condemned by the Military Commission." But in the same letter Riggs had expressly asked for clemency for five of the convicted.

Lincoln shuffled through a note from Jane Williamson of Doctor Williamson's family. She pleaded for the life of Chaskaydon, Robert Hopkins, saying he had saved her family at the Yellow Medicine Agency.

Lincoln picked up a telegram from Governor Ramsey. "Nothing but the speedy execution of the tried and convicted Sioux Indians will save us from scenes of outrage. If you prefer to turn them over to me, I will order their execution."

The president opened a resolution from "The People of St. Paul." "The blood of hundreds of our murdered fellow citizens cries from the ground for vengeance!" it read over hundreds of signatures.

Lincoln glanced at a stack of newspapers from Minnesota that condemned his delay and demanded immediate executions of all those held in Mankato.

But the words of Whipple grabbed him again. "We cannot hang men by the hundreds."

Lincoln ran his fingers through his wiry black hair and mumbled to himself, "Ruggles and Whiting are still reviewing the convictions. I've got time."

Seeking a way out, he scribbled a note to Judge Advocate General Joseph Holt. "I wish your legal opinion, whether if I should conclude to execute only a part of them, I must myself designate which, or could I leave the designation to some other officer on the ground."

Then Abraham Lincoln leaned back in his chair, stretched his long legs beneath his desk and closed his eyes. "So many times," he whispered to himself, "so many times I get hold of something that I can't let go of. I wish there was a way to let go of this."

◦ 59 ◦

I T WAS EVENING WHEN CHARGER led the Fool Soldiers and the
white captives away from White Lodge's camp. They had nego-
tiated for nearly twenty-four hours and had not eaten since the
feast with the Santee, which had opened the bargaining.

They were all exhausted, hungry and cold, but the Tetons were
determined to put as much distance between them and the Santee as possible.

"I do not trust them," Charger said. "White Lodge has our horses now. He might try to retake the captives."

"Of all we brought with us," Kills Game added, "we have one
horse, four rifles, and a small tipi. It will be hard to defend if they attack
us."

"They may not fear us," Charger rejoined, "but they do fear our
Teton brothers if they harm us. We have that. But we must be careful.
Swift Bird, take a rifle and follow behind. If the Santee come, you are
our guard."

As they trudged through the gathering darkness, the wind
brought up a blizzard. Snow stung like sharp needles on their backs as
the careworn party blindly struggled on. Several of the younger children

256

were seated on the horse. Pretty Bear carried Eldora Wright on his back. Emma Duley held tight to her mother's hand and guided her as Mad Bear lent support. Julia Wright was losing ground and kept falling behind. Finally Emma left her mother and turned into the icy wind to reach Julia. Together they painstakingly walked to Charger.

"You must stay with us," he told the woman.

"She can't," Emma informed him, "she aint got no shoes."

"Stop and rest," Charger shouted above the howling wind. Then he knelt down with Julia. "I should have seen your bare feet. I'm sorry." He sat in the snow and removed his moccasins, handing them to Julia.

Julia looked into Charger's face, her eyes wide with astonishment. "Your feet will freeze!" she exclaimed.

"My feet are tough like leather." He smiled as he ripped strips of blanket and wound them around his feet. "I will be fine."

"There's no way we can ever thank you. You saved our lives," Julia proclaimed as an emotional torrent broke loose. "I was sure that we'd be kilt. We'd already lost my son George and the Duley baby. When I called to the people in the boat, White Lodge was red-hot mad. He beat me, and I thought we'd all be punished. We din't have no hope 'til you came. How'd you know?"

"Galpin from the boat told us, but I knew. I knew before you came into Dakota country that you were on the way."

"How?"

"I had a vision, a dream. Wakan Tonka sent us to rescue you. You were our destiny. We are young, and we must show courage by doing a brave man's deed."

Julia looked at the boy thoughtfully. "I've spent time with the Santee. I learned some of their language. But you speak in English. Where did you learn to speak so good?"

"I often visited the trading posts on the river. I went to Primeau's and even learned a little French. Some of my people say that because I am part white I learned your language more easily."

"Part white?"

"My grandfather passed this way on the river many years ago. He was one of the first whites to ever come this way."

"Who was he?" Julia wondered.

"They called him Lewis, I believe his other name was Meriwether."

Julia looked at Charger in amazement. "The great explorer? Lewis, of Lewis and Clark?"

"You have heard of him? I did not think his name was known."

"Almost all Americans know his name. He's famous."

"To my people he was just a white man who came through our land."

"Thank you, Waanatan, will you bring us to your people? Will they welcome us?"

"My people call us Fool Soldiers for helping white people. But it is not foolish to do a good thing. We must get you to Fort Pierre, where your people are. It is nearly 100 miles downriver."

"Can we make it?" Julia asked as she looked at the others huddled together for warmth nearby.

"Wakan Tonka did not bring us this far to fail."

"Waanatan." Little Emma Duley leaned closer to Charger to be heard above the wind. "I don't hate the Santee. After we left home, they treated us like their own children. The old woman who took us, she made her face black and cut her hair when they traded us to you. Like we was dead."

Four Bear, hunched against the wind, approached Charger, Julia, and Emma.

"We must stop," Four Bear pleaded. "True, we must put miles between us and the Santee, but they will not travel in a blizzard either."

Charger considered for a moment and then acted. "Set up the tipi, put the women and children in it. We will watch through the night."

As the wind howled and the snow pelted into the blankets that they clutched around their shoulders, the Fool Soldiers walked in a tight circle around the tipi.

258

"We must keep moving," Charger ordered, "to keep us from freezing and to watch for White Lodge."

The next morning the snow stopped, and the Teton reached Bone Necklace's camp. The chief stared with disbelief at the bedraggled party.

"You did a brave thing," he told the young warriors. "I will help you. Take this ox cart that we found along the river. It will hold the children. Here are more blankets and food that should last until you reach Pierre. You have done a good thing."

Thanks to Bone Necklace's gift, the Teton and their white refugees moved more quickly, but Laura Duley's injured foot continued to slow them. Riding in the cart with the children made it too heavy for the horse to pull, so Charger divided his men into three groups who took turns aiding the horse by pushing the cart from behind.

When they were only miles away from the friendly camp, a gunshot echoed from behind the party. Charger and Kills Game rushed back to where Swift Bird stood poised, his rifle aimed at a distant form.

"It is White Lodge. A few Santee are with him. He wants his woman back."

"We will all fire," Charger said. "Shoot high, above them, not to kill."

The three fired a ragged volley at the distant Santee.

Then Charger shouted, "We will fight you, and we will not give up any of the whites. Come to us if you want to die!"

White Lodge waved a rifle in disgust and cried, "You *are* fools! Don't you know who your people are?" Then the Santee turned and walked away.

On the morning of the fifth day since leaving the Santee camp, a weak winter sun strained to penetrate through thin clouds. The children despaired of leaving the warmth of the tipi. All were sick, coughing with dripping noses. The two Ireland girls were feverish.

Julia Wright asked Charger, "Are we close?"

"Yes, and I know an easier route. It is just a little longer, but it will take us away from the river and onto the prairie. The route is not so hard, and the wind will be strong at our backs. When we turn back to the river, it will take us to the ford and Fort Pierre on the other side. We will be there before the sun sets."

"Have you heard anythin' more 'bout Shetek? Of any other survivors?"

"No, my vision was only of you."

The sun was high in the sky when they returned from their detour and reached the Missouri. First winter ice covered the stream.

Kills Game announced, "I will cross over to find the best place to cross. The ice seems thick." He stomped his foot several times.

"Here by the shore maybe," Charging Dog cautioned, "but not out there." He pointed across the river. "The ice is thin and will crack."

"I will try," Kills Game answered as he gingerly slid his feet over the ice. Indians and whites alike watched with concern as the Teton reached near midstream. Then a loud crack like the splitting of a lightning-struck tree reverberated to the shore. An instant later Kills Game was shoulder deep in the frigid water.

He took his hatchet and pounded at the ice before him and tramped ahead toward the opposite shore. He stumbled onto the riverbank and into the arms of Primeau, who wrapped a blanket around him.

"I haf beeen watching each day for you. My fool soldiers haf come back."

In minutes Primeau was poling his boat through the trail in the ice left by Kills Game. Where the ice stuck tight, he rammed an axe into it. Soon the Fool Soldiers and their captives were safe in the comforting warmth of Primeau's trading post.

As the owner handed out food and hot drinks, he turned to Charger. A broad smile split his bearded face and he pounded the young Indian on the back. "You did it! Charger, by God, you did it!"

"I have delivered the captives as I promised," he replied.

"You've done your part. Dupree and LaPlante here," he gestured at two French traders standing with their backsides to the fire place, "they've agreed to take theese people to Fort Randall and the soldiers."

"Are we home?" Laura Duley spoke for the first time since the rescue.

"No, Laura," Julia said gently, "but thanks to these young men, we soon will be."

❧ 60 ☙

OE WEISER WIPED HIS HANDS on a stained white hospital coat as he leaned over a patient and placed his hand on the man's forehead. His gruff exterior and short brown beard didn't hide the warmth and concern that shone in the doctor's blue eyes.

"Jimmy, you're getting better. No fever, and the red splotches are about gone. I think your measles are nearly licked."

"Good, doc," the young soldier answered, "I kinda miss the fellas. Can I get outta here soon?"

"'Soon' is a relative term, private. Yes, soon you'll be released. But not immediately. What we've found from cases of measles in the east is that when men are sent back to their regiments too quickly, it too often relapses and sometimes results in death. We don't want that. Do we, Miss Miller?"

JoAnna smiled as she looked up from beside a nearby bed. She patted the soldier upon whose forehead she was applying a cold compress. "Certainly not. Not when things are going so well here. There have been no deaths in three weeks. Just look around. Everyone's improving."

JoAnna swung her arms expansively around the makeshift log building that served as a hospital. Ten of the twelve beds were occupied.

262

Eight of the patients had varying degrees of the telltale red rash of measles. The other two men, one with croup and the other with dysentery, were in corners away from the others.

"Hey, Doc," Jimmy called, "I know I'm gittin' better. But can I have a little more medicine?"

Weiser laughed and held up a whiskey bottle. "Weren't you just medicated about half an hour ago? I'm afraid that'll have to do. We have to keep enough medicine for everyone."

In a low voice, JoAnna asked the doctor, "What about quinine?"

Weiser chuckled. "JoAnna, out East they've tried it all on measles. Quinine, chloroform, ether, morphine. Two things seemed to work. Keeping them separate from everyone else and giving them a shot of whiskey every now and then. I don't know if the whiskey really does much, but at least it seems to make them feel a little better. Another thing they've learned is to keep new recruits together for a while and away from the other soldiers. If measles is present let it just infect those that brought it.

"One other thing, Jimmy wanted to report to duty. Like I told him, letting soldiers go back to work too early has been found to lead to relapses and complications like pneumonia. We've been lucky here, and, JoAnna, you've been a big help."

"I'm glad I could assist you," she replied.

Captain Will Duley burst through the hospital door, a blast of chilly air on his heels, and strode purposefully to Dr. Weiser. "Dr. Weiser," Duley said crisply, "We've just received news from Fort Randall and I've orders for you from General Sibley. My wife, children, the other Lake Shetek captives. They've been found!"

"What!" Wesier exclaimed. "How are they? Are they. . . ?"

"Eight of the ten are alive. A Wright child and my baby didn't make it. Two women and six children are alive and at Fort Randall. Some are in pretty bad shape and need help. My . . . wife . . . Laura, there's something wrong with her. She's not right in the head."

"What does Sibley want with me?" Weiser asked.

"He wants you to go with a company of cavalry to Fort Randall in the Dakota Territory and bring the survivors back."

"But, Captain, I'm needed here."

"There are missionaries who can tend to matters here, and Dr. Mueller can come up from Fort Snelling to help out if he's needed. In Dakota they don't have anyone to spare to send here with them."

JoAnna looked warmly at Duley. "Captain, I'll go with you. The women will need another woman with them to lean on after what they've been through."

"I'm not sure what your father will say to that," Weiser added.

"I'll tend to the colonel," JoAnna said. "Captain, will you be leading the troop?"

Anguish spread across Duley's face. "Miss, I'd give anything in the world to be the one to get them. But I'm torn by a higher duty. The execution. General Sibley promised that I would be the one to cut the rope. What if the order comes and I'm in Dakota?"

A silent rage churned just below the surface as Duley proclaimed, "Bringing them back is a duty others can do. There is no one else but me destined to kill those murdering savages."

ॐ 61 ॐ

N November 28ᵀᴴ a company of fifty cavalry accompanied by three horse-drawn wagons set out from Mankato for Fort Randall and the Dakota Territory.

The early morning was cool and the sky slate gray. JoAnna rode beside a teamster in the first wagon. Named Russell, he was gray-haired with not much to say. The only sounds he made were an occasional command to the horses or a harsh hack as he spat tobacco.

Left to her thoughts, JoAnna turned two recent conversations over in her mind. One with her father and the other with Jesse. She had known that Colonel Miller would object, but she had once again asserted her independence. Ruefully but with growing respect, he had given in.

"JoAnna, you're growing before my very eyes," he said. "Not physically like when you grew from a little girl into a woman, but inside. You're different than you were in August. Most is good, but I'm not sure I like this reckless streak."

She had smiled. "Wandering for a week alone on the prairie, fighting for my life at the dugout and tending to men near death leads to change or death. I'm your daughter, I changed."

Surprisingly her talk with Jesse had been more difficult. "JoAnna, this is a foolish risk. Stay in Mankato or go back to St. Paul."

"Jesse," she had answered, "you take risks. Mine is much less than yours. I hear of men who don't want to be left behind as great events pass them by. I don't want to be passed by. I want to do my part."

"What about us?" Jesse asked. "Before, you wanted to marry just as soon as possible. I said that we could once this Indian thing was over."

"Jesse, you also said it wasn't fair to me because of the uncertainty. I love you, but you were right. This war will continue. Father tells me that an expedition to the Dakotas to find Little Crow and others is already being planned. They'll either send you there or to fight the rebels in the South."

She rested her hand on his cheek. "I so dearly want to be your wife. But I'll wait. Both of us must follow our destiny until fate brings us back together. I wish that Sibley had sent you with us to Fort Randall."

"I tried. Because of my duties with Reverend Riggs, they want me to stay in Mankato. But the man given the command is good. Tim Sheehan will get you back safely."

Jesse reached out and held JoAnna in a tender embrace. "Please, come back safe," he had whispered.

The memory brought tears to her eyes that JoAnna hastily wiped away as a horseman trotted to her.

Lieutenant Tim Sheehan, aged twenty-five, another of the heroes of the defense of Fort Ridgely, touched the brim of his hat and smiled at JoAnna. His sandy-colored beard framed bright-blue eyes. "Miss Miller," he smiled, "I've been given special orders from two officers, your father and Lieutenant Buchanen, to watch out for you. If there's anything you need, don't hesitate to ask me."

"How long until we get to Fort Randall?" she asked.

"If we can make fifteen to twenty miles a day, we'll be there in ten to fifteen days with good weather. That means we start early, before dawn, and set up camp about mid-afternoon."

"Can't we go longer in the day?"

"The men could, but the animals can't. They need to eat and rest. We'll get there all right. Pick up the eight and be back by Christmas. At least that's my hope. You're a brave young lady to take this journey."

"Dr. Weiser needs me. I want to help."

"Let's hope all goes well." Sheehan nodded, again touched his hat brim and then spurred his horse toward the head of the column of wagons and men.

The troop turned south away from the Minnesota River and over the rolling hills and prairies of southwestern Minnesota into the Dakotas. They made good time staying slightly ahead of Sheehan's schedule. Once in the Dakota Territory, they continued to the southwest and the Missouri River. On December 11th they rode into Fort Randall.

The fort was located nearly one hundred miles down the Missouri River from Primeau's trading post at the old Fort Pierre. Randall was about one-half mile south of the Missouri, only three miles north of the Nebraska line.

Constructed in 1856 to protect fur traders and miners between the Missouri to the north and the Platte River to the south, Fort Randall consisted of twenty-four buildings. Outside of the fort compound, just to the east, stood the post hospital. It was there that the Lake Shetek survivors were housed.

The post commander directed Sheehan, Weiser, and JoAnna to the hospital. A tall man in white doctor's coat greeted them from the front porch of the building.

"I'm Doc Sawyer, welcome to Fort Randall. Dr. Weiser, I presume?" Sawyer extended his hand to shake Weiser's.

"Yes," Joe answered, "I'm Joe Weiser and this is Lieutenant Tim Sheehan and JoAnna Miller, my nurse. If you knew we were coming, you must also know why. Are they all here?"

"Yes," Sawyer replied. "The six children are resilient and recovering nicely. All were malnourished due to a general lack of food in the Indian camp. The women are recovering more slowly. Mrs. Wright had been beaten about the face and upper body shortly before rescue, and her toes were frostbitten. Mrs. Duley also has physical ailments, a broken foot, but her illness is more in the head, mental. She's . . . Hell, it's better if I show you. Come in."

Sawyer turned and opened a door on his right. They entered a large room with three windows. Four beds and several chairs were crowded into the room. The six children immediately stood and edged timidly toward the visitors. Julia Wright sat up in her bed. Her eyes widened, her face tinged with fading bluish-yellow bruises. In the corner Laura Duley peered out a window, seemingly oblivious to their company.

"Here they are," Sawyer announced, "all of them. We've got room to have spread them out into other quarters, but they wanted to stay together. It seemed best. The women are Laura Duley over there in the corner and Julia Wright on the bed. These are," the doctor pointed at each as he called their name, "Emma Duley, Jefferson Duley, Eldora Wright, Lilly Everett, Rose Ireland, and her sister Nelly."

Slowly the children formed a circle around the two doctors, Sheehan, and JoAnna. Julia Wright struggled from her bed and joined them.

"We've just got to know what's happened," Julia said. "What about the others? All they could tell us here was that fifteen died at Shetek. What happened to our loved ones?"

Joe Weiser choked and cleared his throat. He wished he could spit, but no spittoon was in sight.

"Mrs. Wright, I understand your husband was absent at the time of the attack. There is no word of him. Mrs. Hurd got away with her children, Mrs. Koch escaped from the reds who took her. Smith and Rhodes, along with Charlie Hatch and Edgar Bently, made it to New Ulm. John Eastlick was killed and several of his children. But Lavina Eastlick survived, and her son Merton carried his little brother fifty miles on his back."

"What about my daddy?" Jefferson Duley asked plaintively.

"Your father made it through the slough," Sheehan said softly. "He's at Mankato now. I'm serving with him. He's a captain in the army. But your brother and sister didn't make it."

Rose Ireland struggled with words as her eyes filled with tears. "I saw them kill our mommy, and our daddy was hurt bad. He was dyin' when we left the slough."

Sheehan knelt on one knee and looked Rose and Nelly in the eyes. "Girls, Thomas Ireland, your father, is alive. He's waiting for you in Iowa. Lilly," he turned his gaze to the little Everett girl, "you know that your mom didn't make it. But your father did. He was hurt bad, but he's better and he's waiting for you, too."

JoAnna had walked to the corner and placed her hand on Laura Duley's shoulder. Dim sunlight on Laura's face highlighted the adversity it displayed. "Mrs. Duley," JoAnna began, "you'll be safe now. Your husband, Will, is in Mankato. He misses you greatly, and we will bring you to him. Do you understand?"

Recognition seemed to flit across the woman's face and a trace of a smile as faint as Mona Lisa's flickered over it. Then it was gone and a blank expression returned.

"She's like that," Sawyer said. "Sometimes it seems like she's with us. She says a word or two, and then she goes away again into some secret corner of her mind."

"Are they fit to travel?" Weiser wondered.

"Yes," Sawyer answered. "When do you plan to return to Minnesota?"

Weiser looked to Sheehan, who replied, "Tomorrow. I think getting back by Christmas might help them."

☙ 62 ☜

THE NEXT MORNING FIFTY Minnesota troopers and their three wagons crossed the Missouri and turned east. All the Shetek refugees rode in the largest wagon. The morning chill was blown by a strong wind.

JoAnna was thankful for the canvas wagon top that kept the breeze at bay as she sat between Julia Wright and Laura Duley and answered Laura's questions. The children curled up in blankets and slept.

"Is is really all over, Miss Miller?" Julia wondered. "There's no more fighting?"

"Call me JoAnna. It's over in Minnesota except for random attacks by marauders. But it's over. Most Sioux are now in the Dakotas."

"We know. White Lodge's band was among them."

"It must have been horrible."

"Yes, but in a strange way they came to care for us. They treated our children like their own. White Lodge valued me as his woman. He treated me well."

"He beat you."

"He felt I mighta caused trouble for the band when I yelled at the miners on the river. I hated him for it, but I understood why he did it."

After a pause Julia asked, "What's happenin' at Mankato?"

"Three hundred three are waiting to die. They've been sentenced by a military commission for crimes committed during the uprising."

"They're gonna execute 303?" Julia was surprised.

"That's how many are convicted. Lincoln has to give the final word. They're waiting for word now. Laura, you'll be interested in knowing that your husband will be the man who cuts the rope that hangs them."

Laura Duley showed interest and recognition for the first time. "Thank God," she snapped. "They should all die for what they done. My man will see it's done right."

JoAnna was shocked at Laura's words but grateful that her conversation with Julia had elicited a reaction. Any response was a good sign.

JoAnna sat back to consider Laura's brief outburst and absentmindedly scratched an itch above her navel. When the itch persisted, she felt a welt through her clothing. She glanced right and left. Julia's eyes were closed and Laura had retreated within herself again. JoAnna unbuttoned her blouse at her abdomen and looked down. Her fears were realized. Weeks of working with the sick at Mankato left no doubt. The raised welt was the reddish telltale rash of measles.

Near noon the company stopped to rest and eat. JoAnna approached Dr. Weiser. After describing Laura Duley's breakthrough to him, she got to the point. "Doctor, I've developed a rash on my abdomen. I checked, and I'm sure it's measles."

His voice betrayed concern as Weiser replied, "Are you certain? Show me, please."

JoAnna blushed and timidly undid a few lower buttons. Weiser examined the rash on her stomach.

"You're right. It's measles. Do you feel warm?" the doctor felt her forehead. "You have a temperature, JoAnna. The second wagon is empty except for some hardware. I'll tend to you there."

He reached into his pocket and took out half a full bottle of amber liquid. "Whiskey," he said. "Drink some."

"But I never . . ." JoAnna began.

"Proper ladies can drink whiskey," Weiser finished. "Especially when it's to help save their life."

JoAnna took the proffered bottle and swallowed like it was poison. Her face pinched together like a dried fruit. "My," she gasped. "Men drink this for pleasure?"

"They get used to it, let me assure you. Now get to the second wagon."

The procession continued east until late in the afternoon. Julia's rash spread and began to appear on her arms and face. Weiser kept her apart from the others and applied cold compresses to her forehead along with occasional shots of whiskey. As the camp rested at night, he spoke with Sheehan.

"Tim, I'm worried about Miss Miller. Her fever is climbing, and we're a long way from home."

"Should we go back to Fort Randall?"

"That won't help her. They'd do what I'm doing except that a bed would be more comfortable than the wagon."

"We've got extra blankets, Doc. Put them under her."

"Might help. But let's get us home as soon as we can."

Throughout the next week Sheehan kept his troop moving at a steady pace. They were back in Minnesota when snow started flying. The first flakes drifted slowly, gentle harbingers of what was to come. The Shetek children hung out from the back of their wagon and stuck their tongues out to capture the fluffy flakes. Julia and then even Laura reached out their hands and watched as the snow landed and melted in their palms.

Then the snow grew heavier and the wind picked up, driving the flakes sideways into them, and everyone pulled back into the wagon.

"We gotta get through this," Tim Sheehan shouted over the howling wind to Sergeant Abel Wardler. "If we stop and the snow piles up, we'll be stuck. We'll only stop if we can't move anymore, but it's better to keep moving. Remember the Donner Party."

"Can we outrun it, sir?" Wardler yelled over the banshee-like wail, with thoughts of the Donners, tragically marooned in a mountain snowstorm, in the forefront of his mind.

"If we're just on the edge of the storm, maybe. Let's try."

Sheehan kept pushing his men and wagons east through the maelstrom of wind and intensifying snow. *At least it's at our backs*, he thought as flakes pelted hard against his long blue coat. He cantered his horse up and down the line, encouraging his men to keep moving.

In the second wagon, a kerosene lantern waved back and forth in time with the bounces of the wheels. Dr. Weiser held JoAnna's hand as she twisted in a fitful sleep. His other hand held the cold compress to her face.

It's cold, he thought. *We're in a blizzard, it's freezing outside, and she's sweating.*

The doctor spoke aloud. "Stay with me, JoAnna. You've got a lot to live for. Think about Jesse. You're strong. You can get through this."

Russell, the teamster, cracked his whip over the backs of his team and screamed, "Gee up! Gee up! Ya gotta keep movin'! Gee up!"

As Sheehan raced by, Russell shouted, "Lieutenant, we're boggin' down in the snow. Whadda I do?"

"Wardler," Sheehan ordered, "get some men and have them push the wagon wheels through the snow. Keep 'em movin'."

Throughout the night, men and beasts struggled forward in the blizzard. Near dawn it stopped. An eerie pristine stillness held the prairie in an icy grip. As the sun rose before them Sheehan pointed into the distance. "Look, Sergeant, Doc, there's brown splotches way ahead. Most of the storm was behind us. We're gonna make it. We'll rest when we get there. Doc, report? How are your patients?"

"The women and children in the first wagon are doing fine. Mrs. Duley is even showing more signs of recognizing reality. But I'm worried about JoAnna. The fever is still high."

"Do what you can, Doctor. I'll get us to Mankato."

ɛᴑ 63 ᴄ⸀

At Camp Lincoln the 303 Santee waiting to die had huddled together for warmth as November turned to December and the chill northern winds blew through cracks in the warehouse wooden jail built to house them.

Two wood-burning stoves fought a losing battle against the draft and frigid temperatures. Long stovepipes ran straight up from the iron heaters through an open ceiling and rafters and through the roof.

The prisoners were chained together and each day were ministered to by several missionaries. Samuel Hinman, Thomas Williamson, Father Ravoux, and Stephen Riggs were saddened but heartened by the opportunity to reach these desperate souls.

Williamson and the others were granted special permission to enter the prison to preach and teach the prisoners. They found Bibles and hymnals and toiled at teaching the Santee to read. With the sentence of death hanging over their heads, the captives were even more eager to learn and accept Christianity than their families at Fort Snelling.

Conferring apart from the Santee, Williamson and Riggs, long-time allies, seemed perplexed.

"I've softened my views, Thomas," Riggs said as he looked at the Indians, some of whom were tracing words with their fingers in worn Bibles. "It was impossible for all of these men to get a fair trial in Minnesota. Yes, some should die, and I've expressed that to Lincoln."

"It isn't that simple, is it, Stephen? Some of these here were my parishioners at the mission."

"My work for the Military Commission told me their stories. Several of the braves denied the charges levied upon them at the trials. While most admitted being present at some of the massacres, they swore they had not used their tomahawks on any victims, and when compelled to shoot, shot wide of the mark."

"But they were there. They fought."

"Like soldiers in a war."

"They killed women and children."

"Not all of them, Thomas. That's what makes this so hard and delays the president's decision. I've sent another letter urging more clemency."

"Stephen, it's unfortunate that some of the worst escaped to the west."

"Yes, but, without question, many of these have murdered and raped and deserve to die. Cut Nose, maybe he is not guilty of the twenty-seven people he claimed to have killed, but certainly some. Justina Kreieger was there. She saw him kill several, including children. Napashue, perhaps he didn't kill nineteen as charged, but there's evidence that he killed enough to hang. It is clear that Tehehdonecha and Dowanea committed murder and rape. There were several witnesses. The victim of Tazoo's rape testified against him. Hapan confessed to shooting at Francis Patoile, and there's no doubt that Mazabomdoo killed an old woman and two children. Others were guilty, too, but still others . . ."

"Like Chaska," Williamson finished, "and Robert Hopkins. They should be set free."

"The task is complicated. Many of the Dakota's names are similar. We have Chaskydon, Chaska, Chaskay, and Chaskastay. I'm glad that the president is taking time to try to get this right. There are degrees of guilt." Riggs reached into a pocket and unfolded a scrap of newspaper.

"This is from a letter Bishop Whipple sent to the *St. Paul Pioneer Press*. 'There is a broad distinction between the guilt of men who went through the country committing fiendish violence, massacring women and babes with the spirit of demons and the guilt of timid men who received a share of the plunder or who under threat of death engaged in battle where hundreds were engaged.'"

"Stephen, let's do what we can for these people now. The decision is in Lincoln's hands. The people want blood."

ON DECEMBER 4, 1862, nearly 150 men gathered at the Mankato House Hotel. Every able-bodied man had been urged to take part. It was time to "take care of the savages." Sibley's early fears about trouble from Mankato were about to be realized.

James Clark shouted above the din of loud conversation as men sought bravery in bottles of whiskey. "Things is gone on too long up there at South Bend, Camp Lincoln . . er, whatever they's callin' it.

"The fact is them's murderers up there. They kilt our friends and our families. And what's happnin'? They's bein' fed, gettin' book larnin', and," he added sarcastically, "comin' to Christ. And Lincoln? He's decidin' iffn' he should let 'em go. Whatcha think we should do?"

A man jumped upon a wobbly-legged table holding a whiskey bottle in one hand and a glass in the other. "I say git on up thar and bust down that thar stockade. We'll do what Lincoln won't. Who's with me?"

With a roar of assent, the men burst through the door of the hotel and onto the road leading to the prison at nearby South Bend. A sentinel saw them coming, quickly mounted and galloped his horse ahead of the mob to dismount in front of Colonel Miller's headquarters.

"They's comin'!" the young rider yelled as he breathlessly pounded on the door.

Miller himself opened it and asked, "What's this all about?"

"A mob, hundreds of 'em, sir. From Mankato. They's comin' fer the Sioux. They's been drinkin' and boastin' 'bout it."

"Captain Austin," Miller turned and looked back into his office at Horace Austin, "take your troopers and meet these citizens on the road before they get here. Avoid violence. These men are drunk fools. Just bring them to me."

In short order Austin and his men encountered the mob from Mankato. They had stopped short of the stockade and were milling around trying to decide what to do next.

"Form a circle around them, men," Austin ordered. As the crowd was encircled, Austin announced, "Men of Mankato, you will accompany me to headquarters. Colonel Miller would like to speak with you."

"What iffn' we don' wanna go?" Clark cried.

"Yeah, we're stayin' right here," another yelled.

"Gentlemen," Austin ordered his men, "draw sabers!"

With a swoosh of metal blades drawn from metal scabbards, cold steel gleemed in the frosty moonlight. "You may reconsider your decision to stay here," Austin warned the mob.

Startled by the sight of the sabers and subdued, they ambled forward, some unsteadily, feeling the effects of alcohol. The cavalry prodded them along until they reached Miller's headquarters.

"Why are you on the road at midnight?" Miller demanded.

"Gonna visit friends over other side a the river," one bearded man responded.

Miller looked over them with a steely gaze. "You can do better than that."

"We jest wanted ta see 'em, Colonel. That's all," someone shouted. "We don't mean no harm."

"Fine," Miller smiled tight lipped, "but you'll do your visiting and staring at them at a reasonable hour, and you'll do so sober. Now all of you, turn around and go back to town or we'll build another stockade and put you in it."

The dispirited crowd returned to Mankato. Miller had prevailed, and his report to Sibley provided the general with another opportunity. He telegrammed President Lincoln on December 6: "Lynch mobs have moved on the camp. It will take 1,000 soldiers to keep us secure. In a few days our troops and the Indian prisoners will be besieged. Should you pardon the Indians, there will be a determined effort to get them in possession and may cost the lives of thousands of our citizens."

∞ 64 ∞

LINCOLN GAZED AT THE GARDENS through the window behind his desk. His glasses were perched on the end of his nose, and he looked down at the sheet of paper in his hands. It was the answer to his inquiry of Judge Advocate Holt.

No, Holt had written, there was no way to designate someone else regarding the execution decision. It was Lincoln's. "Mr. President, you have to do it personally."

The day before, Senator Wilkinson had introduced a resolution demanding that Lincoln account for his handling of the Sioux prisoners. The clamor was echoing all the way from Minnesota. Mass execution was the only answer.

Lincoln had already reprieved Robert Hopkins, due to Miss Williamson's plea. He had reviewed all correspondence to him over and over in his mind. He didn't need to read any more. The review of the convictions by Whiting and Ruggles lay open upon his desk.

"Hay!" he called to his secretary, who immediately appeared. "I've made my decision in the Sioux matter. Bring me paper, I wish to write."

Foremost in his mind was his conversation with Bishop Whipple and the comment, "We cannot hang men by the hundreds."

279

John Hay handed sheets of stationery to the president and stepped back.

"John, this may not make the people of Minnesota happy, but after reviewing the report on convictions I have decided to allow thirty-nine to be executed. After reviewing the analysis by Whiting and Ruggles I have concluded that these were guilty of individual murders and atrocious abuse of their female captives. The others, those guilty of solely participating in battles will remain in detention until further notice."

"There will be an uproar, sir. I've read the correspondence from Minnesota and heard from their congressmen. Just as you have."

"It is wrong to kill those who fight as soldiers. Would we want everyone held in Confederate prisons who had fired a shot in battle to be executed? There is a similar principle here. I have identified what seems to be the worst of them. But, John, it isn't easy. The names are confusing. I want no mistakes, so I will write the names in my own hand. I will hyphenate the pronunciations and number them."

"I'm sure you've considered the politics of this, Mr. President," Hay cautioned.

"Yes, John, politics has always been a rough and tumble game that I've enjoyed. But, as I've said before, I will not hang men for votes. If the people disagree they will express their feelings at the ballot box. I fear that with the miserable progress we are making in this war to preserve the Union, they will have many other reasons to show disapproval besides my handling of Sioux Indians in Minnesota."

Lincoln sat at his desk, affixed his glasses and begin to write. He dated the letter to Sibley, December 6, 1862, and instructed Sibley to "cause to be executed on Friday the nineteenth day of December, instant, the following names, to wit."

Then he carefully inscribed, "Te-he-hdo-ne-cha," Number 2 by the record. That was followed by "Tazoo" alias "Plan-doo-at," Number 4 by the record. Thirty-seven names followed written in a similar fashion.

The President concluded, "The other condemned prisoners you will hold subject to further orders, taking care that they neither escape, nor are subjected to any unlawful violence. Abraham Lincoln, President of the United States."

❧ 65 ❧

ord reached Minnesota on December 9th that President Lincoln had made his decision. Thirty-nine were to be hanged. Fear of violence and mob rule if all 303 were not executed was unfounded. Many were disappointed, and anger was expressed in newspaper editorials, but the predicted mob action never materialized.

In his headquarters at South Bend, General Sibley gathered officers to discuss the execution. "Thirty-nine is an affront to the people of Minnesota," Sibley told Miller. "But we will carry it out promptly. I want a gallows built capable of hanging them all at one time."

Will Duley interjected, "Sir, remember . . ."

"Yes, Captain, you may cut the rope," Sibley finished. "I was very happy to hear that your wife has been rescued along with two of your children."

"Praise the Lord," Reverend Riggs said.

"Praise him for what?" Duley rejoined bitterly. "The word I got from Fort Randall is that Laura has been abed since she got there. She's barely coherent and not of sound mind. I'm thankful that Emma and Jefferson are safe, but remember I've lost three other children to the savages. I'll gladly send them all to hell."

"You'll get your chance on the nineteenth," Colonel Miller said.

"Not quite so fast on that," Captain Austin corrected. "We seem to have a little problem."

"What's that, Captain?" Sibley asked.

"We don't have enough rope to hang them all at one time. In all of Mankato there isn't enough rope."

"Impossible!" Miller cried. "Get more rope."

"I'm trying, the countryside's deserted. Mankato is a town. They don't have rope."

Sibley shook his head. "How much more do you need?"

"I've put in requests to St. Paul. Special made rope, too. They say they can get it here in a couple of weeks."

"All right, Captain. I'll ask for a delay until, oh, the 26th. I think the day after Christmas would be appropriate. A late gift for the people of Minnesota. Once the new date is confirmed, separate the thirty-nine from the others."

"Where, sir?" Austin asked.

"The stone Leach building in Mankato will hold them. The president has been very specific in who he authorizes us to hang. Major Brown, Reverend Riggs, you have lived among these people. You know many of them by face as well as name. Make sure we get the right ones to the gallows."

"General," Brown replied, "even for us this won't be easy. Many of the names are the same or sound alike. Each Santee was given a number during the trials, but no one remembers which number belongs to which Indian."

"I'm sure you can sort them out, Major."

"What about their spiritual needs?" Riggs wondered.

"Colonel Miller, be sure that our men of the cloth have access to the prisoners. You have done remarkably well saving souls, Reverend. Baptisms and even communions in the prison. Robert Hopkins as an altar boy. To think, if not for Lincoln's reprieve, we'd be hanging him."

"We still should," Duley urged vehemently.

"One other thing, Colonel," Sibley concluded. "I'll declare martial law. We will close all bars and prohibit the sale of alcohol before the hangings. Troops will patrol Mankato, and order will be maintained."

By December 17th word had been received from President Lincoln allowing the execution date to be postponed to the 26th. Colonel Miller issued the order and set the time for 10:00 A.M.

Final pleas for clemency were sent to Lincoln. Bishop Whipple reminded the president that Sibley had ruled that the right to assistance from counsel did not apply to military commissions. He asserted that many Santee had not even understood that they'd been on trial for their lives.

Sibley countered, "Every man who was condemned was sufficiently proven to be a voluntary participant, and no doubt exists in my mind that at least seven-eighths of those sentenced to be hung have been guilty of most flagrant outrages."

The names of those to die were published in Minnesota's newspapers. Dismay and disgust were expressed by many because of Lincoln's reprieves, but no violence ensued. However, one woman in Red Wing, Minnesota, greeted the list with joy and relief.

Chaska's name was not there and Sarah Wakefield told friends, "I noticed the name of Chaskadon but knew it was not Chaska's number, and that he was not guilty of the crime that Chaskadon was being punished for. I will not go to Mankato now."

The thirty-nine sentenced to die were to be taken from the others and placed in a stone building in Mankato. Joe Brown and Stephen Riggs called out the names of the condemned and separated them from the rest. It was the morning of December 22nd.

The two were to examine the Indians and make sure that they got the ones who were on the president's list. Brown stared intently at each as their name was called and each Santee stood.

Then he huddled with the pastor. "Reverend, this is harder than I thought it would be. We've got four Chaskays and three Washechoons, the numbers the Commission gave 'em are mixed up, and some, well, I just don't recognize. But I think we got the right ones."

"I hope God guided you. Captain Austin, take them to Mankato."

At 2:30 that afternoon, Colonel Miller and Reverend Riggs entered the room that confined the thirty-nine Santee. Jesse stood behind them. The Indians were all fastened to the floor by chains, two by two. Some were sitting up, smoking and conversing, while others were reclining, covered with blankets and apparently asleep.

Most of them were young men, though several were quite old and gray-headed. The youngest looked to be about sixteen. They all appeared cheerful and contented. None seemed to anticipate the certain doom which awaited them.

They looked as innocent as children. They smiled as the men walked in and held out their hands to shake.

Miller told Riggs, "I have the order. We'll do this twice. First I'll read it in English and then you can translate into Dakota."

Miller straightened up, adjusted his blue collar and cleared his throat. Then in a clear ringing voice he began to read, "I speak to you on a very serious subject this afternoon. Your Great Father at Washington after carefully reading what your witnesses have testified in your several trials have come to the conclusion that you have each been guilty of wickedly and wantonly murdering his white children; and for this reason he has directed that you each be hanged by the neck until you are dead on next Friday, and that order will be carried into effect that day at 10:00 o'clock in the forenoon.

"Good ministers, both Catholic and Protestant, are here from among whom each of you can select your spiritual advisor, who will be permitted to commune constantly with you during the four days you are yet to live. Say to them now that you have so sinned against your fellow men, that there is no hope for clemency except in the mercy of God, save through the merits of the blessed Redeemer and that I earnestly exhort you to apply to that, as your only remaining source of comfort and consolation. Translate, please Reverend Riggs."

The Dakota listened with seemingly little emotion or interest. Some grunted and calmly smoked their pipes. An older man knocked the ashes from his pipe as the time and date of execution were announced. Another rolled the reddish-brown kinnikinnick into his hand and prepared to stuff it into his pipe.

When Riggs concluded, the room was silent for a long moment. Then the half-breed Henry Milord shouted from his sitting position. "Damn you all! I wish we had killed more!"

Miller glared an icy stare and left the room to Riggs. "Many of you sent letters to family at Fort Snelling before. I will take down your words again if you wish. Let me pass among you."

Tazoo the juggler, condemned for raping Mattie Williams, was the first to confide in Riggs. "Tell our friends that we are being removed from this world over the same path they must shortly travel. We go first, but many of our friends may follow us in a very short time. I expect to go direct to the abode of the Great Spirit, and to be happy when I get there, but we are told that the road is long and the distance great. Therefore, as I am slow in my movements, it will probably take me a long time to reach the end of the journey. I should not be surprised if some of the young, active men we will leave behind us will pass me on the road before I reach the place of my destination."

Washechoon, called Frenchman, held out his hands to Riggs. "Help me. I did nothing. I killed no one. I know nothing of killing white people."

"Quiet!" Hapan snarled, "Die like a brave Dakota. We killed hundreds of white people. We knew we would pay if we lost. It is time to pay with our lives."

Rdainyanka had spoken eloquently in favor of continuing the war. His father-in-law, Wabasha, had urged him to surrender to Sibley at Camp Release. Now he bitterly had Riggs write to Wabasha:

You have deceived me. You told me that if we followed the advice of General Sibley and gave ourselves up to the whites, all would be well; no innocent man would be injured. I have not killed, wounded, or injured a white man, or took any plunder of their property, and yet today I am set apart for execution, and must die in a few days, while men who are guilty will remain in prison.

My wife is your daughter; my children are your grandchildren. I leave them all in your care and under your protection. Do not let them suffer, and when my children are grown up, let them know that their father died because he followed the advice of his chief, and without having the blood of a white man to answer for to the Great Spirit.

My wife and children are dear to me. Let them not grieve for me. Let them remember that the brave should be prepared to meet death; and I will do as becomes a Dakota.

๑ 66 ๛

HE NEXT MORNING BROUGHT a great contrast in emotions to
Mankato. Cheers greeted Tim Sheehan and his party as they rode
into Camp Lincoln. Despair still hung over the condemned like
the thick cloud of a prairie sandstorm.

Jesse raced to Sheehan. "Where is she? Which wagon?"

"The second, and, Jesse, she's been sick."

Jesse grabbed onto the tailgate of JoAnna's wagon and hefted himself in. JoAnna was lying on blankets, white as the snow and obviously
weak. Faint red rash remained on her face along with several small scabs.
She smiled wanly at him. "I prayed to see you again. It's kept me alive."

"Measles?" Jesse looked questioningly at Weiser.

"Yes, and she had a tough time of it. But she got through it.
Fever just broke when we hit the Minnesota River. She'll be all right as
long as she gets some more rest."

Jesse moved to JoAnna and gently held her in his arms. "Your
father's in town. I've sent for him. He'll be here soon. Everything's going
to be all right."

In the front wagon Will Duley hugged his children as they cher-
ished their reunion. Then he tenderly wrapped Laura's hand in his. She

288

looked at him and, for the first time in months, a smile curled her lips. He smiled lovingly.

Later that day, Christmas Eve, the condemned men were allowed to send for friends and relatives from the log prison at Camp Lincoln where the other prisoners were still detained.

The scenes varied. Some of the Santee were so grief stricken that they could not speak. Others asked that messages be carried to loved ones at Fort Snelling. One told a friend, "Tell my mother that I saved the life of Mrs. Wakefield, now she lives, and I will die."

Some wished their children to learn from their mistakes and, looking to the future, urged them to become Christians and live like the whites. Strangely, some were able to talk and joke as if they were on a hunting trip.

Thomas Williamson later called the event, "The saddest experience of my life."

That night JoAnna drifted into a deep, peaceful sleep in a room off her father's quarters. Jesse and Colonel Miller looked in on her repeatedly with prayerful thanks.

On Christmas Day, the Indian women who had been made to work as cooks for the prisoners were permitted into the cell. There was no wailing or show of emotion from the men this time. To do so in front of women would show weakness.

The men gave to them locks of hair, moccasins, blankets, whatever possession they knew they would never use again.

Late that afternoon Williamson, Ravoux and Riggs offered the Santee braves once last chance at Christian salvation. Dr. Williamson stood before the men with his friends on either side.

"Soon you will go to another place. Will it be a better place? God knows. But today you still can choose. He who believeth and is baptized shall be saved, sayeth the Lord. If you accept the Holy Spirit here today through Holy Baptism, you will have eternal salvation. It is your choice to make. Father Ravoux is here if you wish to be baptized into the Catholic faith. I represent the Protestants. Because of his involvement with the military commission, Reverend Riggs does not feel that it is proper for him to do more than assist. Choose now if you wish."

Baptiste Campbell urged his companions, "I am Catholic. Choose the priest."

About thirty of the Santee followed his advice. Williamson turned to Riggs. "All these years working with them, and they choose the Catholics. I'm disappointed."

"Don't be, Thomas. It's because of Campbell. Baptize the few that are left."

Some of the Indians were baptized by Ravoux and then came over to Williamson.

"If one baptism will get us to heaven," Round Wing said, "then two will make it twice as sure."

Williamson and Riggs obliged.

That afternoon a message came from Washington. The last-minute pleas of Riggs and Thomas Williamson had been heeded. Lincoln granted a reprieve to Round Wind. The president had reviewed the testimony that claimed that Round Wind was ten miles from the woman he was accused of killing at the time of her death.

The old Indian was freed. The next morning the day of execution was at hand.

ঙ 67 ଔ

JESSE BUCHANEN TIGHTENED the worn leather reins as his black gelding skittered beneath him. "Easy, boy," he said as he leaned forward and whispered in the horse's ear. "Stand easy." The animal snorted a cloudy mist in the frosty morning air as he calmed down.

The lieutenant wished he could dismount and stretch his long legs, which were cramped. But he was in formation and had to remain at attention. His blue eyes squinted at the sun, bright in spite of the cold. The young officer judged that the appointed hour was near.

Buchanen patted the horse gently alongside its neck. Then he straightened in the saddle and gathered his heavy blue coat closer around his neck. "Dang, it's cold," he mumbled. Then he gazed at the thousands of impatient people gathered before him. Not too cold for them, he thought. Men, women, even children stomped their feet on the snow-packed ground to keep warm. A fog from their breathing drifted above them into a clear blue sky.

The young lieutenant gazed at what had led thousands of Minnesotans to turn out on a frigid morning, the day after Christmas, 1862. A gallows stood before him. Not just any gallows, but the largest ever constructed in America.

Built of heavy oak timbers, it was located on a levee across from army headquarters in Mankato. The structure was twenty-four feet on each side, in the form of a diamond and about twenty feet high. A large rope was attached to a pole in the center of the frame. A scaffold was supported by heavy ropes centering on the pole. Thirty-eight ropes, each threaded with the thirteen knots of a hangman's noose, swung gently in a light breeze. They awaited thirty-eight men, Dakota or mixed-blood.

Jesse was one of just over 1,400 soldiers directed to oversee the execution. The men stood at attention, ringing the gallows in rows. Jesse sat at the end of a long line of mounted soldiers.

The civilian spectators were there for revenge, retribution, and morbid curiosity. Many could tell horror tales from the previous fall. They had lost friends or relatives and had been uprooted from their homes.

The horse moved forward under him. Jesse pulled him back into line again. *Everyone's getting impatient*, the soldier thought, *even the horses.*

It was nearly ten now. Jesse's bright-blue eyes watched the doorway intently. Inside Father Ravoux led the condemned men in prayer. The Santee had painted their faces and braided their hair in preparation. Then soldiers knocked off their leg irons and bound the wrists of the Indians.

The Santee smiled and bid the soldiers farewell. One pointed his finger skyward and said, "Me going up." Tazoo began to wail a mournful, low chant. Others joined in. It was their death song. Some began to chant, "Nothing lives long, only the earth and the mountains." Gray canvas sacks were placed upon their heads but not pulled over the Indians' faces. The cell doors opened. The Santee filed toward the door.

Standing upon the gallows platform, another officer also waited impatiently. His dark eyes focused on the jail exit. Will Duley was ready. He couldn't wait for the execution to begin.

Sarah Wakefield watched intently from near the front of the crowd directly in front of the gallows. She planned to stay in St. Paul once Chaska's name was left off the list of condemned. But she wanted to be sure and had made the trip to Mankato.

Her eyes riveted on each face as they climbed the thirteen steps up the platform to stand beneath the waiting nooses swinging in the gentle breeze.

The condemned continued to sing as they took their places and clasped the hands of their brothers on either side.

Sarah's eyes widened in horror. It couldn't be. One of the last up the steps was Chaska! She screamed at the soldiers, "No! There's been a mistake! Chaska . . . he's not supposed to be there!"

She pushed through the crowd to the line of soldiers before the gallows still shouting, "No, there's been a mistake!" But when she tried to push through the soldiers, a sergeant grabbed her roughly from behind.

"There ain't been no mistakes," he growled. "This is who we got orders to hang."

Sarah wrenched, swung her arms and kicked as she tried to free herself from the soldier's grasp.

"Take her away," he commanded two privates. "Get her out of here and don't let her come back."

Still screaming, with tears flowing freely down her face, Sarah Wakefield was dragged away as Chaska took his place under a noose.

JoAnna Miller searched the faces of the soldiers from an upstairs window in the headquarters building across from the gallows. She turned to her father. "There's Jesse, at the end of the line of cavalry. Oh, I wish this would be over with. I want to be with him."

Colonel Miller walked to the window and gazed out. He would give the final signal for execution. "It'll be over soon enough, JoAnna. And the wedding will take place when the time is right. The fact is, you shouldn't be here at all. This isn't fitting for you, to say nothing about the fact that you're still recovering."

"There are thousands of people here. This is one of the biggest events in Minnesota history. I want to be here. Besides, Jesse's here, and I'm feeling stronger."

"Lieutenant Buchanen is a soldier. This is where he belongs. You, my precious daughter, belong in St. Paul."

JoAnna's voice softened as she turned her eyes toward her father. She twisted a curl in her hand and replied, "I missed you. For months both of you have been traipsing around western Minnesota chasing Indians. It was a horrible war." Her tone became harder remembering her own experience. "And the savages slaughtered so many innocent people. They deserve to die here today. More of them should. I'll never forget the look in Laura Duley's eyes."

"I'm afraid Jesse wouldn't totally agree with you, JoAnna. You got much closer to this war than you should have."

JoAnna didn't answer as she stared down in fascination at the spectacle below.

Major Joseph R. Brown was the signal officer. His eyes were riveted on Miller, who was standing behind an open window. The nooses had been affixed to thirty-eight necks and the canvas bags pulled down. The colonel looked past his daughter to the clock on the wall and then to the scene below. Brown nodded his head. All was ready. The clock slowly began to chime as the hour hand struck ten.

Miller raised his finger and touched it alongside his nose. Brown gave three rhythmic raps on a drum head. On the third, Duley cried, "This is for my children!" and slammed a hatchet down hard on the rope. It failed to slice through. He raised the axe again, "This is for Laura!" and drove the axe down with all his might.

Instantly the platform beneath the Santee fell away. Thirty-eight forms were suspended in air. As they swung, some tried to grab the blankets of those nearby. Others continued to clasp hands. The knot on one noose slipped and the Santee brave strangled. Another, Cut Nose, actually fell to the ground and had to be rehanged as the crowd chanted, "Put him up! Put him up!"

Round Wind watched from a bluff nearby. As the suspended bodies twisted and kicked, loud screeching screams sounded from behind the old Dakota. He turned and looked above at the sky. A flock of eagles descended over him from the bluff to fly just over the gallows. Quickly, Round Wind counted.

"Thirty-eight. There are thirty-eight of them. They cry out like warriors and come for the spirits of my brothers. The Great Spirit has not forgotten us."

Tears formed in his eyes, but Round Wind didn't know if they were from joy or grief. He gathered his blanket around his shoulders and turned to the west. He would go now to Sitting Bull and the Teton.

Within ten minutes not one of the thirty-eight was breathing.

A woman in the crowd smiled and pulled her young boy close. "It doesn't get us even, Merton," Lavina Eastlick told her son. "But I hope your pa, Freddie, and Giles are looking down at this. You saved Johnny, carried him near fifty miles before we caught you. I'm just glad God let us live to see this day."

JoAnna hurried across the square to Jesse, a woolen shawl held tightly against the chill. Jesse dismounted and held her close.

"I wanted them to die," she said softly. "They did so many awful things, but it was horrible to watch."

"It was horrible for more reasons than you think, JoAnna. Not everyone who died here today was a killer. You do know this isn't over. Sibley wants me to go west with him in the summer, into the Dakotas after the Sioux."

"Yes, I expected it. Father said as much. I'll wait for you, Jesse, and I'll be there for you when you get back."

They held their close embrace as thirty-eight bodies swayed from the gallows behind them.

Four teams of horses were driven to the scaffold, and the wagons were loaded with the bodies of the dead. An armed detail of soldiers accompanied the wagons to a wide trench dug between Front Street and the river. There the Santee were placed in a double row, some four to five feet deep.

That night nearly all the bodies were removed by neighboring medical doctors who needed cadavers to study. Cut Nose wound up in the office of Dr. William Mayo. Later, his sons would learn about bones and anatomy by studying the contents of the large jar that held the Santee chief's remains.

Sarah Wakefield received the following letter from Stephen Riggs: "Dear Madam, In regard to the mistake by which Chaska was hanged instead of another, I doubt whether I can satisfactorily explain it. We all felt a solemn responsibility and a fear that some mistake should occur. . . . When the name Chaska was called in the prison on that fatal morning, your protector answered to it and walked out. I do not think anyone was to blame. We all regretted the mistake very much." Stephen Riggs.

ᔂ Epilogue ᘓ

Measles did ravage Fort Snelling in the winter of 1862-63. Over two hundred died from the disease. In May about 1,300 Fort Snelling Santee were herded like cattle onto riverboats and transported down the Mississippi to the Missouri River and then up to Crow Creek in southeastern Dakota Territory.

The reservation was dry, dismal and drought stricken. Farming there was a failure. By late 1863 some few Santee had managed to return to Minnesota. The forty-eight who had been acquitted were released at Fort Snelling to be transported with the other Santee to Crow Creek.

The remaining prisoners from Mankato were sent to Davenport, Iowa. In April of 1864 Lincoln issued a pardon for twenty-five men. In October he ordered the release of Big Eagle. The order was not obeyed and the President tried again, "Let the Indian, Big Eagle, be discharged. I ordered this some time ago." Big Eagle was one of the few who did return to Minnesota. For forty more years he lived on a farm near Granite Falls, not far from Yellow Medicine.

In April of 1866 President Andrew Johnson pardoned the remaining 247 Santee at Davenport. They were sent to Crow Creek. One hundred and twenty of them had died in prison.

The treaties with the Santee were abrogated by the United States government and the land turned over to farmers. Some of the treaty money due the Santee was paid to white victims and their families.

In February, 1863 Congress set up a commission to consider damge claims from Minnesota and by March the Interior Department reported it had paid out $1,370,374 to claimants. Traders and merchants got most of the money.

Stephen Riggs and other missionaries continued to minister to the Dakota, even on the Crow Creek Reservation.

The Fool Soldiers returned to their village. Some found their homes had been white-washed by sarcastic Indians. Martin Charger's Fool Society exists to this day.

Thomas Ireland survived his wounds at Shetek and was reunited in Iowa with his daughter, Nelly. He was the only member of the original settlement to return to Lake Shetek to live.

Charlie Hatch recovered from his wounds and went south to fight the Confederacy.

Lilly Everett married a man named Keeney.

Will Duley traveled into the Dakotas on Sibley's expedition. After the Minnesota Indian wars Will, Laura and their two surviving children moved to Alabama.

Lavina, Merton and Johnny Eastlick all survived their ordeal and continued to live in Minnesota.

Julia Wright and Eldora stayed in Minnesota.

Mrs. Hurd and her two children escaped Slaughter Slough and eventually joined up with the Meyers family, Lavina, Merton and Johnny Eastlick, Will Everett, Tom Ireland, Edgar Bentley and Charlie Hatch on the road to New Ulm.

Mariah Koch was taken captive by the Santee and escaped. She reached New Ulm safely.

Joe Godfrey served three years of his ten year sentence. He was then released to live on the Dakota reservation in Nebraska. There he farmed until he died in 1909.

John Other Day was given a $2,500 reward from the State of Minnesota for his service. He continued to live and farm in Minnesota.

Governor Alexander Ramsey became a United States Senator from Minnesota.

General John Pope commanded the Department of the Missouri from 1870-1883. He led several campaigns against the Dakota but tried to avoid conflict. Pope never recanted his hard attitude toward the Minnesota Santee, but his attitude toward the western Indians was much more salacious. He thought they had a natural talent for raising live-stock. He was wrong.

Abraham Lincoln was assassinated and not able to fulfill his pledge to reform the Indian system. President Grant took up the cause when he became President.

The hanging of the thirty-eight in Mankato is still the largest public execution in the history of North America.

Abraham Lincoln received a letter from Sarah Wakefield com-plaining about the death of Chaska, "Who saved me and my little fami-ly. He was executed in place of the guilty man." She recalled that Reverend Riggs had called it "a horrible affair" and of those convicted and held at Davenport Sarah wrote, "I am in favor of the majority of the poor fellows being pardoned. I cannot deem them guilty as many per-sons, as they were so very kind and honorable to me while I was with them."

Lincoln answered, "In spite of my best efforts it is clear that in this case the wrong man was executed." He turned his full attention to the war with the southern Confederacy. In the election of 1864 Lincoln carried Minnesota.

Shakopee and Medicine Bottle fled to Canada, Will Duley and Jesse Buchanen went west with Sibley while Jo Anna waited. Henry Sibley led an expedition in 1863 to track down and punish Santee who had fled into the Dakotas. There they earned the lasting enmity of a young Sioux warrior, Sitting Bull. Little Crow traveled west and then returned to Minnesota. Nathan and Emily traveled to Crow Creek with the Dakota. All their stories will be continued in the upcoming book, Pursuit.

ᛞ Sources ᛰ

Lincoln and the Sioux Uprising of 1862 by Hank H. Cox, 2005, Cumberland House Publishing.

Over the Earth I Come: The Great Sioux Uprising of 1862 by Duane Schultz, 1992, St. Martins Press.

The Dakota Indian Internment at Fort Snelling 1862-1864 by Corinne L. Monjeau-Marz, 2006, Prairie Smoke Press.

The Lake Shetek Indian Massacre in 1862 by Lavina Eastlick, 1890, Minnesota Historical Society.

The Sioux Uprising of 1862 by Kenneth Carley, 1976, Minnesota Historical Society.

Mary and I: Forty Years with the Sioux, by Stephen Riggs, 1969, Ross & Haines, Inc.

Let Them East Grass: The 1862 Sioux Uprising in Minnesota, Vol. 3, *Ashes* by John Koblas, 2006, North Star Press.

The Sun and the Moon: A History of Murray County by Maxine Kayser Luehmann, Star Press.

Through Dakota Eyes by Gary Clayton Anderson and Alan R. Woolworth, 1988, Minnesota Historical Society Press.

Grandpa Was a Cowboy & an Indian & Other Stories by Virginia Driving Hawk Sneve, 2000, University of Nebraska Press.

History of the Sioux War by Isaac V.D. Heard, 1863, Harper Brothers.

What They Might Have Said by Ryman LeBeau.

Interview with Harry Charger by Dean Urdahl, 2008.

Fort Snelling in 1838 by Helen White and Bruce White, Turnstone Historical Research, St. Paul, Minnesota, November 1998.

Return to Shetek, Courage of the Fool Soldiers, Video produced by Barbara Britain.